MEJI

BOOK ONE

A NOVEL BY

MILTON DAVIS

ISBN 13: 978-0-9800842-0-7
ISBN 10: 0-9800842-0-2

Cover Art by Thomas Richard Davis III
Cover Design by Marion Designs
Layout/Design by Uraeus

Manufactured in the United States of America

Second Edition

MEJI

INTRODUCTION

Ndoro and Obaseki. Warrior and mystic. Twin brothers rescued from ritual infanticide, only to be separated not long after their birth. Two paths to follow. One destiny to fulfill.

In *Meji*, Milton J. Davis has created an African-oriented fantasy epic that is wide-ranging and deeply engrossing. The novel is set in Uhuru, an Africa that is not the same as the one we know. Uhuru is a continent in which the cultures of our world's Africa developed in different directions, leading to a setting that is at once familiar and exotic.

Meji is a huge tapestry of a tale that encompasses a multitude of characters and a vast variety of cultures, tribes and kingdoms. Yet for all its twists and complexities, the story is tightly knit – told the way an African *griot* would tell it, strumming his *kora* as his audience listens raptly in the flickering glow of firelight …

As you join Obaseki and Ndoro on their separate and ultimately converging journeys through the heart of Uhuru, you will see how deeply the author has immersed himself in the ocean of African history, folklore and mythology, and how he has rearranged those elements in an entirely new way.

I know how Milton felt as he was writing *Meji* – for I've swum in that ocean myself. Many years ago, I studied sources similar to the ones Milton has perused, and invented an alternate Africa of my own: Nyumbani, the continent though which the heroic warrior Imaro wanders. My woman-warrior character, Dossouye, lives in yet another parallel version of the Bright Continent.

At that time, I knew the potential existed for the conception of many other variations on classic African themes. A limitless number of stories were waiting to be written by other authors. Consider the dozens, if not hundreds, of ways the legend of King Arthur has been retold. That's just one story, from one culture. Africa, with its hundreds of cultures stretching back to the beginning of humanity, offers infinite opportunities for stories of fantasy and sword-and-sorcery – or, as I prefer to call it, sword-and-soul.

In *Meji*, Milton has made full use of those opportunities. From the *kraals* of the Sesu to the desert stronghold of the Ihaggaren; from the cosmopolitan city of Mawena to the river kingdom of Tacuma, the author's vivid prose sweeps the reader along on a wave of pulse-pounding action, vivid description and agonizing moral dilemmas.

You will meet a wide array of characters as you accompany the twin protagonists on their quest to transform the Two into One – from the haughty to the humble, from the virtuous to the vicious, from the divine to the demonic. And the women of Uhuru are equal to – and sometimes more than a match for – the men.

When I first read *Meji*, I was profoundly impressed by the sheer scope of the endeavor and the narrative skill of the author. *Meji* is a story that needed to be told – and for Milton J. Davis, it is only the first of many.

Read on, and become One with the Two …

— **Charles R. Saunders**

To Vickie

Your love inspires my dreams

1

A yellow moon shimmered above Sesuland, casting its hue across the rolling grasslands. Atop a low rise overlooking the Kojo River, the inhabitants of Inkosi Dingane's kraal attempted to sleep despite the unusually bright night. Restless cattle crooned at the sky, their wild brethren answering in agitated tones. Dry season had come early and pushed away the shroud of moisture obscuring the stars in the expansive sky. Soon it would be time for the Sesu to pick up their shields and assegais and march against their enemies. Dry season was war season, and the Sesu had a way with war.

The sound of cowbells and drums exploded from the royal compound beyond the cattle pen. Royal messengers dashed among the huts with wavering torches, their voices filled with excitement. The day the Sesu waited for was finally at hand; inkosi Dingane's great wife Shani was in labor.

Dingane squatted outside the birthing hut, his mind in turmoil. Every scream sent a wave of fear racing through him. Though his other wives had borne him many children, this would be Shani's first and his most glorious. This child, this boy would be his successor. Dingane took great pains to make sure he did nothing to offend the spirits during the pregnancy, lest they curse Shani's unborn child. He spent many nights awake imagining how he would raise his heir, teaching him the ways of a Sesu warrior and the secrets of the inkosi. By the time he was of age, the elders of the tribe would dare not select anyone else to succeed him. He would be by far the one most capable of leading the Sesu to future greatness.

A strange cry escaped the hut. Dingane jumped to his feet and ran to the entrance. A hand reached out and stopped him; no man, not even the inkosi, was allowed into the birthing hut. Themba, Shani's maid, emerged.

"Send for Mulugo," she said urgently. "Something is wrong."

Dingane turned to his bodyguards and pointed to a young looking man who leaned against his spear.

"Go find Mulugo and bring him here quickly!" he ordered.

He turned back to Themba. "Is the baby in trouble?"

"I do not know," Themba replied. "Only Mulugo can answer that question."

The warrior returned with Mulugo. The medicine-priest wore one of his many masks, his mayembe clutched in his bony right hand. His brown eyes locked on Dingane, and the inkosi took a step away. He did well to hide his fear of the old priest before his warriors, though he knew his façade did not fool Mulugo. The priest gestured toward the hut. Dingane pulled aside the cloth covering the entrance, careful not to look.

Dingane crouched beside the entrance, rocking back and forth on his heels as he offered his prayers to Unkulunkulu. His son was being born and the turmoil inside sent his stomach churning in pain. Every scream sent him reeling. Any more and he would have to send his warriors away. He must not show weakness, no matter how much he felt it.

Shani screamed again, pulling Dingane to his feet. He rushed into the hut, his heart pounding like a celebration drum. Three faces met his; the cowering gaze of the midwife, the scowl of Mulugo and the exhausted smile of Shani. Dingane smiled until he saw what his wife held. Shani had given birth to twins.

"You are cursed," Mulugo said. "You prayed for sons and Unkulunkulu has given them to you.

The joy faded from Shani's eyes. "What does he mean, Dingane? What is he saying?"

Themba placed a cool rag on Shani's forehead. "Calm yourself, my queen. Do not worry."

"Twins are an abomination, a bad omen to the tribe," Mulugo

announced. "They must die."

"No!" Shani screamed. She clutched her crying babies close to her breast.

"They are my sons!"

Her desperate eyes sought Dingane. "You cannot let him do this."

Dingane looked away from his Great Wife and glared at Mulugo. What the priest said was true, but he would not be denied a son. The fear he held for the priest dissipated.

"My sons will not die," he declared.

Mulugo held his mayembe out to Dingane, the ornate spirit-filled animal horn inches from the inkosi's face.

"You are a fool!" Mulugo replied. "You stand here naked to Unkulunkulu and deny his will for your own vanity. The Sesu chose you to lead us for your strength and wisdom, and you return our favor by damning our souls!"

"Be quiet, old man!" Dingane spat. "Do you read the mind of the Eye now?" Despite his anger he felt Mulugo's words. The Sesu followed him only as long as he protected them and their beliefs.

"No, Dingane, I do not know the mysteries of the Eye. But I know the heart of the Sesu." Mulugo shook his mayembe, and then let it drop to his side.

Dingane felt trapped. He looked into Shani's terrified eyes, at his sons searching their mother's breasts, at the ancient wisdom carved in Mulugo's face. He could not deny the Sesu, yet he could not deny Shani and himself.

"Will the spirits be satisfied with one?" he asked.

"Dingane, no!" Shani exclaimed.

"Ukulunkulu's favor is not open for barter," Mulugo warned.

"This is no bargain. Take one of the boys. The other shall live as I please."

Mulugo glared at Dingane and stormed from the birthing hut. Shani did not give up so easily.

"You can't do this, Dingane!" she pleaded. "These are our children!"

Dingane looked into Shani's damp eyes, his face set hard. Over the years he had given in to his sweet flower many times. Now there was no room to give.

"Shani, you must try to understand. This is a terrible but necessary thing. I have already asked too much when it comes to your wishes. I cannot ask anymore."

"It is so easy for you," Shani said. "You did not carry them. You did not feel your body grow plump with life. You did not feel the love grow as well."

"You are not the only one grieving," Dingane said. "But Sesu ways are strict and necessary, just as those of your people."

"The Mawena do not kill their twins," Shani snapped.

"But the Sesu do," Dingane replied.

Shani looked away from Dingane. For a long moment they both were silent, but finally Shani spoke.

"I will do as you wish, but I will choose which child will live."

Dingane nodded his head, relieved to be released from such a burden. He stood to leave the hut, but Shani raised her hand.

"I want one week to make my decision."

"It must be tonight." Dingane's voice was stern.

Shani's eyes narrowed. Her small mouth formed a rigid line as she spoke. "My son will not die a stranger to me. If he does, I will, too."

Dingane's hard look softened with fear. "Whatever you wish."

"I will see no one but Husani and Themba."

"No one," Dingane replied. "But if you choose which one to keep, I will choose his name."

Shani lowered her head. "As you wish my husband."

Dingane turned and left the hut. Mulugo waited as he emerged.

"Where is the child?" Mulugo asked.

"You will have him soon enough," Dingane replied.

Mulugo scowled, spun and stomped away muttering. Dingane

refrained from imagining what curses the medicine priest weaved against him. His first priority was to fulfill Shani's demands. He beckoned one of his warriors.

"Bring Husani to me," he ordered.

The warrior ran into the darkness and returned quickly with Husani. Shani's personal bodyguard was a tall, broad man, characteristic of the Mawena. He carried a shield and short spear, his hair cropped short in the Mawena style. There was no doubt where his loyalties lay.

"The Great Wife has asked that you stand guard of her hut during her recovery," Dingane said to Husani. "No one is to enter or leave except you or Themba."

Husani nodded in acknowledgement. With that Dingane turned away and went to his kraal.

"Husani," Shani called out. "Are you there?"

"Yes, inkosa."

"Enter, please."

The warrior stooped low and entered the birthing hut. Shani sat in the background, cradling her babies. She looked up, and then struggled to her knees.

"My queen!' Themba exclaimed, 'you mustn't!"

"Help me," Shani demanded. Themba went to Shani and helped her to her feet. Shani swayed, the pain burning through her loins.

Themba grabbed her. "Please, inkosa, you must rest!"

Shani looked past her midwife to Husani. "You have always been faithful to me."

Husani's eyes narrowed. "What do you wish, my inkosa?"

Shani looked at them both, the fear radiating from Themba's timid eyes, the strength of Husani's stare. They would do anything she asked, each for their own reason. But they would do it. She handed the twins to Themba.

"Take them," she said. "This is Ata, and this is Atsu. Tonight you will take them to Mawenaland."

Fear took hold of Themba's face. "We cannot do this!"

"It is what our queen wishes," Husani said, reminding Themba of her first loyalties.

Themba paced. "We will be caught. Dingane will kill us all."

"You must leave tonight," Shani said, ignoring Themba's comments. "Dingane will not visit this hut for one week, nor will anyone else."

"Not even Mulugo?" Husani asked.

"Especially not Mulugo."

Shani saw the concern in Husani's eyes. "I will be fine. I have enough food. All I need is rest."

"And after a week?"

"That is in Olodurmare's hands," she replied. "Now go. Take my sons to our people."

Husani bowed and went for the hut entrance. Themba did not move. Her eyes pleaded with Shani, but the inkosa was unmoved.

"Come, sister," Husani urged. "We waste precious time."

Themba gave Shani one more glance then hurried out of the hut, Husani close behind.

Shani stared for a moment where Themba stood holding her babies in her trembling arms. She could not cry or mourn, for the fatigue finally overcame her and she collapsed where she stood.

Mulugo sat naked in his hut surrounded by the swirling grey smoke of a smoldering dung fire. His eyes closed, he concentrated with every speck of his being to control the anger and fear threatening to break the mental dam holding back the dangerous emotions. This was not the time for random action, he thought to himself; he must marshal the weaknesses invading his mind and transform the useless energy into decisive action.

He saw his death in the eyes of the twins, just as the babalawo foretold. As a young medicine priest visiting the city of Abo, he humored himself by seeking his fortune from a decrepit babalawo. The toothless man sat at the edge of the marketplace that long ago was shared by Sesu and Mawena, offering fortunes and remedies for a handful of kola nuts.

"Two kola nuts, young Sesu," the man coughed. "I see Fate's web in the bones."

Mulugo remembered how he laughed at the man, an arrogant sound expressing his contempt for everything Mawena.

"A fortune from a Mawena is worthless," he told the old man.

The babalawo's face went from smiling to stern. "For you, young warrior, I will read the bones for free." He tossed the bones at Mulugo's feet, his eyes rolling back to white.

"A great medicine priest you will become, but your path will be cleared by treachery and deceit. Power without respect shall be your reward until that day when the one who is two brings an end to your dark days."

Mulugo felt the fire in his veins as if the words were uttered moments ago instead of the countless seasons passed. He chanted, the rhythmic words soothing the anger that lapped at the rim of his control.

"I ask for a fortune and you give me a curse," he spat at the old man. Mulugo shoved the man into the dirt and threw the kola nuts in his face. The old man looked at Mulugo, managing to grin.

"Your life is a curse, young Sesu," he replied. "It will be a long life, a very long life."

The heat rose in the hut and Mulugo sweated. His life had been long. His climb to the high priest of Sesuland had been a journey of deception and cruelty, but he had done no different than any ambitious man seeking power. He never experienced the touch of a woman; the chance of eternity through children was never to occur. Still he thought the words of the beggar fortune teller mere coincidence until saw Dingane's twins.

"The One Who is Two," Mulugo whispered.

He had to kill them soon. Every moment they lived they grew stronger. The blood of a chief flowed through their veins, two souls blessed by a lineage superior to his own. Though twins, he saw the difference. One cried with the soul of the world, his only concern the hunger in his belly. The other sat quietly, his eyes drinking in the new world about him, seeing everything within and beyond a normal Sesu's sight. He was the one who had to die first, the one Mulugo would have chosen if given the chance. Dingane's weakness ruled once again and the Mawena cow had her way.

The swirling smoke became less random, moving with a pulse that claimed life from nothing. Faces appeared before Mulugo, faces of the spirits to which he offered his dark libations nightly in hopes they would strengthen him in his time of need.

"The Weak One calls," they whispered. "He has seen his death and is afraid."

"Silence!" Mulugo shouted. His ancestors mocked him, but the truth was that he was more powerful than they had ever been when they were alive. It was this new borne force that summoned his oldest uncles from the Zamani to serve him in the life they would never know again.

"The abomination is here, borne with the blood of chiefs and the power to see beyond seeing. How do I stand against this power?"

"Only one of twins can bring your demise," they sang. "Make the herbs that bring the sleeping sickness and serve it to Shani. The child eats what the mother eats. An adult will sleep, but a child will die."

Mulugo smiled. It was a simple task, something well within his powers to perform. The abomination would die like many other new born, and no one will be the wiser. Mulugo sprinkled the leaves into his worn stone mortar and began his work, humming a chant as he prepared his freedom.

* * *

The sun rose impatiently over the Sesu pastures, eager to get about its celestial business. Warm rays of light pierced the hut in which Dingane slept. One sliver touched the chief's face and he sprang from his cot as if burned. He bolted from the hut, spurred by the message sent to him from his ancestors while he slept.

In his dream Mulugo had defied him. The old wizard had taken matters into his own hands, invading the birth hut and killing both babies with his jagged metal knife. Shani's screams rang in his head as he neared the hut, his breathing heavy and desperate. He looked about for Husani but the warrior could not be found. Dingane yanked the hut door aside and charged in. Shani's head rose slowly from her cot, her eyes wet and red. The babies were gone. He ran, headed to Mulugo's abode, his eyes wide with anger. Striding into the wizard's hut, he found the old man sitting before a small stone table, his ancient hands slowly grinding a collection of herbs.

"Damn you, Mulugo!" he shouted. He attacked the medicine priest, wrapping his hands around the old man's neck. Mulugo struggled to speak, pounding Dingane's arms feebly. He stopped suddenly, throwing his hands out behind him and finding his cane. His breath escaping him, Mulugo touched Dingane lightly on his leg. Searing pain rushed through the inkosi's body; he released the priest and fell away, clutching his calf. Mulugo leaned against the stone table in the center of his hut, gathering his breath.

"The night has driven you mad!" Mulugo gasped.

"You killed my sons!" Dingane shouted.

Mulugo looked at Dingane. "I have not touched the abominations. I have been doing what I could to deflect whatever evils your decision has brought to us."

Dingane stood. "But they were not in the hut! Shani was crying and I dreamed..."

Dingane fled the hut, Mulugo following as closely as he could. By this time the commotion had passed throughout the village and everyone crowded about the birthing hut, curious to know what was afoot. Dingane's warriors cleared a path as the chief returned and charged inside.

Shani waited for him. She sat erect, covered in fresh clothing Themba brought her the night before, her composed face hiding her pain.

"Where are my sons, woman?" Dingane shouted. "Where are Husani and Themba?"

"Gone," Shani replied, her voice strong and firm. "The Mawena do not kill their twins."

"Do you know what you have done?" Dingane shouted. He grabbed her by the wrists and yanked her to her feet, ignoring her grimace.

"I bent the rules for you, Shani. Yesterday I defied Mulugo and the elders for you. And this is how you repay me?"

"You did nothing for me," Shani replied. "If that was so you would have spared both my sons."

Dingane let her go, his face a mirror of disgust. "I expected you to be a Great Mother worthy of this tribe. My dowry to your father was more than he asked because of what I thought you were worth. I was wrong."

"I am Mawena," Shani said. "I will not let my children die."

Dingane spat on the floor of the hut and left Shani sobbing. When he emerged Mulugo was waiting.

"What has happened?" he demanded.

"Shani sent the twins to her people."

A gasp rose from the crowd. Mulugo threw his medicine stick to the ground and pointed a crooked finger at Mulugo.

"See what has happened so soon, inkosi of the Sesu! The evil befalls us quickly."

Dingane ignored Mulugo's gesticulations, turning his attention to Gamba, the leader of his personal guard.

"Gather an impi of my finest warriors and send for my weapons."

"Where are you going?" Mulugo asked.

"After them," Dingane replied. "The boys are with Husani and Themba. They had a head start, but Themba will slow Husani down."

"I will go with you," Mulugo decided. "We must wait no longer. When we find them, we must kill one immediately."

"I will not slow down for you, old man"

"You will not need to," Mulugo replied.

Gamba returned with the warriors. He helped Dingane don his headdress and strapped his shield and assegais across his back. Dingane looked over his men and was satisfied with Gamba's choices.

"Impi kimbia!" he shouted and they set off at a warrior's pace. Mulugo followed close behind, resting in his litter as his porters kept pace with the warriors. They ran through the streets of Selike, urged on by the chants of the Sesu. Men, women, girls and boys all shouted for their success. The throng followed them to the edge of Sesuland, and then watched as their inkosi and his warriors disappeared into the grassy horizon.

* * *

Husani gazed on the grasslands from his perch, searching for signs of pursuit. He and Themba reached the hills just before dawn, and found a place to rest before continuing their journey to Mawenaland.

He looked back, watching Themba suckle the twins, absorbed in the nurturing of Shani's children. Though she did her best, they would never reach the Mawena. An impi was surely pursuing them by now, an impi with no woman or babies to slow them down. He had to do something if the twins were to make it to Mawenaland. What, he did not know.

"How are they?" he asked Themba.

"As well as can be expected," she replied.

Husani crouched closer to Themba. "We must go now."

Themba glared. "The babies need more rest. I am not even

finish feeding them!"

"They will have all the time they need to feed in Mawenaland," Husani replied harshly.

Themba pulled the babes from her breasts. Their feeble cries tore at her heart; she pleaded with Husani once more.

"Just a few more minutes," she begged.

Husani said nothing for a moment, his mind elsewhere. When he finally turned his attention back to Themba, his expression echoed his resolve.

"Take your time, Themba. We can wait."

Themba fed the babies until they were full then placed them in the basket. She looked about for Husani but could not find him. Themba sang, more to soothe herself than the sleeping twins. Death was following her; she felt its press upon her back, its putrid breath cold against her flesh. She should have fled Shani's hut as soon as the inkosa stated her intentions. But now she was part of this foolish scheme, too afraid to say no when asked.

Husani reappeared suddenly from the bush. "Are you ready?" he asked. Themba checked the babies one last time. "Yes I am," she answered.

"Good," Husani said. He took his wrist knife and handed it to Themba.

"Mawenaland is not far from the base of the hills. If you follow this path, you should reach it by sunset."

"What are you talking about?" Themba replied.

Husani placed his hand on Themba's shoulders. "Listen to me. Dingane has surely discovered the babies are gone by now and an impi has been sent after us. Together we are too slow."

"Then we will die!" Themba exclaimed.

"No, woman, listen to me," Husani insisted. "Just inside the woods of Mawenaland is Koso. When you come across the Kosobu, show them my knife. They will make sure you and the babies get to Abo."

Themba realized what Husani was going to do. She never doubted his bravery, but to see him, his handsome face resolved, she then knew what a true warrior he was. She took the knife, placing it in the basket with the twins. She touched Husani's cheek.

"I will pray for you," she whispered.

"And I for you," Husani replied. "Now go."

Themba picked up the basket, trotting down the path Husani showed her. Husani watched until she disappeared, then covered her tracks. He returned to his perch and waited.

The sun hung low on the western horizon when Husani spotted the impi. They were moving fast; at their current pace they would reach the hills in minutes. Their chant reached his ears and made him smile.

"Come for me, Sesu," he said. "You will surely get me."

He rose and set off, climbing up a path in the hills that ran opposite of the trail leading to Mawenaland. He ran long enough to make sure the Sesu warriors would not overtake him before he reached his destination. Once he was sure of his distance he walked, saving his energy for what lay ahead.

* * *

The impi picked up the trail not far from the village. There was no rest, no easing of the pace; the Sesu had been defied and revenge was demanded. But Dingane would make sure that revenge only went so far. He would have his son.

By midday the hills that separated Sesuland from Mawenaland were in view. Dingane increased the pace, knowing the longer they traveled without seeing their prey the better their chances at reaching Abo. The warriors responded with a war chant, beating their assegais against their shields. We are coming, they chanted. We are coming for you.

Dingane led his warriors into the hills, their stride still strong despite the miles they'd traversed. It did not take them long to find the Mawena camp.

"The ashes are still warm," Dingane remarked. It only took a moment to find the trail leading away from the Mawena camp.

The impi set off again, their energy renewed.

The trail snaked upward through the hills, meandering like the gemsbok which created it. The natural growth of grasses faded with each step, usurped by low shrubs and weak trees as they drew closer to Mawenaland. The Sesu paused at the top of the hill then plunged into a dense tangle of bush and trees. The path narrowed, and the Sesu were forced to travel single file.

The slim path slowed them down considerably, the thistles from the encroaching bushes slashing their bare arms and legs. A wicked thorn bit into Dingane's calf and he dropped to his knees in pain, his hand grasping his wounded limb. No sooner had he descended that he heard a wet thump behind him. He turned to see the warrior behind him fall, an assegai buried in his chest. The others raised their shields and formed the tortoise around their inkosi, protecting him from the deadly missiles raining down on them. As suddenly as the barrage began it stopped. Dingane broke free of the formation, running at full speed through the narrow path. Fury consumed him as he looked for Husani, promising himself the Mawena would die a painful death when he was finally captured.

Husani leaped in his path. He slammed into Dingane, knocking the inkosi off his feet and into the brambles. Dingane scrambled to keep his balance, but Husani pushed him further into bush, the thorns tearing into his face and sides. The biting of the bush was punctuated by a searing stab into his right thigh. Dingane held back a scream as Husani leapt back, a look of grim satisfaction on his face.

"You will die, fool!" Dingane shouted.

"I know," Husani replied. The Mawena jumped over Dingane and charged the approaching Sesu warriors. Dingane watched Husani plunge into his men, using the narrow path to his advantage. Five Sesu fell before Husani was finally overwhelmed, his large frame disappearing under an avalanche of Sesu blades.

The warriors freed Dingane from the shrubs. As soon as he was clear he shoved them away.

"Come! We must go."

"Inkosi, your leg," Gamba said.

"Are you a healer now, Gamba? Follow me!"

Dingane place his full weight on his wounded leg and shouted. Determined to go on, he took another step. The pain overwhelmed him and he collapsed into the arms of his men.

When he awoke, he was stretched out on a hide cot, Mulugo squatting beside his leg, busily pressing the wound with a poultice. The medicine priest raised his eyes slowly to meet Dingane's.

"It is happening as I foretold," Mulugo said.

"Be quiet," Dingane ordered. "I will not stop until I have my son back."

Mulugo looked exasperated and turned his attention back to the wound. "We must go back to the kraal. Your wound is bad and I do not have the proper herbs to heal it. I did not expect to be saving a life, only taking one."

Dingane gritted his teeth. "We are not going back without my son. Do the best you can." He rose up on his elbows and called for Gamba.

"Make me a litter quickly," he commanded. Gamba trotted off to do his job.

"Even you cannot deny what is happening," Mulugo said. "Can't you feel the unbalance? Both boys must die!"

Dingane glared at the medicine priest. "Listen to me, old man. One son will die; the other will live. If you mention this to me again, I will cut your throat."

Mulugo looked stunned. He backed away from Dingane. "I am returning to the village. I will no longer be a part of this evil."

"You will do no such thing," Dingane said. "You came this far, you will go all the way. Do you understand?"

For once Dingane was privileged to see fear in Mulugo's eyes. Maybe the medicine priest thought him mad; it didn't matter to Dingane. The only thing that mattered was his son.

Dingane tried walking but the pain was too great. Gamba

returned quickly with the litter. Dingane struggled in and nodded to Gamba. "I am ready."

Gamba bowed to Dingane. "Impi kimbia!" he shouted. With the command the impi fell into ranks and began the run to Mawenaland.

* * *

Themba scrambled down the goat path leading to the forest. The fear that had been held in check by Husani's presence was upon her in full fury, riding her more heavily than the babies she bore against her breasts. The sun was setting, the long shadows of the nearby forest creasing the hills. Themba would give anything to be among them, hidden in familiar darkness. But as soon as she reached them she realized she'd been too long among the Sesu. The forest engulfed her, the sky above becoming an ominous canopy of leaves.

"Oya protect me!" she prayed as she ran on.

The trail widened as it progressed into the trees, the signs of human habitation growing more numerous. Themba knew she was close to a village, but her legs would carry her no longer. She would never make it before dark; she would have to sleep in the forest. She stopped and then gingerly stepped from the trail into the bush. She found a good spot, a large tree surrounded by a stand of saplings. She put the babies down and cleared a spot to sit. The twins slept, exhausted from the journey and lack of milk.

"Poor little ones," she whispered. "Your lives begins so hard."

She woke them and offered them her breasts and they suckled eagerly. She sang to them, knowing that any sound might attract danger but too tired to care. When the babies were finished she laid them on the blanket then lay beside them, clutching Husani's knife in her small hands.

It seemed only moments had passed when Themba jumped up, startled by harsh clanging. Sunlight broke through the canopy, stinging her eyes and frightening her even more. She found the babies and calmed somewhat, then leaned against a tree to orient herself. The clanging came from a herd of goats passing along the path, shepherded by a group of young boys. One of the boys approached her, his eyes searching the bush for the source of the scream.

"Habare!" she called out. The boy looked suddenly in her direction.

"Umzuri," the boy replied. "Who are you, mother?"

"I am Themba, handmaiden of inkosa Shani, daughter of Oba Noncemba. I need your help."

The boy bowed respectfully.

"Wait here. I will go back to my village and bring help."

"What is your village?" Themba asked.

"Koso."

The boy ran through the brush and back to the path, calling his cohorts. Two younger boys appeared, and the eldest pointed to Themba. The boys nodded then went to her.

The younger boy took off his shoulder pouch and handed it to Themba.

"Here, eat. Paki said you looked hungry." Themba had not thought about food until that moment. She accepted the pouch eagerly.

"Are these your babies?" the other boy asked.

"No," Themba replied, her mouth stuffed with food. "They are the sons of inkosa Shani, Great Wife of inkosi Dingane and daughter of Oba Noncemba.

The boy stepped away from the sleeping children, showing his respect.

"We will protect you until Paki returns."

Themba smiled. "We are honored to have such fine warriors protecting us."

The boys made fine company, sharing their food and conversation. It seemed only a moment passed before the eldest boy returned, bringing with him a group of warriors from the village. The younger boys moved aside quickly, leaving Themba to confront the warriors alone. The eldest of the men stepped forward, a graying beard bordering his cherubic face, his stomach protruding past his waist belt. His left hand carried a worn shield, his right an assegai with an extremely long blade. In other circumstances Themba might have found him amusing, but the threatening look on the man's face emphasized the seriousness of her situation.

"Paki says you are Shani's handmaiden."

"I am."

"And these are her children?"

Themba nodded.

The man smirked. "Then where is the Great Wife?"

"These babies are twins," Shani replied. "The Sesu consider them abominations, and the medicine priest said they must die. Shani did not want this so she sent Husani and me…"

One of the younger warriors came forward. "Did you say Husani?" he asked.

"Yes, yes. He gave me this to show anyone who found us."

She revealed Husani's knife. The old warrior looked at the young man.

"It is his knife," the young man said. He looked at Themba. "Where is he?"

Her eyes watering as she replied. "He stayed behind to slow down the Sesu pursuing us."

The young man's face became somber, his fingers absently rubbing the cowry shells about his neck. The older warrior motioned to Themba.

"Come with us."

Koso bordered the Bose, a wide, lethargic river shadowed by trees bent lazily over its muddy waters. Cone shaped houses of wood and mud lined the narrow streets leading from the river's edge into the forest. The entire village smelled of fish. For Themba it was a welcomed change from cow dung. The warriors took her to the meeting tree, a huge ancient plant surrounded by the village elders. The chief sat in the center, his head covered by a crown woven in the kente of his family. He seemed young for a chief, but his bearing reflected his position. Each elder wore his family kente, signifying a group of great power. She knelt, placing the basket with the babies before them and touched her head on the ground.

"I am Olatunde, chief of the Koso. You carry the children of Dingane?" the chief asked.

Themba felt fear in her throat. "Yes, father."

The chief rubbed his chin. "We are not friends of the Sesu. They raid our farms and steal grain for their cattle. I have no reason to save the sons of an enemy."

The thought of harm coming to the infants forced Themba's fear aside. "These boys are not Sesu. They belong to Shani, daughter of Oba Noncemba, your oba. I have promised to take them to him and I will, with or without your help."

Olatunde held up his hand. "I didn't say we wouldn't help you. I wanted everyone at this council to understand why we will help. We are, after all, Mawena. We are proud of the blessing Shani sends us."

He raised his hand and the younger warrior came forward.

"Jelani will take you and the babies to Abo by boat. Dingane chases you, but the boats will take you faster. You must leave now."

Themba bowed to the chief. "I thank you for your kindness. Shango keep you."

Jelani led Themba to the awaiting boats. A tall, beautiful woman met her, her head wrap and dress signifying the chief's clan.

"I am Zuwena, wet nurse for the chief's family. I will care for the children."

Themba clutched the babies, reluctant to give them up.

Zuwena gave the handmaiden a sympathetic smile. "It is all right. You are tired and your milk is weak."

"Will we take the same boat?" Themba asked.

"Yes," Zuwena replied. Themba handed the babies to Zuwena slowly, still wary despite being surrounded by people willing to help her.

"They are fine boys," Zuwena remarked. "They will grow into great men."

"If they live," Themba replied.

Jelani helped Themba and Zuwena into the boat. There were three boats in all, the front and rear boat containing oarsmen and archers. Jelani prepared a place for Themba, a cot with a lambskin blanket.

"You can rest here," he said. "If I know Husani, your journey was hard.

"He was a brave man," Themba replied.

"I know. He was my brother."

Themba smiled at Jelani, the resemblance now apparent. She lay down on the cot as the boats got under way. Knowing of Husani's brother calmed her. Everything would be fine; of this she was certain. Once in Abo, Oba Noncemba would handle the situation and the babies would be safe. She closed her eyes and let the rhythm of the boat lull her to sleep.

* * *

Oba Noncemba slept fitfully in the bedchamber of his palace, unaware of the crisis approaching his city. He had a youthful look about him despite the gray speckled hair on his head and the white beard. The privileges of higher status had not contributed to his waistline; he was as fit as his days as a warrior oba leading his armies in conquest of the kingdom now known as Mawenaland. The last decade he spent not as a warrior but a diplomat, securing the borders of his realm through trade, negotiation and marriage. Shango blessed him with few sons but many daughters and these had married the princes of the many surrounding lands, making them family. All had married well except Shani. Noncemba stirred in his sleep as he recalled his youngest daughter which he had not seen since she married Dingane, chief of the Sesu. He did not like the young Sesu, but it was a marriage he could not avoid. The Sesu were growing numerous and powerful under Dingane's rule, rising from a small tribe of cattle raiders to a unified force. Though still not a kingdom, the young chief was powerful enough to request a bride.

Noncemba sat up in his bed just before the messenger entered.

"My oba, forgive my intrusion. You are needed urgently at the meeting tree!"

Noncemba did not question the messenger's summons. He dressed and followed the messenger through the palace and into the courtyard. The wide area brimmed with people; spectators sat upon the bleached white walls, a curious murmur drifting into the enclosure. The elders sat below the branches of the enormous baobab, a tree older that the ancestors, its canopy shielding the entire courtyard. They were flanked by his generals dressed in red kapok and chain mail, each wearing their headdress rank except Kumba, their leader and Noncemba's closest friend. Before them all a small group knelt, their heads touching the ground. Noncemba's anxiety increased as he recognized them as Kosobu. This was definitely a Sesu matter; the Kosobu lived along the river separating Mawenaland from the Sesu grasslands. As he approached them a woman lifted her head and struck the oba still. It was Themba, Shani's handmaiden, and she held twins in her arms.

"What have the ancestors blessed us with?" he whispered.

"A blessing and a curse," Kumba commented.

Noncemba walked up to Themba and knelt before her. The spectators gasped while the elders frowned at such a break in protocol.

"Are they my grandsons?" he asked.

"Yes, my oba. This is Ata and this is Atsu. The inkosa sent them to you for your protection."

Noncemba was well aware of the Sesu attitude towards twins. Many of the Kosobu were orphaned Sesu hidden among the reeds of the river by their desperate mothers. The Kosobu found them and took them in without question.

"The Sesu will be angry," Elder Kosoko said. The elder stood, a tall, thin man twice the age of Noncemba. His family was among the First of Mawenaland and had produced its share obas in the past.

"They will demand that we kill them."

"Killing twins is not our way," Kumba snarled.

"Everyone here knows this," Noncemba replied. "This is a serious matter, one that could lead to war if not handled carefully."

"Then let war come," Kumba said. "For the past ten years we have danced with the Sesu. It is time we crushed them and their ambitions like dung flies."

A whisper of approval meandered among the spectators. Noncemba's royal stool was brought to him by his attendants. He sat before his people, returning to tribal protocol.

"One hunts the lion with skill, not anger," he said. "The Sesu are a concern, but so are the Kossi, the Burundi and the Fah. Mawenaland is strong enough to defeat any of these lands alone, but defeating one makes us vulnerable to another. We must consider our response carefully."

"How can we appease the Sesu without killing the twins?" Elder Kosoko asked. "They know Themba brought them here. They will come to you and ask for justice."

"Inkosi Dingane does not want to kill them both," Themba said.

Noncemba eyes widened in time as a gasp rose from the throng.

Themba dared to lift her eyes again. "Dingane wished to keep one for him. It is his first child from Shani. The medicine priest insisted they kill them both but the inkosi refused. Inkosa Shani told Dingane she would choose which one would live, but she sent them both to you."

"You didn't make this journey alone," Kumba said. "Who helped you?"

Themba's head sagged. "Husani."

"Where is he?" Noncemba asked.

"He stayed behind in the hills to slow the Sesu impi pursuing us. He told me to go to Koso. He said they would bring me to you."

Noncemba nodded. "You have served my family well. You and the others may go to my palace and rest."

Noncemba's servants led Themba and the Kosobu into the palace. Noncemba turned to the elders.

"Dingane's desire for a son is our advantage," he said. "Come, let us prepare for our visitors."

* * *

The Sesu impi had been on the trail since morning. Despite the burden of carrying Dingane they made good time, arriving at the outskirts of Mawenaland by midday. They rested briefly, long enough to eat and quench their thirst. Then they marched again, their chants muffled by the encroaching forest.

The trail ended its meandering and widened into a well-used road. Wooden huts peered through the trees, but no people were visible. Word of the impi had preceded it, and the Mawena were staying clear. Dingane rose from his litter as they climbed a heavily forested hill, anticipating the scene about to unfold before him.

They reached the crest of the hill and Dingane raised his hand, halting the impi. Below them was the city of Abo, the heart of Mawenaland. Cylindrical wooden houses topped with conical thatch roofs peppered small plots of farmland. The plots grew smaller as the homes pushed closer to the city. In the city the dwellings consisted of stone and were grouped according to clan. Each clan enclosed its homes with white clay walls painted with the family kente. The center of this magnificent sprawl was filled by the royal compound of Noncemba. A massive stone fence encircled a large pasture filled with cattle, the wealth of many tribes before Dingane's eyes. Noncemba's hilltop palace marked the nucleus of the royal compound. The extravagant homes of his clan members peppered the hillsides. Beside the palace the meeting tree thrived, a massive plant older than the ancestors. Below its branches the elders of Mawenaland waited.

"Put me down!" Dingane demanded.

"But Inkosi, your leg!" Gamba replied

"Down!" Dingane ordered. He was eased down slowly and stood immediately. The pain throbbed in his leg, but he ignored it. Noncemba would not see him as a cripple.

The Sesu proceeded, their wary eyes noting every movement and shadow. The streets were completely deserted; the Mawena had obviously been warned of the impi's arrival and were prepared. As they entered the inner city, a commotion drew their attention. Mawena warriors appeared behind them and quickly closed ranks behind the Sesu, careful to stay out of spear range. Though they outnumbered the Sesu intruders, their advantage didn't lull them into foolishness. A lion fights more ferociously when cornered; no less would be expected from the Sesu.

The gates to the royal compound were open. Mawena elders sat patiently below the branches of the meeting tree, each man draped in his family cloth pattern. In the center sat Noncemba on a gilded stool with a leopard skin cushion. He was draped with a kente robe adorned in elegant patterns of red, purple and green. A black cap studded with thick gold buttons covered his head. He wore a thick serpentine gold bracelet on his right wrist; a cluster of gold cubes tied together by a leather cord circled his left wrist. More gold cubes dangled from leather bands surrounding his ankles, spilling over his sandals. Golden rings shaped in the patterns of animals and proverbs decorated every finger. There was a time when Dingane was in awe of the Mawena. Even now it was hard for him to suppress his admiration. But time taught him the meaning of true power, which did not lie in elaborate clothing and trinkets. He was Noncemba's equal in every way. The Sesu had become strong under his rule, strong enough for Noncemba to offer Shani to him as his great wife.

Dingane halted his warriors outside assegai distance of the meeting tree, a sign that he meant no violence.

"Mulugo, come with me," he said to the medicine-priest.

Mulugo's litter was lowered and the old man took his place beside Dingane. As they neared the tree, Dingane recognized Themba kneeling beside Noncemba. She had shed her Sesu garments for Mawena clothing. In her arms was the bundle that Dingane sought.

It was Dingane who spoke first. "Habare, baba."

"Umzuri, Dingane," Noncemba replied. "It's been a long time, my son."

"I am not here to chat," Dingane replied. "I want my sons."

"You mean your son," Noncemba replied. On the oba's signal Themba rose and walked to Dingane, extending the bundle. Dingane took it and turned back the cloth. There was only one child.

"What have you done?" Mulugo demanded. "Where is the other child?"

"What difference does it make?" Noncemba replied. "The child was to be killed, so we saved you the trouble."

"Where is the body?" Mulugo asked.

Noncemba scowled. "What are you implying, magic man?"

Mulugo's face twisted with skepticism. "You are the boy's grandfather. Would you really kill the son of your daughter?"

Noncemba glared at the medicine priest, his hand tightening on his staff. "The blood of the Mawena is strong in my grandsons. To waste it sickens us all. But our tribes are bonded; my grandsons are Sesu and subject to your ways. Shani was wrong to send them here. We carried out your deed because of this disgrace."

Noncemba stood, raising his staff. The Mawena warriors stormed forward, surrounding the Sesu. Noncemba smiled.

"Do not push this issue, my son. We have suffered enough with your ways this day."

Dingane trembled with rage. He stared at Noncemba, his strength occupied by keeping his assegai in his hand.

"I need someone to nurse the child during the journey back to Selike," he finally said, his voice trembling.

Noncemba nodded and turned to Themba. She walked to Dingane, staring directly into his eyes, her loathing for him apparent to everyone. But she was not alone. A warrior stepped forward with her, a young man Dingane quickly recognized as being related to Husani.

"Themba and Jelani will return with you," Noncemba said. "I trust you will make sure no harm comes to them?"

"I will," Dingane replied.

"I wish you a safe journey home," Noncemba said.

Dingane turned away without a reply. He stormed through his warriors, the pain in his leg insignificant against the rage in his head. The Sesu warriors followed with Themba and Jelani the last of the group.

"He insulted you!" Mulugo exclaimed. "He dishonored the Sesu!"

"The Mawena are strong," Dingane replied. "Do you see?" He waved his hand to acknowledge the numerous warriors shadowing their retreat.

"Our time will come, Mulugo," he continued. "Mawena bone will one day shatter beneath Sesu feet. That I promise you."

* * *

Kumba came to stand before Noncemba and fell to his knees.

"What is your command, my Oba?"

Noncemba rested his chin on his fist. "Follow them until they leave our land. I don't want anyone doubling back. If any of Dingane's warriors break rank, kill them."

A wicked smile came to Kumba's face. "It will be our pleasure to serve the Oba."

Kumba stood and marched to his warriors, shouted the order to march. They formed ranks and trotted from Abo to catch the Sesu.

Noncemba watched until the army left the gates of the city.

He turned to his closest servant.

"Bring me my grandson."

The servant returned with the infant wrapped in a blanket of royal kente. Shani's son looked stared into his grandfather's eyes with intensity beyond his few days of life.

"You must name him," Elder Kosoko advised.

"You have your grandfather's face and your mother's eyes," Noncemba said. He raised the infant over his head for all around him to see.

"Behold my grandson," he announced. "He will be known as Obaseki Noncemba."

The elders bowed their heads, whispering the name to the ground that held the bodies of their ancestors. Noncemba lowered the baby and smiled.

"I hope you live up to your name, little one." Noncemba handed his grandson back to the servant then with a wave of his staff, lead the procession of elders and warriors back into the walls of the Inner City.

2

Ndoro crouched beside the thorn fence surrounding Shani's kraal, swinging a gnarled branch back and forth. On the other side of the fence Sitefu attacked Amanzi relentlessly as the other herdboys looked on, his zinduku smacking Amanzi's head repeatedly. Amanzi backed away, clearly giving up the fight.

"Say it!" Sitefu shouted. "Say it!"

Amanzi looked desperate. He tried to fight back, but Sitefu was just too fast. He finally dropped his sticks.

"You are my master," he said.

With that Lungile stepped between them. He was the inqwele, the leader of the herd boys, the best stick fighter among them. He was in charge of sparring.

"It is over," he said. "Sitefu, tend to Amanzi's wounds."

Ndoro knew Sitefu would win. Amanzi was afraid of him like the other boys his age. Ndoro wasn't afraid. He wanted to join them and spar with them, but his world ended at the thorn fence. Momma would take a switch to him if he tried to venture outside the Royal Kraal, so he would sit and watch the other boys filled with longing and anger.

A strong calloused hand lifted him and he laughed.

"Put me down!"

Jelani's other hand went under his other arm and he laughed again.

"Look, another monkey in the kraal. I guess I'll throw this one out, too!"

Jelani swung him over the brambles and spun him around.

"Let me go! Let me go!" Ndoro squealed.

"I do and your momma would skin me," Jelani replied. "Come,

little monkey; it's time to eat."

Jelani let him go and Ndoro landed on his feet. He looked up at the burly bodyguard, grinning and lifting his eyebrows. Jelani grinned back.

Ndoro sprang like a gazelle, bounding to the hut. Jelani ran after him, surprised at how hard he had to run to catch up with the boy. He caught him only a few paces from the hut, grabbing him under the arms again and lifting him up.

"You're faster than you ought to be, little monkey."

"I'll beat you soon, big monkey."

Jelani put him down. "You probably will."

Shani emerged from her hut with a smile for her son.

"Ndoro, were you at the fence again?"

"Yes, momma. Sitefu and Anzani sparred today and Sitefu won. He's fast like the cheetah, but I'm faster. I could beat him."

Shani looked at Jelani and he looked away.

"Don't spend so much time watching those boys. You have chores to do. I need your help."

"The other boys don't help their mommas. They watch the herd and stick fight. The girls stay at home."

He folded his arms across his chest. "I am not a girl."

Shani turned her back on him. "Come inside. The food is ready."

Ndoro trudged into the hut, his head low. He sat cross-legged before the fire and Shani handed him a bowl of uPhutu porridge. He stared into the bowl.

"Momma, inkosi Dingane is my father," he said.

Shani stopped eating, her face pensive. "Yes, Ndoro, he is your father."

"Then why aren't I in an intanga?"

"You are too young."

Ndoro scooped a spoonful of porridge and chewed slowly. Shani watched him nervously.

"Amanzi is my age, I think. He is in an intanga," he said. "His father is not inkosi, but he is in an intanga."

Jelani frowned at Shani and left the hut with his bowl.

"We won't talk about this tonight," Shani said. "Eat you uPhutu and go to sleep."

Shani waited until Ndoro slept before leaving the hut to look for Jelani. He sat by his hut eating his porridge. She marched up to him and gripped her amble hips.

"Is there something you wish to say?" she asked.

"You are his mother and I am your servant," Jelani replied. "It's not my place to comment on the raising of Ndoro."

"But you disapprove."

Jelani sat down his bowl and stood, towering over her. He had grown into a man since leaving his people eight years ago to serve Shani as his brother had years ago. Unlike his brother, he was not one to hold his opinion.

"You can't continue to hide him from the facts," Jelani said. "It's time he understood his place."

"He's just a boy," Shani protested. "I want him to enjoy his life as long as he can. He will have plenty of time to suffer."

"Ndoro will be a Sesu warrior one day. It is a hard life of struggle for respect and status. The sooner he begins to make his place among his own, the better his chances will be to remove the curse that looms over him."

"He's just a boy!"

"You will do what you want, inkosa," he said. "If you want Ndoro to have any kind of chance among his own you must let him go. It will be hard and painful, but it will make him the warrior he must be to endure this life."

"What if they don't accept him, Jelani? What if they deny him his place?"

"Then he will have to force acceptance on them," he replied. "The world of men is merciless, inkosa. No man is given status. He must earn the respect of his peers. If Ndoro can accomplish this he has a better chance of being acknowledged by Dingane."

Shani sat in the dust and dropped her head in her hands. "Will you help him, Jelani?"

"It is not my place," Jelani replied unhappily.

"You are the only man he knows. You must help him."

"The Sesu won't approve."

Shani lifted her head, her lips bunched in anger. "This is a Mawena decision. The Sesu will not recognize my son so they have no say in his upbringing. Train my son, Jelani. Make him a warrior, a Mawena warrior."

Jelani looked at the inkosa, a smiled forming on his handsome face. "Is this your command?"

Shani sat up, straightening her back and raising her head. "It is my command."

"I will start tomorrow." Jelani finished his bowl. "Good night, inkosa."

Shani smiled. "Good night, Mawena."

* * *

"Ndoro, wake up."

Ndoro struck at the hands shaking him, kicking out his legs against his cot.

"Come on, little monkey. It's time to rise."

The voice calling him wasn't the soothing tone of his momma. His eyes snapped open to Jelani's face.

"Jelani?"

The warrior stepped away, folding his hands across his chest. "Stick fighters rise early in the morning to practice their skills."

Ndoro jumped off the cot. "I'm a stick fighter!"

"Come then. Let's see what you know."

Ndoro chased Jelani outside. He ran to the thorn fence, fishing out the sticks he'd hidden the day before. When he turned around Jelani held two sticks of his own.

Ndoro let out a yell, charging and flailing. Jelani laughed, stepped aside and tripped the boy. Ndoro fell on his face, jumped to his feet, found Jelani and charged again. After the third fall and a bloody nose, Ndoro stopped charging. He glared at Jelani, his face caked with dirt, blood running out his nose and over his lips. His narrow shoulders rose and fell with his heavy breath.

"You're...not...supposed...to...move!"

"That's the Sesu way," Jelani replied. "Two fools smashing at each other until someone gets tired and the other one cracks his head. The style favors the strongest man."

Ndoro dropped his arms, confused by Jelani's words.

"It's the way the boys fight and the way the men fight. It's the right way."

Jelani crossed his arms. "If it's so right, why didn't you hit me?"

"Because you're a big monkey!"

Jelani laughed. "You're almost right. I am bigger than you. Sitefu is bigger than you, too."

Ndoro dropped his sticks and sat hard. "Then I'm not big enough to beat Sitefu."

Jelani came to him and pulled him back on his feet. "Yes you are little monkey. Come, let's clean you up and start over. This time I'll show you the right way to fight."

Jelani led Ndoro to the river. The warm water soothed his wounds and lifted his mood. Jelani had beaten him bloody and never raised his sticks. He dodged like the springbok evading the simba.

He dunked his head underwater and shook it.

"I am ready," he announced.

They walked back to the kraal and practiced the rest of the day, stopping only for a bit of food and water. Ndoro was relentless, listening to Jelani every word, repeating every motion as best he could. As the sun disappeared behind the undulating horizon their practice ended. Man and boy slumped to the ground, arms sore and but spirits high.

"Shango, boy!" Jelani exclaimed. "Do you ever get tired?"

Ndoro lay on his back, gazing at the emerging stars above. "I am a stick fighter. I never get tired."

He didn't remember falling asleep. He didn't feel Jelani lifting his limp form and carrying him to the hut, humming to him like a baby. He woke for a moment when he felt the familiar contours of his cot and the voice of his momma.

And so it went for a month, early rising, day long practices, then tired dreamless sleep. Shani suffered for her little man as she watched Jelani stern but careful training. He pushed the boy without sparking his anger. Ndoro seemed to enjoy the punishment, his well of energy challenging Jelani's endurance.

Jelani's touch woke Ndoro. He sprang up in his cot ready for another day of practice.

"No practice today, little monkey," he said. "Today you take our goats to the pasture across the river."

Ndoro mouth gaped.

"You do know how to do this don't you?"

Ndoro nodded.

"Then get to it, little monkey. The goats are hungry."

Shani was waiting with a bowl of uPhutu. She smiled, but her eyes expressed her worry.

"Be careful, Ndoro."

"I will mamma."

Ndoro finished his porridge and ran to the kraal, sparring sticks in his right hand, his herding stick in his left. Shani held the gate open for him and he drove the goats down the hill and across the river to the grasses below. He felt the boys' eyes on him, their faces unreadable. Most of all he noticed Sitefu. He watched Ndoro, his mouth in a slight frown. Ndoro's stomach rumbled in nervous excitement. Sitefu would have to approach him to establish his place among the other herd boys. The older boys, the ones watching cattle, seemed not to notice him at all. They talked among themselves, teasing and laughing, a few of them threatening each other to sparring.

He found a good spot of grass and halted his goats. Ndoro sauntered to a nearby acacia and sat beneath its thorny branches. He placed his sticks at his side, leaned against the smooth tree trunk and waited.

It wasn't long before a procession of boys came in his direction, each one herding his goats before them. Sitefu led them all, his eyes focused on Ndoro in a way that made the younger boy nervous. His feelings dissipated as Sitefu drew closer; he wasn't as big as Ndoro thought. Ndoro was actually taller than the boy, although at only eight seasons old his physique was just a thin layer of skin and muscle. Sitefu's body was lean and muscular like a leopard, but like a leopard he could be powerful. Ndoro witnessed that in Sitefu's fight against Amanzi. But Ndoro was no Amanzi. He was a stick fighter, a Mawena stick fight, and he was anxious to find out where that would take him among his peers.

Sitefu wasted no time. He strode up to Ndoro, fighting sticks in his hand and touched the boy on his head.

"I am you master," he announced.

Ndoro picked up his sticks and stood. "No one is my master."

Ndoro did not see Lungile until he stepped between the boys.

"You can't fight him," Lungile said.

"Why? He is in my intanga. I must prove to him that I am his master."

"Mulugo said we should not talk to him. He is cursed."

Ndoro's eyes widened. "Cursed? I am not cursed! I am the son of Inkosi Dingane!"

"The inkosi is not above the ancestors," Lungile replied. "You shouldn't be alive."

Ndoro's hands tightened around his sticks. No matter what Jelani taught him, he would not strike at Lungile. He wasn't afraid of him; he knew he couldn't beat him, at least not yet.

"If I was supposed to be dead I would be," Ndoro retorted.

"You need to learn respect, dead boy," Lungile said. "Sitefu, if you want to fight him, go ahead."

Lungile smirked and walked away. Ndoro's mouth opened in shock. The inqwele was not watching the match, which meant if he won it would mean nothing.

Sitefu didn't care. His stick flew at Ndoro's head, barely missing as Ndoro stumbled away. He staggered away, Sitefu flailing at his head and knees. Ndoro avoided most of the blows but the ones that landed stung his pride more than his skin. He sidestepped, dodging Sitefu's charge and giving himself time to settle down. Sitefu's stick smacked against his blocking stick and Ndoro swung at his attacker's head. Sitefu was quick; he pulled his head back and the stick missed. Ndoro brought the stick down, feinting at Sitefu's knees then swung at his head again when the boy dropped his blocking stick. Stick met skull and Sitefu winced. Ndoro frowned; there was no blood so the fight was not over. He dodged a wild swing and smacked his stick against Sitefu's ribs, followed by another blow to his head. There was blood this time; Ndoro grinned in triumph and stepped away, his hands raised in victory.

Sitefu did not stop. The stick smashed against Ndoro's ribs, knocking the wind out of him. He fell to his knees gasping. Sitefu beat him on his back and head while the other boys cheered. Ndoro scrambled about on hands and knees, blackness blotting out the pain. Lungile would not stop his beating; Jelani was too far away to help him. The rules of sparring did not apply anymore. Jelani had warned him but he did not believe him.

Ndoro flipped around and kicked Sitefu's ankles, knocking him down. He came to his feet and kicked Sitefu in the face. The boy rolled onto his back, blood pouring from his nose. Ndoro raised his stick and struck him again across the forehead, raising a welt.

"I am your master!" he shouted.

A hard stick struck him across the back. Ndoro spun around, swinging his stick. Pain exploded in his stomach; he doubled over and the pain appeared across his back. Ndoro gritted his teeth, fighting back the tears struggling to escape his eyes and the darkness seeping into his head. The blows came so quick the pain felt continuous, cascading over him. The blows ceased amid yelps and the thump of feet against the grass. He felt himself rising.

"I'm here, little monkey," Jelani whispered

Ndoro smiled as he let the darkness take over, happy to be

away from the pain.

He didn't open his eyes when sound finally came back to his ears. He couldn't understand the words floating over him but the anger in them was clear. He stayed still, listening as the words began to make sense.

"This is your fault!"

"How can you blame me for this? You are the one who has disowned him. Did you keep him alive for this? His own intanga did this to him!"

"They will be punished."

"I don't care what happens to them. I care about our son."

Ndoro opened his eyes to the dim interior of his momma's hut. Her back was to him, the faint light from the dying fire illuminating her familiar outline. Jelani stood beside her, his arms folded across his chest. Dingane stood in front of momma, his features hidden by her body. Ndoro tried to move to see his father's face but he didn't want them to know he was awake.

"What do you want me to do?" Dingane raised his hands. "I told you to keep him in the kraal. Mulugo spreads his lies every day. Everyone either hates him or fears him."

"I tried, but he insisted," Shani said. "Jelani said it was best."

Dingane rushed to confront Jelani. "So this is your doing, Mawena."

Jelani did not move.

"Jelani is trying to make him a man," Shani said.

Dingane glared at Jelani a moment longer then looked at Shani.

"Shani, you must understand. I am bound by tradition. There is only so much I can do. He must do the rest himself."

"Then let him," Jelani said. "You can't make them accept him, but you can make them follow tradition. Ndoro is Sesu and should be treated so. He should be with his intanga. He should earn his place among them with his stick fighting skills. Anyone who violates Sesu law should be punished. If you refuse to treat him as your son, at least treat him like a Sesu."

"So be it." Dingane walked away from Jelani. He moved Shani aside and approached Ndoro. Ndoro opened his eyes fully, staring into his father's eyes.

"Baba," he said.

Dingane cradled Ndoro's head in his hands and smiled. He leaned towards Ndoro and their heads touched, then he pulled away, turned and left the hut.

Shani rushed to Ndoro and held him close.

"Momma, where is baba going?"

"Don't worry, little monkey," she said, using Jelani's pet name for him. "How do you feel?"

"Good, momma," he lied.

"You must rest now," she said. "In time you will feel better."

"Baba said I can be with my intanga."

Shani's face turned solemn. "Yes, he did. But you must understand, Ndoro. Many Sesu don't think you should be here. They will do whatever they can to disgrace you. Some will try…they will try to…"

"Kill me?"

Shani's eyes glistened. "You must be strong and wary. Your father cannot help you."

"Jelani will," Ndoro said.

"Yes I will," Jelani replied. "Now sleep. Tomorrow will be an early day."

Ndoro smiled at them both. Dingane was his father, but momma and Jelani were his family. He could deal with any challenge as long as they were with him. He hugged momma, her smell soothing his mind. He lay in his cot, closed his eyes and once again fell into a peaceful slumber. The next time he awakened, he would wake as a Sesu.

3

Adesina cried, his legs tangled beneath his narrow bottom, his arms hanging at his side. His small brown head hung back so far only his chin and nose could be seen above his neck. He wailed from deep inside in his throat, a sound that should have echoed between the family compound walls of Abo. But only one person heard his cry, and that person had had enough.

"Shut up, Adesina!" Obaseki shouted. The young prince lay on his bed, his eyes clinched, hands over his ears. His feet dangled over the edge of his bed, kicking at Adesina.

"Don't do that!" Lewa scolded. She looked at both boys with sympathetic eyes too beautiful to belong to a twelve year old girl.

"He misses his momma," she explained.

"Why doesn't he miss her somewhere else?" Obaseki fussed. "I'm sleepy!"

"Salako performed a cleansing spell and drove him away."

Obaseki slammed his fist like hammers against the bed.

"I hate Salako!"

"Seki?"

Dara opened his door and stepped into his room, concern and fear in her eyes.

"Who are you talking to?"

Obaseki opened his eyes to his aunt and sat up on his bed. Adesina continued to wail, but Dara didn't here him. She didn't see him either, nor did she see Lewa frowning at her. Obaseki learned long ago that some of his friends were special. Only he could see them, but Salako could feel them. He hated Salako.

"No one," he answered.

Dara saw the lie in his face and shrugged.

"I don't believe you, but I don't want to know. Do whatever you need to do and get some sleep. Kumba is leading weapons training tomorrow and he will hear no excuses."

"I will, aunt."

Dara looked around the room one more time, rubbing the charm bag around her neck and whispering before she left.

Obaseki put his hand over his ears again. Adesina continued to cry despite Lewa's cooing.

"Okay, Adesina, I'll do it," Obaseki said.

Adesina looked at him, his shoulders trembling. "You will?"

Obaseki let out a defeated sigh. "Yes. Now stop crying!"

Lewa folded her slim arms across her budding chest. "Don't play with him, Seki. If you're not going to do it, don't offer."

"I said I would."

"How are you going to get out of the palace? You're an heir."

"I'll figure something out after I get some sleep!"

He fell back on his bed with a thud. When he looked up Adesina was gone. Lewa remained.

"You didn't go."

"I never do."

Obaseki shrugged. "You can stay as long as you're quiet."

He lay back down on the bed and closed his eyes.

"Seki?"

Obaseki sprang back up. "What?"

"Good night."

* * *

The morning sun rose into a clear blue sky, its brilliant light reflecting off the stark white walls of the royal palace. Servants swept the royal courtyard clear of debris, preparing for the Oba's daily conference with the elders. Outside the palace walls other servants prepared meals, white smoke rising from the short chimneys protruding from the tops of the rotund ovens. The smell of fresh bread seeped into Obaseki's room, stirring his senses and waking him. He rose, looking about for Adesina and was pleased in his absence. Lewa was still there, staring at him from her corner.

"You slept well," she said.

Obaseki nodded as he put on his kente robe. He reached over his bed to the shelf and took down his sparring stick and shield, his face curled up in a frown. He hated weapons training; he would rather go to the ovens and help the cooks prepare the meal. He was fascinated by the preparation, the way the flour rose into tasty hard bread loaves, the aroma of the goat stew and the constant singing of the servants as they worked. Sometimes he wished he was just another boy, following his father to work in the fields or into the forest to hunt, or better yet pushing a canoe into the Kenji to cast the net for fish. But instead he was the grandson of Oba Noncemba, son a mother he never met and a father whom no one spoke of.

He trudged out of his room into the morning brightness. His cousins emerged from their rooms, bright and eager for the day's lesson. They separated, seeking their favorites among the crowd, every one of them avoiding Obaseki. He glared at the ones brave enough to look at him and they glared back, shaking their sticks in his direction. He didn't bother to return the threat; they knew they couldn't beat him despite his apathetic attitude. It was his luck to have ability in something he despised.

He was the last to line up. Kumba stood under the ironwood tree shielding the practice courtyard, his dark hard face wrenched in disgust. His wide bare chest bore the scars of battles fought and won, his thick arms showing stretch marks made by muscles larger than the skin was meant to sheath. A leather kilt wrapped his narrow waist; thick thighs emerging from the hem, narrowed briefly at the knees then spread into muscled calves almost as thick as his thighs. Some said Kumba could crush the skull of a buffalo with one blow of his right fist while ripping the horn from a charging rhino with his left hand. Obaseki believed them.

"Oba Noncemba is cursed by the ancestors!" he growled. "His daughters have given him weaklings instead of warriors!"

His stared passed through the others, focusing on Obaseki.

"So you finally decided to join us?"

"Yes, uncle." Obaseki's words were more respectful than his tone.

"Save your defiance for sparring," Kumba snapped. "Your cousin's are eager to show you what they learned since last we met."

Kumba turned his broad back to his pupils and commenced the drill. The boys followed him the best they could, their movement weak shadows of the warrior's precise execution. Still, they were improving. The drills continued until noon before Kumba raised his hand. The boys stopped and fell into the dirt, everyone except Obaseki. He was too angry to be tired, because Adesina had returned and brought his wailing with him.

"You said we'd see mamma today!" he screamed.

"Will you leave me alone?" Obaseki shouted back before he realized what he had done.

"So, young prince, I'm bothering you?" Kumba loomed over him, blocking the sun with his massive frame.

"No uncle, I…"

The stick still hit him despite his quick block. He rolled in the dirt, his head hurting more than his body. He kept rolling until he bumped into the ironwood.

"You are fast, I grant you that," Kumba commented. Kumba grabbed him by the arm and dragged him away from the others. He shoved him down, and then folded his arms across his chest.

"I know about the ghosts," he said. "Personally, I don't believe it. You are not a medicine priest. You are a prince, and you have the potential to be a damn good warrior, but you must concentrate, Seki.

Obaseki glanced away towards Adesina who continued to cry. He brought his eyes back to Kumba.

"I will try, uncle."

Kumba sighed. "Go home, Seki. You've done enough today. Think about what I said."

Obaseki stood and trudged back to his room. He was halfway

back when Lewa appeared at his side.

"You promised, Seki."

"He promised he would stop."

"He won't stop until you take him home.

Obaseki stopped walking, looking around to make sure no one was watching before he answered.

"It's not that easy. I'm not supposed to leave the palace. It's forbidden until I become a man."

"You can sneak out."

"How?"

"I can show you."

He looked at Lewa, her face confident. Adesina cried.

"Okay," he said. "Let's go."

Lewa turned and led them to the cooking pots. The servants were busy with the midday meal, swirling about the open fires and smoking ovens as they sang one of their many work songs. The aroma of simmering goat reminded him of his hunger and he rubbed his stomach.

"The little prince is hungry!" the servants sang. A large man with a greasy smile grabbed his hand and led him to a stool beside one of the largest ovens. He opened the iron door, extracted a bread loaf and handed it to Obaseki.

"Thank you, Omope." He bounced the treat from hand to hand while it cooled, then took a big bite. The bread melted in his mouth and he moaned.

Lewa's expression was not a happy one. "Seki, let's go."

"Not until I finish my bread," he mumbled.

"Now!" Lewa swung and smashed her hand against a calabash on the table beside Obaseki. The water splashed his face and soaked his bread. Everyone turned, their eyes fearful. Omope scrambled to him with a towel.

"I am sorry, my prince. Please forgive us!"

"It's not your fault." Obaseki glared at Lewa who stood with a smirk on her face.

"The bread was good. I must go."

Obaseki wiped himself and followed Lewa. He pretended not to see the servants clutching their talismans and whispering prayers.

Lewa led him to the commissary area behind the kitchens. All the food for the palace was received, inspected and sent to the kitchens from the area.

"We'll hide in the storage hut until the next wagon of grain comes," she said. "We can sneak inside while the others are unloading. We'll have to make sure we jump off in the city. If not, we'll end up in the countryside outside the main gate."

Obaseki nodded. His defeat complete, he opened the door to the hut and walked inside. The smell of rotting grain attacked his nose and he stumbled back.

"It stinks!"

Adesina's abrasive wailing overpowered his repugnance and he went inside. The trio sat patiently, Adesina's crying subsiding to whimpering. The clatter of ox hooves and wooden wheels finally reached their ears and they sat up straight. The door swung wide and grain poured into the hut like water. The torrent hit Obaseki, pushing him back into the hut. Grain dust filled his nose and lungs, choking him. Before he could cry out the grain flood halted. He tried to move, but couldn't.

"I'm stuck," he whispered.

Lewa wasn't paying attention to him. "The wagon is leaving!"

Obaseki dug himself free as fast as he could. He peeked outside to make sure no one else was looking then dashed out of the hut after the wagon. Lewa and Adesina were on the wagon, holding up the canvas that once covered the grain. He grabbed the back of the wagon and jumped on, crawling under the canvas before the farmers noticed.

This was too much for a crying spirit, he thought. He'd almost died in the grain hut, and now he was violating a sacred rule older than any elder alive. He didn't dare imagine what kind of punishment awaited him if his grandfather discovered him gone. He lifted the canvas slightly, peering out onto the scene fading behind him. He could see the palace spires rising over the commissary and the kitchens, their gold caps glistening in the blue sky. Someone might be looking for him right now. Soon the Atuegbu would be scouring the palace grounds, Dara following them with worried eyes and wringing hands. She would be blamed and punished. Dara didn't deserve punishment, though. She was afraid of him, but she did her best to ignore his friends and had covered up for him when others thought his behavior strange. She even defended him before his grandfather, something that most didn't have the courage to do.

He was going back, he decided. He would find another way to get Adesina quiet, one that didn't involve someone else getting punished. He lifted the canvas and saw the palace gates, the high wood and iron doors that closed the Royal Palace from the rest of Abo in mysterious splendor. He was outside for the first time in his life.

Lewa's voice killed his astonishment.

"Get ready, Seki. We're almost there."

"Where?"

"The main market," Lewa replied. "Adesina's mother comes here every day with bushels of yams. Her stall is in the center of the market."

"I should go back," Obaseki said. "This isn't right."

"It's too late now," Lewa said. "We're here."

A confusing bouquet of smells and sounds penetrated the coarse fabric hiding him, enticing him to look. A crush of people surrounded the wagon, some buying, others selling, all engrossed in a daily ritual that existed long before Abo claimed to be a city. He jumped from the back of the wagon, his body filled with wonderful energy as he watched the Mawena selling their goods. He was lost in the crowd immediately, pushed and jostled by the constant torrent of sweating bodies. A familiar whine penetrated the noise, accompanied by the same annoying face.

"Momma is not here!" Adesina screamed.

"Yes she is," Lewa assured him. "Come, follow me."

Obaseki followed Lewa, pushing through the crowd as they inched their way to the central courtyard. He was so focused on keeping up with Adesina and Lewa that he didn't notice the curious stares transforming into shocked faces as the Mawena recognized the royal pattern of his kente robe. No one could remember seeing a member of the royal household outside the palace at such a young age; no one had ever seen a member of the royal family outside the royal palace alone. When they reached the central stalls everyone knelt, their heads touching the ground.

Obaseki had just realized the commotion he caused when Adesina shrieked.

"Mamma! Mamma!"

The woman bowed before them, a basket of yams resting beside her. A colorful scarf covered her head, helping to obscure her face. Obaseki walked to her and squatted before her.

"Please, aunt, rise and face me. I have something to tell you."

Adesina's momma lifted her head just enough to look into Obaseki's eyes. He smiled and she smiled back. She was a handsome woman with a comforting smile.

"What do you wish of me, young prince?"

"I have come to speak to you of your son."

Adesina's momma sat up straight. "My son? My son is dead."

"I know, but he is not happy. Salako drove him from his home. He misses you."

Anger seeped into the woman's face. "You have no right to torment me even if you are a prince. Whoever told you these things did not mean for you to use them this way."

"Adesina told me," Obaseki replied nervously. Others raised their heads to listen to the conversation.

"Tell her I miss my tum-tum," Adesina whispered.

"He missed his tum-tum," Obaseki said immediately.

The woman's hand clamped over her mouth as tears welled in her eyes. "Where is he? Where is my Adesina?"

"He is here. He wishes to come home."

The woman was about to answer when a broad man with the face of Adesina appeared, grabbing her by the arm and pulling her away.

"Who are you?" the man demanded. "You are no medicine priest. Adesina's spirit tormented us day and night with his wailing. He is gone. It is time for him to move on."

"But he wants to go home," Obaseki pleaded. "He will be quiet if you lift the spell and let him come home."

The man rushed Obaseki and pushed him to the ground. The crowded gasped, many falling back to their knees and hiding their faces in the dirt.

"No, Olujimi" the woman exclaimed. "He is a prince! You mustn't touch him!"

"I don't care who he is. He has no right to tell us our business. Salako told us what to do and it worked."

Olujimi pulled his orinka from is waist belt, brandishing the war club over his head. "Go back to the palace, young prince. Leave us common folk alone."

The assegai struck Olujimi with a force that spun him around, knocking the orinka from his hand. Adesina's father grabbed the shaft protruding from his arm in reflex; his teeth clinched in anger and pain. The man who threw the spear walked up to his victim. He was clad in a leather shirt covered by chain mail, a conical helmet on his head. A curved sword hung from his waist belt that held his leather kilt around his narrow waist. He placed a sandaled foot on Olujimi's wounded arm and jerked the spear free. Olujimi passed out.

The man approached Obaseki and knelt before him.

"Prince, I was sent to bring you back to the palace."

Obaseki nodded. He was relieved that an Atuegbu had found him, but he knew what it meant. His grandfather was angry.

The warrior glanced back at Olujimi. "Did he harm you?"

"No!" Obaseki blurted. "It was I who harmed him."

He went to Adesina's mother. She hovered over her husband, her voice soft as she prayed.

"I am sorry, aunt," he whispered. "I was only trying to help Adesina."

"He was a selfish boy," she replied. "It is why the ancestors took him so young. Tell him to go. This is his fault. He has caused this by not respecting us. He is no longer wanted."

Obaseki looked about him. Lewa stood beside him, looking sad enough to make him want to cry, but Adesina was gone. Obaseki knew he was gone for good.

"He is gone, aunt. I am sorry."

Obaseki returned to the warrior. More warriors had arrived, forming a wall between Obaseki and the others.

"I am ready," he said.

The warrior nodded and they marched away from the market, Obaseki in the middle of the ranks, his head down in sorrow and shame. He did not understand this strangeness about him, this ability to see spirits as if they live, to talk to those long since dead as if they still existed. But he would try; one day he would discover the purpose of it all. He would do it for himself. He would do it for Adesina.

4

Inaamdura sauntered through the central courtyard of the Yellow Palace, her delicate hands folded behind her back. Her dark brown face was a sculpture of composure, her strong cheekbones and narrow nose similar to her mother. A collection of colorful beaded necklaces rose from her slim shoulders to just below her chin, each one a token of admiration from a hopeful suitor. Her shapely body was covered by a thick yellow robe that fell to her sandaled feet, protecting her from the cool winds that blew down from the towering mountains watching over Kampera. She was her mother's eldest and most beautiful daughter, and she was well aware of her status.

Inaamdura halted before the ornate wooden door leading to her mother's personal garden. She was about to enter when a familiar giggle drew her attention.

"Bikita, how many times have I told you not to spy on me?"

Little Bikita hugged Inaamdura from behind, pressing her cheek into her sister's back.

"Where are you going?"

"You know where I'm going and you know you can't follow."

Bikita worked her way around Inaamdura and gazed into her eyes. She was as much as her father's daughter as Inaamdura was her mother's, a handsome child with a round face and dancing eyes. Her beaded braids played about her high forehead as she nuzzled her sister.

"You could take me if you wanted."

Inaamdura knelt, looking her precious sister in the face. Her mother taught her to conserve her emotions in all relationships, but she could not deny Bikita. Her effervescence wore away the hardest barrier she could ever erect, so she gave in and loved Bikita like she loved no other.

"Look, Kita, do you want to see me in trouble with mamma?"

Bikita frowned. "No."

"That's what will happen if I take you in the garden. Momma will take a switch to me and beat me until I bleed."

Bikita gasped. "No! Momma wouldn't do that to you. You're her favorite."

"Favorite or not, I can't take you into the garden. Now go and play. Your time in the garden will come soon enough."

Bikita clasped Inaamdura's face between her hands and kissed her on the nose.

"Bye, Rah-rah."

She skipped away across the courtyard and into the palace. Inaamdura watched her with a bit of joy and sadness. Her time in the garden would come and her childhood would end. It was the price she would have to pay for the privilege of being the daughter of Azana.

Inaamdura opened the door of the garden and was rushed by the heavy scent of flowers. The garden bloomed constantly, populated with flora that displayed their enticements in an unending sequence of colors and aromas. She followed the granite path to the acacia tree dominating the center of the garden, its seductive white blooms a contrast to its sharp thorns. Below its broad canopy Azana sat on her cushioned ironwood stool, staring at her daughter with her intense black eyes. Their likeness was disturbing , a resemblance so close that those looking at a glance might mistake one for another. But where Inaamdura's face and body expressed the softness of youth, Azana's suffered with the hardness of age.

Azana gestured for Inaamdura to sit and she did so, folding her legs beneath her as he sat at her mother's feet.

"You are late," Azana said.

"I am sorry, momma."

"You must handle Bikita sternly or she will ruin you."

"I know momma. I will try harder."

"You will not try; you will do. You have no more time, Inaamdura. Events are moving faster than I expected."

Inaamdura stiffened. It was not her mother's way to rush into action.

"What has happened?" she asked.

"My eyes have seen the Sesu moving towards the border with intent. My ears have heard inkosi Dingane talk of empire, of building a city to rival Abo of the Mawena and of making the grasslands the home of the Sesu."

"What of our overtures?"

"Dingane has agreed to take Amadika as his Great Wife, but only because of the disfavor Great Wife Shani suffered from the birth of her twins and her defiance of Sesu tradition."

"It is not right to ask a woman to choose between her children," Inaamdura said, letting her anger slip.

"That was an unnecessary comment," Azana scolded her. "It is not our concern of what is right or wrong among the Sesu."

"If Dingane has agreed to marry Amadika, why are you concerned?"

Azana reached out her hands and Inaamdura helped her mother to her feet. They walked along the path, their feet crushing the colorful collage of petals scattered before them.

"Dingane may be too strong for Amadika. She may not be able to fulfill her duty as a Bonga wife."

"So what do we do?"

"I don't know. Dingane has invited us to attend the Mkosi ceremony. Your father thinks it is a waste of time, but I insisted that we attend. My ears tell me the Mkosi ceremony is the most important of all Sesu festivals, one in which all the Sesu attend to confirm the soul of their nation. We will have a chance to see what the Sesu have to offer the Shamfa. Besides, if would be an insult if we did not attend."

They walked together silently, enjoying the coolness of the day. Inaamdura found her mother's company best when they didn't speak. She felt close to her in those quiet moments, sharing the love that she knew her mother would never express verbally for it was not her way. She was the perfect Bonga wife, bred to lead her husband to greatness. While her father performed the ceremonies and made the speeches all men desired of their kings, it was Azana who bore the burden of running the nation as she ran her home. She made the decisions of the kingdom; Muchese made sure they were carried out. The nation wore a Shamfa face, but it was ruled by a Bonga hand.

Her mother broke the silence as always.

"You will accompany your father and me to Sesuland. Amadika will remain here."

"Shouldn't she go as well?" Inaamdura asked. "It is she he is to marry."

"The Sesu are not like us, daughter. Their way of life is simple and hard. It is not the life for a Bonga wife, but we all must make sacrifices for the pride of our family. If Amadika sees what her future holds too soon, she will cause difficulty."

Inaamdura stopped to watch a thorn bird land in the acacia, working its way through the dangerous thorns with ease.

"We will leave in two weeks," Azana said. "Make sure you handle your affairs."

"I will, momma."

"Good. Now leave me to my garden. I wish to feed the birds."

Inaamdura happily withdrew, leaving her mother to her joy. Her relief was short-lived. Twaambo waited for her draped in Shamfa warrior regalia, his thick legs spread in a powerful stance and his right fist pressed into his hip. He was as serious as her mother, but held none of her solemn ways. In fact, Twaambo was very un-Shamfa like. His dark brown eyes were intense; his brows always close together as if in constant contemplation. She could not deny that he was handsome, but there was no difficulty in reserving her emotions towards him. Of course she would marry him, but she did not like him and she suspected she never would.

"Hello, Twaambo," she said.

"Inaamdura, it is good to see you."

Inaamdura walked past Twaambo and he followed.

"What are you doing here?" she asked.

"There is something I wish to show you."

Inaamdura turned to look at her fiancé, flashing a wicked smile.

"I cannot see that until we marry."

Twaambo looked shocked. "I did not mean..."

Inaamdura laughed. "I know, Twaambo. Now what is it you wish to show me?"

"It is not here. I must take you there. It will require a week's travel. I have talked to Muchese and he has given his permission. The proper escorts will accompany us, of course, and a company of my finest warriors will join us as well."

"I cannot go," Inaamdura said.

"You haven't asked what I wish to show you."

Inaamdura stopped in the courtyard, grasping Twaambo's hands in hers.

"Our family had been invited to attend the Mkosi ceremony in Sesuland. My mother asked that I accompany her."

"It is not your place to go," Twaambo said angrily.

"It is not you place to question the decision of the Queen Mother," Inaamdura snapped.

Twaambo backed down, but only slightly.

"I agree, but isn't it odd that the daughter destined to marry the inkosi does not attend his people's most sacred celebration?"

"Amadika will attend many Mkosi celebrations in the future."

"The Sesu are not worthy of the Shamfa's attention," Twaambo spat. "Give me two regiments and one dry season and the Sesu would no longer be worth our time."

"You are the perfect diplomat," Inaamdura said with a smile.

"I would be angry with you if you weren't so beautiful," Twaambo replied. He squeezed her hand and Inaamdura feigned a blush.

"You should leave, Twaambo. I have much to do before I leave and you are a distraction; a pleasant distraction, but one just the same."

Twaambo bowed. "You will go with me when you return?"

"Yes, Twaambo, I will. Now go."

Twaambo left the courtyard. Inaamdura watched him, trying her best to summon some kind of emotion towards her future husband with no success. She understood the words of her mother and she saw the wisdom in them, but she knew her mother did not always heed her own words. She loved her father. She would not admit it, but she saw it in her mother's eyes when she looked at him.

She stepped into the dim light of the Queen's House, the living quarters of the Yellow Palace, following the carpeted floors to the ironwood staircase leading to her room. She had chosen the smallest room of the palace as her own, preferring the small space to a large expanse begging to be filled. Her taste were modest, her room possessing a small bed, two chest of drawers for her small wardrobe and an elaborately carved mahogany chest. The one window of the room looked out to the mountains where she would gaze at the cloudy peaks for hours. She sat before the portal, looking out onto them again. She wondered how long they had watched indifferently over the coming and going of men and beasts, witnessing the world change while they remained the same; silent, powerful and unmoving. One day she would rule an empire as strong as the mountains, a dynasty that would outlive its founders. Twaambo was a strong and ambition man, although she worried about his aggressive streak. It would take time, but he would eventually carve out his own land to the east of Shamfa among grasslands and forest of the highlands. They would rule together, in time challenging the Shamfa and the Bonga for dominance of the valley. This was her secret ambition, to sit in the garden with her mother not as an obedient daughter, but as an equal.

"Inaamdura?"

Amadika stuck her head into the room, her worried frown ruining an otherwise pretty face. She stepped inside, shuffling to her sister's bed to sit. Amadika was the sister that looked like the child of Muchese and Azana, possessing the sweet, child-like face of her father and the feminine voluptuousness of her mother. Her ways were a mix as well, sometimes playful and energetic, sometimes solemn and serious. She also possessed a sense of dread which was uniquely hers, a trait that annoyed Inaamdura to no end.

Inaamdura turned and smiled. "Hello, little sister."

"Don't use your charms on me," Amadika snapped. "I'm not one of your dogs sniffing about. Twaambo told me you going to Sesuland with mamma and baba."

Inaamdura sat silent while she fought to control her anger. Twaambo would pay for this, but first she would deal with Amadika.

"Inkosi Dingane has invited mother and father to the Mkosi ceremony. Mother asked that I accompany them."

Amadika slammed her fist on the bed. "Why was I not told? I'm the one promised to marry Dingane. I should go, not you!"

"Listen to you," Inaamdura admonished. "You sound like Bikita. That's the reason mother did not ask you to go. The last thing she needs is for you to get in front of the inkosi have one of your fits."

"And what if I do? At least he'll know I don't want to marry him."

Inaamdura felt pain rising in the back of her head. "You would jeopardize the alliance between Shamfa and Sesuland?"

"Twaambo says we don't need the Sesu," Amadika answered. "He says we could break them like sticks if they attacked Shamfa."

"Twaambo is no expert on war," Inaamdura replied. "How many battles has he won? How many lands has he conquered? If mother believes the Sesu are necessary allies they will be so. Don't let Twaambo's ego infect your reason. Remember your duty."

Amadika face became composed. "Twaambo deserves a woman that believes in him."

So there it was. She always knew of Amadika's infatuation with Twaambo as a child, but apparently that infatuation had lingered. She was not about to be dragged into a fight with her sister about a man, let alone Twaambo.

"If I tell you something, you must keep it a secret," Inaamdura said.

Amadika looked skeptical. "What?"

"Promise me you won't tell anyone, not even Twaambo."

Her sister hesitated. "I won't tell him."

"The purpose of our journey is to determine whether the Sesu are worthy allies. Most of all, mother wishes to meet Dingane face to face to determine whether he is a suitable match for you."

Amadika's eyes brightened. "Really?"

"Yes. It is important for any alliance to be as strong as possible. If you and Dingane are not a good match, the alliance will fail."

"I hear the Sesu are savages," Amadika whispered. "They still live in grass huts and the men have as many wives as they can afford. It's disgusting."

Inaamdura place a light touch on Amadika's shoulder. "I will look out for you, little sister. If Dingane is just one speck less the man Twaambo is, I will speak strongly against him."

"Thank you Rah-Rah," Amadika said as she hugged her.

"Now go," Inaamdura ordered. "I need a nap."

Amadika hugged her again and pranced from her room. Inaamdura waited until she knew her sister was far away before snatching up a brush from her vanity and hurling it across the room. Amadika tried her patience to no end. She refused to accept the fact that her future had been decided. She would marry Dingane no matter what mother thought of him. The deal had been struck; there was no going back. Twaambo was not an option. It was time for her to grow up and face facts; maybe her marriage to Dingane would be the slap to bring her to her senses. Inaamdura left her chair and fell into her bed face first and arms spread, embracing the mattress like a long lost love. She tried to sleep but her stomach fluttered as she thought of seeing the Sesu for the first time. Were they the savages everyone thought they were, or were they equal to the Shamfa in culture and power? She hoped for Amadika's sake the latter was true.

The days leading to their journey passed quickly for Inaamdura. Azana decided to put her in charge of selecting the entourage that would accompany them to Sesuland. It was a test to determine if she was astute in Shamfa politics and Inaamdura approached the task carefully. She kept the group small, 10 families total. The Shamfa families outnumbered the Bonga as a reminder to the Bonga of their lower status. She selected three members from each family; an elder, a warrior and an attendant. Her only difficulty was Twaambo's family. His father, Sipole Sishokwe was an obvious selection. He was her father's closest friend and ally. By right the warrior should have been Twaambo, but he would not go. He would be as volatile as Amadika and sure to cause trouble. She left the task of Twaambo's refusal to her mother who handled the situation calmly yet stern, leaving neither father nor son in a position to argue the decision. In the end her mother showed her approval by sending her a flower from her garden, a beautiful protea that she placed in a jade vase on the chest by her window.

The caravan assembled at the stone road surrounding the Yellow Palace outside the King's Wall. Each family supplied its own ox drawn wagon, each transport covered by a canvas depicting the family patterns. Muchese's wagon was yellow, the only wagon constructed entirely of wood strengthened by protective metal strips. The huge vehicle was tied to six oxen bred especially to pull the tremendous weight. During war the wagon served as Muchese's command hut, but on this day its stark interior had given way to a woman's touch. The supply wagons had been loaded with enough provisions to feed them for the entire journey even though they expected Sesu hospitality once they reached the ceremony. If that occurred they would share what they had left with the less fortunate on their return trip through Sesuland. The gesture would not be forgotten and would leave a good impression on the common folk from which many of Dingane's warriors originated. One company of warriors was selected to provide protection for them. They were the Twon, her father's personal company consisting of warriors from the main Shamfa clans. Each man brought three mounts; a stallion, a mare and a donkey for provisions. They were impressive in their leather caps and breastplates, the chain mail sleeves extending beyond the short sleeved protection. Metal studded strips of leather hung down over most of their riding pants, with leather boots protecting their legs up to the knees. Half the company was positioned at the head of the train, the other half at the rear. They sat stoically, waiting with the others for Muchese and Azana to emerge from the palace.

A formal announcement had not been made concerning the journey but the throng appeared just the same, lining the eastern avenue originating at the King's wall. The road passed through the main market, the merchant district and Bonga district before emerging through the Eastern gates out into the grasslands. People jostled for position on the road's edge to see the train, fist fights erupting as tempers grew short and the temperature rose.

Muchese stood in the window, looking down on the agitated crowd. Inaamdura watched her father for the indication that they should leave but he seemed in no particular hurry. He looked down at the restless crowd and smiled.

"Can you hear them?" he asked her. He turned to show the brilliant smile that was the trait of his clan, a countenance that Bikita had inherited and Amadika tried to imitate.

"They call for you, baba," she said.

Her mother sat on the lounge, her face showing her displeasure.

"Are you done toying with your people?"

Muchese smiled at his wife despite her remark.

"You are a brilliant woman but you know nothing of ceremony. The people need spectacle. They need to wait impatiently to see their king, for they know their king blesses them with his presence."

"Then bless them, my husband. The day grows short and we have much ground to cover before nightfall."

Muchese pouted then left the window. He was dressed in parade garments, a golden headring with a bull head symbol in the center. He was bare-chested with braided golden armbands encircling each bicep. Gilded rings adorned every finger, each shaped in the symbol of the Shamfa clans. His black toga fell to his sandaled feet. He left the room; Inaamdura and her mother close behind. Twon escorts met them as they entered the courtyard, leading them through the palace gates and to the awaiting wagon. They opened the doors but Muchese refused to enter.

"You two get inside," he commanded. Inaamdura was puzzled, which showed on her face.

"Ceremony, my daughter," he said.

Azana rolled her eyes and entered the wagon. Inaamdura followed, sitting on the calfskin bench closest to a viewing port. She watched as her father walked up to the ox driver and took his whip. He snapped the whip and the wagon lurched, Inaamdura falling onto the bench. She looked at her mother and she shrugged.

The families saw them approach and their warriors banged their shields in approval. A roar rose from the crowd and the people surged forward to view Muchese. The line of warriors held firm, keeping the East Road clear for the train. Drummers played furiously, accompanied by a host of bembira players and the voices of thousands of Shamfa and Bonga. They followed the train through the King's market where the merchants had closed their shops in honor of the day. The train crept deliberately through the city, eventually passing through the massive iron doors of the fortified wall. Muchese continued to lead his wagon until they were out of sight of the city. The caravan halted and he returned the ox driver's whip. His warriors helped him into the wagon.

"We can make good time now," Azana said.

"My lovely wife is always so serious," Muchese said as he approached her. He sat hard beside her and kissed her full on the mouth. Azana shoved him away playfully, slapping him lightly on the shoulder.

"Muchese! This is no time for play!"

Muchese kissed her again then fled to Inaamdura's side.

"Look, Dura. You are looking at a sight as rare as a hyena with a beard. It is a Bonga woman that truly loves her husband!"

"Sometimes I wish I didn't," Azana replied. "I would leave you and watch this village you call a kingdom crumble."

"That it would without your stern hand," Muchese admitted. "Inaamdura, ride with our warriors. Your mother and I have things to discuss."

"Yes, father." She signaled the ox driver from the portal and the wagon halted. A horse waited for her when she exited the wagon, held in place by Sipole himself.

"Come," he said. "I was looking forward to riding with you."

"Thank you, uncle." Inaamdura climbed onto the mount and rode off at a trot with her future father in law.

"You know I am angry with you," he said. "Twaambo should be here protecting you and serving me."

"It was my mother's decision," Inaamdura replied.

"Nonsense. I know Azana well, and she could care less if Twaambo accompanied us. You told her he could not go."

Inaamdura decided not to play coy. "Yes, I did."

Sipole sniffed. "Twaambo told me of his conversation with you and Amadika. I admit my son talks too much, but it was not your place to punish him. You should have come to me."

There was a hint of anger in Sipole's voice which told her she had made the right decision. Sipole only demanded Twaambo's council in matters of war.

"I apologize for my rashness," she said. "I miss Twaambo's company as much as you, uncle. I will make it up to you both when we return to Kampera."

Sipole nodded then changed the subject. "This journey will not be so pleasant once the road ends. The grasslands are not as smooth, and Sesuland is filled with hills, rocks and rivers. You'll be glad you took a horse by the time we get to Selike."

"Is that the capital city?"

Sipole laughed. "City is a relative term. To the Sesu it is a metropolis, but to you it will appear a maze of villages. The Sesu have no need for cities. They have no goods to trade and their craftsmanship is limited to their clothes, weapons and trinkets. They value nothing but their cattle and their honor. I still don't understand why an alliance with them is so important."

"Weren't the Shamfa once the same as the Sesu?" she asked.

Sipole glanced at her with a respectful eye. "Yes we were, but that is why Disingwayo broke away and led us to where we are today. He saw the potential in us and knew it would not be fulfilled adhering to the old way."

Inaamdura had listen to her father tell the story of Disingwayo, "The Banished One," and how he forged the Shamfa in the shadow of the mountains and on the backs of the Bonga. It must have been an exciting time, full of danger and uncertainty. She often imagined herself living in those times as Disingwayo's Great Wife, fighting side by side with her husband and helping him build an empire between the mountains and the river. She hoped the same future waited for her with Twaambo.

"Twaambo has found his destiny on the other side of the mountains," Sipole continued.

"What?" Inaamdura eyes went wide.

Sipole looked at her then laughed. "Oh, I'm sorry. He wanted to show you himself. I guess I spoiled the surprise."

"He said he had something to show me," she said.

"I will speak no further," Sipole finished. "I have said enough."

By nightfall they were near the frontier, the land claimed by both Sesuland and Shamfa. The road had faded away hours ago but so far the ground was smooth enough to continue at a steady pace. The wagons were circled and camp set up for the night. Inaamdura returned to her father's wagon exhausted but happy. Sipole's slip had her mind racing as she thought of the possibility of a new land, an unexplored country open to the rule of Twaambo and herself. She wished she had stayed in Kampera and followed her fiancé to this new world and her new future. Sesuland suddenly felt vile in her mouth, like a sour fruit that once held the promise of sweetness. She would be sure to visit Twaambo as soon as she returned. There seemed to be much they needed to discuss.

She found her mother and father sitting outside the wagon on their stools, both holding long sticks in their hands. They seemed to be doodling in the dirt, drawing lines and circles with exuberant gestures and excited voices.

"Who in their right mind would want to take this road?" her mother said.

"The smart warrior," Muchese replied. "The key to victory is to do the unexpected. History is replete with leaders who thought their people were safe because of a false belief. The raging river is always passable, the impenetrable forest is penetrable, and the highest mountain will someday be climbed."

Inaamdura saw a crude map of Uhuru traced into the dirt, the major cities marked with a simple dot. Muchese was attempting to draw a line through Sesuland to Mawenaland, but Azana kept erasing the line with her right foot.

"Why must you always disagree with me?" her mother asked. "Haven't I given you great council since the day we joined?"

"Yes you have, Azana. But you must understand that war is as much about chance as it is about logic. Sometimes one must take a chance to be victorious."

Inaamdura cleared her throat to announce her presence.

"Come to me, child," her mother said. "Your father is teaching me the science of insanity."

They spent the rest of the night feasting, discussing, arguing and laughing. Inaamdura tired before them both and went to sleep early. The sun was weak in the clear sky when a sudden jolt of the wagon woke her; she sat up to see her mother and father were not in the wagon. She dressed quickly and went outside. The ox driver was hastily hitching the oxen to the wagon.

"Where are my mother and father?" she asked.

"They are ahead with the others. They went out to meet with

the Sesu."

"The Sesu are here?"

The ox driver smiled. He was naked except for his loincloth, a narrow short man with hard muscles and wrinkled skin.

"The Sesu always come in the dawn," he said. "They believe their magic is stronger then. It is also the time they choose to attack."

Inaamdura ran to the center of the wagon circle. Her father sat on his royal stool flanked by her mother and Sipole. The other nobles stood behind them, their attendants holding their family icons. The Twon formed two lines on either side of the nobles, fully armed and emotionless.

Inaamdura came to her mother's side and finally saw them. She counted ten warriors, each man covered in elaborate outfits of cow tails that hung from their necks, arms, waists and legs. Each man wore a plume of feathers on their heads, some large enough to obscure their faces, other with a simple arrangement in the back and a single feather in the front. The man in front was a towering figure, his broad chin shadowed with a grey-black beard. His balding head barely held his head ring, the remaining hairs woven around it to hold it in place. His garments were understated compared to his companions; a single stork feather rose from the front of his leopard head band, a cluster of lourie feathers adorning the back. A leopard claw necklace encircled his neck. He regarded Inaamdura for a moment then turned his attention back to Muchese.

"As I said, your wagons will slow us down. Dingane sent us as an escort, but we do not wish to be late for the ceremony."

"I understand your concern, Madikane," Muchese said. "We are honored that Inkosi Dingane chose to send an induna of such a high rank to escort us to Selike. We would feel terrible if our cumbersome caravan should delay your arrival. But our wagons contain tribute to your inkosi that we would be embarrassed to enter your royal kraal without."

Madikane stood silent, rubbing his grizzled chin. "You can bring the wagons, but we must leave now. We're two days from

Selike, but with the wagons it will take us five. Send a messenger when you are ready to depart. We will await you at the Mpaza."

Madikane brought his right hand across and hit his chest with his fist. Muchese and the other men returned the gesture. The Sesu sprang to their feet and Madikane led them away, but not before taking another glance at Inaamdura.

"Well, that was interesting," Muchese said as he rose from his stool. "I didn't expect them so soon."

"They have probably been following us for days," Sipole replied. "They were waiting for the right moment to approach us."

"The Twon have that effect on people," Muchese said. "They are a fearsome group."

Sipole laughed. "We are at the border of Sesuland. Madikane could care less about the Twon."

"Enough of this," Muchese said, clearly irritated by Sipole's words. "We must break camp. Our hosts are waiting."

Inaamdura was so involved in her father and Sipole's squabbling she did not notice her mother until she spoke.

"What did you think of the Sesu?" she asked.

"Oh, mother, I didn't see you."

"What did you think?"

Inaamdura could not hide her feelings. "They were impressive."

"Madikane seemed to think the same of you."

"He noticed that I was late, nothing more."

"I don't have to tell you the effect you have on men," her mother said. "Stay close to your father and the Twon. I don't trust these Sesu."

Sipole's words were proven true as they approached the Mpanza River. The massive Sesu encampment sprawled on both banks. Naked children shouted as the train was spotted and the warriors broke away immediately. Inaamdura was fascinated with how fast they ran, charging up the hill and surrounding the wagons before the Twon could take position around Muchese's wagon. Madikane was the first to reach them.

"You must stay among yourselves," he advised. "The Mkosi is a proud time for the Sesu, and nothing would be prouder than a warrior killing an enemy on his way to pay respect to the inkosi."

"What of your men surrounding us?" her father asked.

"They will obey my orders as long as you do. Stay with your people until we reach Selike."

Madikane was about to leave when he saw Inaamdura. This time his stare was deliberate.

"This is my daughter, Inaamdura," Muchese said, his voice tight.

"Is this the one promised to Dingane?"

"No."

Madikane smiled. "Good."

He turned and marched away. His men formed a perimeter around the wagons.

Muchese turned to her, his face serious. "Get inside the wagon, Inaamdura. I want you to stay there until we reach Selike."

"But baba, the wagon is hot and I cannot see well."

"Get inside the wagon!" he shouted.

Inaamdura was stunned. She couldn't remember the last time her father yelled at her. She backed away from him then turned and ran to the wagon. She clamored inside and was greeted by her mother.

"Your father is doing what is best for you."

"I am not afraid."

"This has nothing to do with being afraid. Madikane is taken with you. I have given one of my daughters to the Sesu and I will not give another."

Inaamdura felt a chill like the mountain winds. She sat, resigned to watch the journey to Selike from inside the royal wagon.

And what a journey it was. The wagons did slow down the procession, but in truth the Sesu didn't seem to mind. They set out in early morning, a chorus of drums and voices calling for the departure. The warriors and their attendants led the way, followed by their attendants. The women followed, the married women covered in cotton cloth dressed with multi-colored beads adorning their necks and ears. The single girls wore only a small beaded skirt around their waists, their breasts exposed. They all walked together and they sang the entire day. The warriors sang first, then the boys, the married women, the single women and the old. As soon as one group was done the other began. Inaamdura did not understand the words, but the feeling was intoxicating. She spied what she could through the wagon vents, but had a better view at night when she was allowed from the wagon. She ate quickly then ran to the wagon perimeter to watch the Sesu celebrate throughout the night, the warriors martial steps athletic and threatening, the single women moving their bodies to attract the attention of the single warriors. She watched them until her mother forced her back into the wagon.

As they drew closer to Selike they met other bands of Sesu heading to the ceremony. The volume of the singing increased as the bands joined together, the clans greeting each other as family. The warriors were the exception. The rivalry between the regiments was immediate. The warrior danced before each other, their movement more threatening and aggressive. The Shamfa were introduced to a more ominous tradition among the Sesu; the stick fight. Warriors from different regiments would face each other in a circle of bodies, brandishing long sticks with small shields. After a round of boasting and dancing they would attack each other in a blur, striking at their opponent's body and occasionally taking a swing at the head. Some warriors dropped their stick and conceded to their opponent, who would help the man to his feet in good spirits. Others would fight until a blow to the head knocked them unconscious. The victor would immediately drop his stick and tend to the defeated one, a gesture that was approved by the losing regiment. Inaamdura watched as much as she could, fascinated by the endless energy of the Sesu. At night when she was allowed outside the wagon she would hurry to the edge of the encampment and sit, watching the Sesu under the protection of a squad of Twon.

By the fourth day their journey to Selike had become a procession of thousands. For as far as she could see in every direction were Sesu men, women and children, walking and singing. The stick fighting had ceased; the warriors, women, girls and boys all sang the same song. They swayed like grass with the wind, each person in perfect time with the person beside him or her. Inaamdura found herself moving with them despite the jolting ride inside the wagon. That night as she sat at the wagon boundary with the Twon, Madikane approached. He was alone and without his weapons, a dagga pipe in his hand. He offered it to the Twon and they refused with their silence. Inaamdura rose immediately to return to the wagon.

"What do you think of the Sesu?" Madikane called out.

Inaamdura halted. She knew she shouldn't speak to Madikane; it was obvious he was interested in her as a potential wife and neither her mother nor father wished to give him any reason to hope.

"I am destined to marry another," she said. "He is man of great standing in our land, and refusing him would cause a rift that would be difficult to repair."

Madikane took a long drag on his pipe and let the smoke seep from his lips.

"You are not one to waste words, are you?"

Inaamdura shared a smile with Madikane that was more generous than he deserved.

"I find myself growing more impressed with your people every day. You seem to possess a joy the Shamfa lost long ago."

"The Shamfa are our cousins," Madikane replied. "The marriage of Dingane and Amadika only legitimizes what is well known."

He took another drag from the pipe and closed his eyes. "The Shamfa have strayed too far from the Untuni traditions. You have gained much, but you have lost much as well. Maybe the Sesu will teach you how to live again."

One of the Twon guards grasped her arm. "Princess, we must go now."

Inaamdura freed herself from his grasp. "You are here to protect me, not give me orders. You forget your place."

Anger flashed across the Twon's face but was quickly replaced by a subservient smile. He bowed and stepped away.

"What is that song everyone is singing?"

Madikane grinned. "We are calling for the inkosi," he replied. "We are asking him to show himself so we know he is still alive and the Sesu are still favored by Unkulunkulu."

"You know Dingane well?"

"I know Dingane very well. I am his senior induna, chosen because my clan is the strongest in Sesuland. I command six thousand warriors and my kraal is second in size only to the inkosi. Not only do I know Dingane well, he knows me very well also."

Inaamdura picked up a challenging tone in Madikane's voice. He was apparently a powerful man in his own right, which was why he showed an interest in her. He was seeking his own alliance with the Shamfa.

"What does he look like?"

Madikane frowned. "You will have to see for yourself tomorrow." He took another drag on his pipe and walked away, disappearing in the darkness.

Inaamdura began to call him back but realized the futility of the effort. She felt weak; it was late and she needed to rest for tomorrow. She turned to her bodyguards, eyeing the one that tried to rush her earlier.

"Now it is time for us to go."

The Twon took up beside her and they walked back to the royal wagon, Inaamdura anxious for the coming of the next day.

The morning came with a chorus of shrill voices just after dawn. The Sesu women sang a song that resonated throughout the grasslands, waking everyone for the final march to Dingane's royal kraal. Inaamdura sprang awake to their call and was met by the angry stare of her mother.

"You spoke to Madikane last night," she hissed.

"I did," Inaamdura replied. "I told him I was promised to another."

"I told you to stay away from him."

Inaamdura sat up. "I thought you trusted me, mother. I have done nothing to make him think there is an opportunity for an alliance with the Shamfa. It is obvious he wishes to raise his status among the other indunas, and a Bonga wife would give him that edge."

Azana smiled. "You are truly my daughter. I knew he was interested, but I underestimated his intentions."

"Don't worry about me, mother. I have your instincts. I am concerned about Amadika. Are you sure she is strong enough to handle Dingane?"

Azana sat beside Inaamdura and placed her hand on her arm. "As much as I would like to hope, Amadika's marriage to Dingane will not help our cause. The union will make us allies by blood and allow us to focus on other more important matters."

"So she is a gift?" Inaamdura tried to hide the disapproval in her voice. Her failure was reflected in her mother's stern gaze.

"Amadika's fate is as it should be. She is too weak to be an asset to any noble man. She will be a good Sesu wife and bear Dingane many sons. She should be grateful that I find any use for her at all."

Inaamdura had enough of the conversation. "I would like to go outside for a moment before our journey begins, mother. The wagon gets stuffy as they day wears on, so I am grateful for any fresh air I can get."

"Your father has lifted his restriction." Azana rose to her feet. "Since we are so close to the Royal Kraal, he feels Madikane will behave himself for the remainder of the journey. You can ride with us."

Inaamdura smiled; the news of her freedom was enough to cool her down. She followed her mother out of the wagon and ran to her mare tethered to the provision wagon. She mounted and rode back to the royal wagon to join her mother and father. They rode to the front of the train and took their place at the center of the Shamfa royal procession.

They were part of a massive human herd, an endless march of

thousands of Sesu headed to a sacred destination. As they crossed the Nzolo River the singing resumed, a song that begged for the inkosi to show himself to his people. They walked up the hill before them, the gentle slope an easy climb for the multitude. Inaamdura felt the excitement rise in her with every step. She was no longer an observer; she was a follower, a part of a ceremony she knew nothing of but anticipated more that anything in her short life. By the time they reached the crest of the hill she thought she might scream to release the tension inside her. When she looked out over the hill at the scene below her, all she could manage was a startled whisper.

Thousands of grass huts covered the land, domiciles so recent they were green with new grass. Columns of smoke spiraled into the sky forming a grey haze over the encampments. Through the smoke she saw the Royal Ikhanda, the kraal of Inkosi Dingane. It covered the entire face of the hill, the outer thorn fence tracing a circle three miles at its widest point and ending at the entrance to the ceremonial grounds. An inner fence encircled the ceremony courtyard. At the north end of the courtyard was the cattle pen holding the famous white cattle of the Sesu inkosi. Above the cattle pen was a smaller cluster of huts, the largest occupying a space close to the entrance to the pen. Thousand of huts rested between the outer kraal and the cattle pen wall.

The Shamfa followed their Sesu companions to a clearing left of the royal kraal. The regiments separated, each claiming an area based on its rank. Madikane's warriors signaled the Shamfa to follow them. They made their way through the multitudes on a ragged road leading to the Royal Kraal. Madikane's clan halted outside the thorn fence and set up camp, the women and children immediately gathering grass to build their huts. The Shamfa circled their wagons and set up their camp.

Inaamdura followed her mother and father to Madikane. The induna sat below an acacia with his senior warriors while his wives labored on the huts. Muchese dismounted and approached the men with great ceremony.

"Induna Madikane, I thank you for your protection during our long journey. I will be sure to share my complements with Dingane when we meet later today."

"You will not see the Inkosi today," Madikane replied. The Mkosi ceremony begins at first light tomorrow and will continue for three days. Dingane will receive you after the ceremony is complete. He has asked that I assist you until then."

Muchese was not happy. "I understand the importance of your ceremony, but I too have a kingdom to rule, and any time I spend away from my duties is a disservice to my people. If Dingane would give us just a moment of his time it will insure that we had the opportunity to discuss important matters if for some reason we must leave before the ceremony's end."

Madikane stood to face Muchese. The Twon moved to flank their leader and Madikane's warriors came to their feet.

"No one can see the inkosi before the ceremony. If your duties are more important than your alliance with the Sesu, leave now and bother us no further. I for one will not try to stop you. I warn you though; Dingane will see your early departure as an insult."

Inaamdura was puzzled by her father's impatience. It was not his way to hurry a diplomatic opportunity, especially one involving someone as important as Dingane.

"I ask your pardon," her father said. "We will retire to our wagons and look forward to our meeting with the inkosi."

They mounted and rode back to their camp. Inaamdura pulled her mare close to her father, hoping he would explain his hastiness. He said nothing, his mouth set in a rare frown as he leaned forward on his stallion. Once they reached the wagons he dismounted quickly and scurried to the royal wagon, closing the door hard behind him.

Inaamdura turned to her mother, her expression asking the question she could not speak.

"He is afraid of them," Azana said. "He has seen enough to realize the Sesu are a larger threat than he anticipated."

"What do you think?" Inaamdura asked.

"I am concerned," she admitted. "It is apparent my eyes and

ears see and hear both ways. I had no knowledge that the Sesu were this numerous. I fear we may have played the wrong hand with these people. We may have to fight them despite the marriage alliance."

The thought of the Shamfa at war with the Sesu made her stomach churn. Her sister would be a hostage among the Sesu if that occurred, and she was not sure the Shamfa could defeat such a large and virile people.

"It might be best we wait until we meet Dingane before we make any assumptions," she replied. "His ambitions may not extend to Shamfaland."

"We have decided as much," her mother replied. "Believe me daughter, if this Dingane reveals himself as a person we cannot trust, there will be no marriage. The inkosi of the Sesu may find himself a head short of his ambitions."

Azana placed a reassuring hand on Inaamdura's shoulder. "Come, Dura. Let us rest. I hear the Mkosi is a long monotonous thing. We must not be caught snoozing by our hosts."

The day crept by like a bush snail. Inaamdura scampered around the wagon camp too excited to sleep as she watched the Sesu go about their daily routines.. Many of the people stared at the wagons, a mode of transportation uncommon among the Sesu. Children ran up to her to play despite their parents protests, but they were run away by the warriors guarding the wagons. The singing was more random, bursting out unexpectedly among the young girls and the warriors. No songs filled the day like those on the march. Inaamdura suspected the Sesu were saving their energies for the next three days. She decided to go to sleep as well. She planned to stay awake for the entire ceremony and knew she needed the rest. The royal wagon was too hot for sleep, so she ordered a servant to make her a bed beneath the wagon to protect her from the sun and the curious. Inaamdura crawled onto her bead and tried to imagine what she would experience over the next three days as the Sesu celebrated these sacred days.

The sound of footsteps woke her. Inaamdura peered from

under the wagon and saw movement in the distance. She crawled out to see most of the camp asleep except for a few Twon on guard duty. The shuffling came from outside their camp; she stood and walked to the perimeter to find the source of the commotion.

She startled the guards as she approached.

Bati, the senior guard approached. "How can I help you, princess?" he asked.

"What is going on?"

Bati shrugged. "Who knows with these monkeys? Some of the warriors are gathering before the entrance of Dingane's kraal."

Inaamdura straightened her back and assumed a regal pose. "Show me."

Bati led her to a place where the warriors were in full view. They were covered in cow tails and feathers more grand than the ones she saw on the march. A bonfire burned in the center of Dingane's kraal surrounded by figures that moved in time to a rhythm that carried on the wind down to her ears. The warriors did not move; they stood like trees, as if their feet held onto the ground like roots. The drumming was joined by a low chant from the figures around the bonfire and the warriors marched into the kraal, swaying from side to side in a trance-like motion. Inaamdura watched them make their way up the avenue into the ceremonial area, holding her breath like a child watching something sacred for the first time.

She never saw the warriors. Her concentration was broken by grunts and she turned away from the spectacle to see her Twon bodyguards lying on the ground grimacing. A band of Sesu warriors stood over them; Madikane stared at her with his hungry eyes.

"This is not for you to see," he stated. "Go back under your wagon."

For a brief moment Inaamdura reeled from true terror. Her protection lay at her feet and Madikane stood before her with his men. He could take her if he wanted; there was no one to stop him. She would have to control the situation.

"You had no right to attack my men," she said. "They did not know this was a sacred ceremony."

"They could have asked," Madikane said, smiling.

"Dingane asked you to watch over us. Is this the way you treat guests?"

Sounds rose from the camp. Inaamdura glanced backwards and saw more Twon coming her way, lead by her father.

"Warn the others," Madikane said. He reached out and grabbed her by the wrist, squeezing until it hurt. "This ceremony is not for you."

Inaamdura managed to snatch her arm away which seemed to amuse Madikane. He raised his assegai and his men followed him into the darkness.

This time her father was more relieved than angry.

"What did that man do?" he demanded.

"We saw a procession of warriors into Dingane's kraal," Inaamdura replied. "Madikane said it was not for us to see. Our Twon paid for their curiosity."

"Are you okay?"

"I am fine, father." Inaamdura strode back to the wagon and crawled back under with as much dignity she as she could display. Once on her cot, she broke out in a sweat, her body trembling. Madikane was beginning to scare her despite her resolve against fear. She decided it would be better for her and the Shamfa party that they get close to Dingane as soon as possible, before Madikane made his own decision on their fate.

The intense morning sun rose with the voices of Sesu. The melody wrapped around Inaamdura and woke her, its beauty a salve to the night's confrontation. Everyone in the camp was awake, preparing themselves absently while the voices of the Sesu women held their attention. Inaamdura's attendants swarmed around her, moving her to a secluded area surrounded by heavy cloth. Inside was her bathing tub, the perfumed wood adding its aroma to the singing. Inaamdura's attendants undressed her and she stepped into the soothing warm water. The attendants scrubbed her quickly, their complements on her beauty barely noticed. She sensed this day; there was an energy that seemed to hang in the air. She was trying to understand what she felt when one of her attendant's voices finally broke through her musing.

My princess, will you wear this?"

Inaamdura looked at the squat woman. She held a small beaded skirt in her hands, the type worn by the single Sesu women.

"Who gave you this?" she asked.

"Induna Madikane," she replied. "He said all must follow Sesu tradition during the Mkosi ceremony."

Inaamdura harbored no modesty, but she was not about to give Madikane a glimpse of what he could never have.

"Take it away," she commanded. The attendants dressed her in traditional Shamfa ceremonial clothing. The beads encircling her neck were uncomfortable, but she was pleased to finally be able to wear a full set like her mother. Massive gold leaf earrings dangled from her ears, presents from Sipole. When she stepped from behind the curtain, her mother and father were waiting.

"My beautiful daughter," Muchese exclaimed. "Come, the warriors are waiting to escort us to Dingane's kraal."

Her mother nodded her approval and they proceeded to the wagon circle edge. Madikane and his warriors waited, donned in their finest cow tails and feathers, their shields groomed and assegai blades gleaming in the morning light. Madikane looked at her and she saw the disappointment in his eyes.

"Induna, we are ready," her father announced. Madikane nodded and signaled his men. They led the way to the kraal entrance, the Shamfa walking in single file behind Muchese. They were among the first groups to enter the kraal, following a procession of warriors and elders of higher rank. The thorn fence walls were higher than she realized, towering easily over the tallest of Madikane's men. Sunlight disappeared as they entered the corridor and Inaamdura felt an unwelcome hand on her shoulder.

"You did not wear my gift," Madikane said.

"I have explained to you my feelings. You would do well to understand."

Madikane laughed. "You are stubborn like a warthog. The man who marries you will bear many scars from your tusks."

When they emerged into the light of the ceremonial grounds Inaamdura was trembling again. The small Shamfa band was surrounded by the might of Sesuland. She realized they were as much captives as they were guests, that any demand the Sesu might impose on them would have to be agreed to or they could be killed. If Madikane asked for her before Dingane, her father could not refuse.

Madikane led them to the front of the gathering. Another thorn fence stood before them separating the courtyard from the royal kraal and Dingane's compound. The inkosi's wives sat on either side of the cattle pen, each draped in leather skirts and shirts covered by exquisite beadwork necklaces, bracelets, and belts. She counted ten wives total, five on either side of the entrance. An empty space was noticeable close to a leopard skin covered stool. This was the position reserved for the Great Wife, the honor her mother and father hoped Amadika would fill. She searched the faces of the other wives wondering if she could spot the fallen wife whose fateful decision had given Dingane the son he craved and condemned him at the same time.

They were led to a clearing to the right of Dingane's stool.

"This is your place of honor," Madikane said. "You should have no trouble seeing the ceremony."

"Many thanks, induna," Muchese replied. The entourage took their seats, a nervousness running through them. No sooner had they seated themselves did the Sesu warriors leap to their feet in unison and began to sing. The song boomed throughout the kraal, ringing in Inaamdura's head. Others on the outside began to sing as well.

"They are calling him," Madikane said, managing to sit beside her. "They are begging him to show himself."

Inaamdura barely heard him. She watched the entrance to the kraal, anticipating Dingane's entrance. She was trembling again, but this time she shook with excitement, not fear. The moment she had waited for was at hand.

Dingane emerged from the royal compound, his entire body wrapped in a suit of woven grass. Only his face was visible and it was a handsome, regal face. His dark brown eyes stared forward as if in a trance, the wrinkles in his forehead giving him the look of wisdom. He held a gilded assegai over his head, the shaft grasped in his left hand, the right hand just below the blade. A single file of elders followed behind him, each covered in white robes decorated by white and red beds. Each walked with a staff topped with a golden figure representing their clan.

Dingane walked past his wives and stopped in front of them. The elders took their places behind him and sat cross-legged on the ground, laying their staffs before them. The inkosi of Sesuland turned slowly to either side, displaying the golden assegai to everyone on the ceremonial ground.

He spoke with a resonant voice that reached down into Inaamdura and grasped her heart.

"Where are my people? Who stands behind me before the ancestors?"

The people responded with the Song of the Inkosi, The Strong Bull. As the Sesu sang the praise of Dingane, Inaamdura knew her life was to change this day. No matter who her parents had chosen, she would marry Dingane. This was the man who would give her an empire. Let Amadika have Twaambo; let the Bonga cry and protest on the broken promise. Her future was not wandering mountain pastures seeking glory. It was in front of her, it surrounded her. Her future was among the Sesu.

Dingane danced, moving his muscular body with the grace of a leopard. He thrust his assegai in mock battle, performing the ritual dance known only by the inkosi. Inaamdura watched him move, drinking in every motion. She wanted to dance with him, matching his martial steps with a dance of joy. When he finally finished she was disappointed. The medicine priests approached him and tore off the grass clothing while chanting. When they were done he stood naked, his chest rising and falling with his exertion.

His wives came to him then, dressing him as they sang, wrapping his leather loincloth around his waist followed by a kilt of bright white brushed cow tails hanging from a belt of red beads. They fastened a breastplate of leopard skin around his chest and clamped golden armbands about his massive biceps. A necklace of leopard claws was secured around his neck. The last of his wives marched to his side, placing his headdress over his head ring, a thick head band of leopard and otter skin, a single stork feather rising from the front. Dingane nodded to her then sat among the elders. He nodded his head and the ceremony continued.

The remainder of the ceremony meant nothing to Inaamdura. The procession of the regiments performing their sacred dances, the homage paid to the ancestors by the elders, even the sacrifice of the black bull by the bare hands of the youngest regiment did not stir her. She could not take her eyes off Dingane. She watched him as he watched the others, fascinated by his every gesture. Somewhere during the ceremony he looked at her for a brief moment, a slight smile on his face. She smiled back and looked away, but she could not deny what she felt. She was so enthralled with him that she did not notice when the ceremony ended. The warriors trailed out of the royal kraal, their voices lifted in song with the other Sesu. The soul of the Sesu had been replenished; Dingane was still favored by the ancestors. The harvest would be bountiful and the raids successful. The Sesu would still be masters of the grasslands.

"Come. It's time to see the inkosi," Madikane ordered.

Muchese was flustered. "Induna, we haven't had time to prepare!"

"It takes no time to say what is on one's heart if those words are true," Madikane replied.

Muchese looked at Azana and his shoulders slumped. "What of our tribute?"

"The inkosi will receive your gifts later," Madikane answered. "Come, we are wasting time."

The Shamfa delegation hastily gathered their possessions and followed Madikane to where Dingane sat with his wives, the elders and his highest ranking indunas. Madikane stood before his inkosi. He dropped to his knees, touched head to the ground then came back to his feet.

"Inkosi, once again the ancestors smile on you and your greatness. I present to you the Shamfa. They have come to pay their respects."

Dingane nodded to Madikane. The warrior took his place behind Madikane with the rest of the indunas. Muchese took this as a sign.

"I am Muchese, inkosi of the Shamfa and friend of the Sesu. It makes me joyous to have been invited to such a powerful ceremony. Surely the ancestors will grant you a bountiful harvest."

Dingane seemed almost annoyed with Muchese's patronizing chatter. His attention went immediately to Inaamdura. Their eyes met and she turned away. Her heart fluttered again and she hid her face behind her hand.

"I am glad you came," Dingane replied. "Most nobles decline our invitation in fear of our land and our people, though you have come despite the warnings. I am honored by your presence."

Madikane leaned forward, whispering in Dingane's ear. Inaamdura went cold inside. He was making his move and there was nothing anyone could do to stop him. Once Dingane made his intentions clear her parents would be in no position to refuse the offer without destroying any chances of alliance with the Sesu.

"Is this the daughter I have heard so much about?" Dingane asked.

"No, inkosi," Muchese replied. "This is my daughter, Inaamdura. She accompanied us as a companion to my wife, Azana."

"Step forward, Inaamdura, so that I might see you better." Inaamdura glanced at her father for his permission. He nodded, his face tight with worry. Inaamdura rose, walking with a grace that only she could display under such circumstances.

"How may I serve you, inkosi?" she asked.

"Madikane tells me you are a smart woman, a true Bonga like your mother."

"I have been raised well," she replied. "Though I cannot say if my strengths are worthy of a noble husband."

"Why is that?"

"My skills have not been tested. I will not have the opportunity until I am married."

Dingane rubbed his chin.

"Tell me about your sister."

Inaamdura hesitated, looking back at her mother and father's anxious faces. She could describe her sister generously, but then she would lose this captivating man sitting before her. She risked causing a rift between the Shamfa and the Bonga if she made her play. She looked at her mother and father one last time before she spoke.

"My sister is a sweet child. She is strong in her likes and dislikes, and she is easily influenced. I am sure she is in love with my betrothed, though she would deny it if you asked her."

"That's interesting, but it's not what I asked you," Dingane said. "Will your sister make a good wife?"

"It depends what type of wife the inkosi wishes. If you wish a woman that will heed Sesu traditions, conform to the ways of her adopted people and bear healthy children, then my sister will make a fine wife. But if you wish a companion, an advisor that will teach the Sesu how build a kingdom in the grass, a wife that can control the operations of the empire that her husband creates, my sister is not the wife for you."

Dingane leaned back on his stool. "Who is this woman that can be such a companion?"

Inaamdura gave Dingane a smile that removed any doubts of her intentions. "I think the inkosi knows the answer to his question."

"Inaamdura, what are you doing?" her father shouted.

Dingane leaned to the side and glared at her father. "I would appreciate your respect while I talk to your daughter."

Inaamdura could not see her father's face, but she was certain it was not pleasant.

"We have settled the marriage arrangement," Muchese protested. "You are to marry Amadika."

Dingane ignored him. "Would you accept me as your husband if I asked?"

"It depends on what the inkosi offered me," Inaamdura replied.

Dingane and his indunas laughed hard at her response. Sipole did not see the humor.

"You are disgracing my son!" he yelled. "Muchese, the Bonga will not tolerate such an insult!"

Dingane jumped to his feet, his face deathly serious. "You may be a man of influence in Shamfa, but you are nothing here. Speak again and my warriors will wash their spears in you."

Again he looked at Inaamdura. "What do you wish?"

"To be your Great Wife," she replied.

"It is yours to have."

Inaamdura knelt before Dingane to cover the weakness in her knees. "If you ask me to be your wife, I will accept."

"Inaamdura, no!" her father pleaded.

"I think your daughter has made her choice, Muchese, and it is my choice as well. I wish to marry your daughter Inaamdura and make her my Great Wife. She will remain among us until the day of the wedding ceremony to learn the ways of her new people."

Dingane stood, passing his gaze among the elders, the indunas and his wives.

"Do you accept the decision of your inkosi?"

A cheer rose among the Sesu, drowning out the protests of the Shamfa delegation. Inaamdura took a deep breath and finally turned to face her people. Her father stared at her, his mouth wide in shock. Sipole glared at her, his intentions clear in his malevolent eyes. She finally looked at her mother. Azana's face was emotionless for a moment, but then her mouth moved and a smile formed on her face. Inaamdura smiled as she read her mother's words.

"Well done, my daughter. Well done."

5))

Obaseki clinched his teeth and closed his eyes, trying his best to hold back the laughter threatening to break free. He sat cross-legged beside his younger cousins on a zebra skinned rug, his arms resting on his knees, his clean shaven head encircled by a thin golden band marking him as a prince. His kente robe hung from one shoulder, the bold yellow, orange and black pattern matching that of his cousins and his grandfather. He tried his best to look regal, but the unexpected grin on his face could not be contained. It wasn't his fault; Lewa was being silly again.

Oba Noncemba cleared his throat and Obaseki managed a few more moments of stillness. His grandfather sat before the royal household flanked by his senior officers. The dry season was coming to an end, the air thick with moisture, the gathering clouds a sign of the coming rains. His grandfather had finally returned from war, but not with the victory he has coveted. For six months he fought relentlessly against the Dumani, driving them from the eastern borders of Mawenaland and into the peaks and valleys of their own soil. He trapped them, positioning his army to deliver the final blow when the plan fell apart. A mistake had been made; a decision that spared the Dumani army from a final crushing defeat and insured that the Dry War would continue into the next year. Worst of all, the blunder had been committed by his own son, Obeseki's uncle Azikiwe.

Lewa sat beside his uncle, making faces at him as he lay prostrate before Noncemba and Kumba. Obaseki snorted and his grandfather jerked his head towards him.

"I am sorry, Grandfather," he said.

Noncemba glared at him then turned his attention back to his son.

"There is no reason to discuss your offense, Azikiwe," he said. "What I and the elders wish to know is why."

Azikiwe raised his head. He was an odd looking man who barely resembled his father. His eyes always seemed locked in a state of shock, giving him a comical look despite his best efforts at a serious countenance. His broad nose was definitely a trait of his father's, but his round face and weak chin was his own. There was no fear in his wide brown eyes as he spoke.

"I positioned my men at the pass as you suggested, but I was concerned about the cliffs over our position. If the Dumani managed to gain the higher ground we would be destroyed. I sent my reserves to cover the paths leading to the cliff tops to prevent such a move."

Kumba, the Mawena commanding general, stepped forward, his large hands folded behind his back. He had removed his tattered kapok uniform and stood before Azikiwe in his leather and steel under armor, his sword still at his side. He was the only person allowed to carry a weapon in Noncemba's presence.

"Your orders were to hold the pass, Azikiwe," he said.

"As I said I was protecting my men from attack from above."

"That's not true," Kumba replied.

"How would you know?" Azikiwe snapped. "I did as I was told."

"You were told to guard the pass with all your men," Kumba retorted. "Why did you send your cavalry away?"

"The cavalry had the best chance to reach the cliffs before Dumani archers could take position."

Kumba paced. "So you made the decision to protect your position?"

Azikiwe shoulders lifted. "Yes I did."

"So you think I am a fool."

"I said no such thing."

"You might as well have," Kumba retorted. "Only a fool would have sent you to block the path without considering the bluffs above you. It was my orders you followed."

"I was not told the cliffs had been considered in the battle plan. If I had been present at the war council, I would have known."

Kumba stopped pacing, looking at Noncemba. He took his position beside the oba and sat.

"You let the Dumani break through to prove a point?" Noncemba asked.

"I did not say that. Had I been privy to the battle plan I would not have divided my forces."

"Your word games are tiresome," Noncemba said. "The ancestors have cursed me with an only son who cares more about his feelings than his family. You are no use to me."

If Noncemba's words stung Azikiwe showed no signs of pain.

"If you gave me the chance to use my talents I would make you proud," Azikiwe responded.

"You cannot display what you don't possess." Noncemba's expression transformed from anger to disgust.

"You've resisted my teaching your whole life, now you jeopardize the existence of our people because of your foolishness."

Azikiwe rose and went closer to his father.

"Let me finish what you began. Give me command of the warriors and I will run the Dumani down and destroy them."

"That opportunity has passed," Noncemba admitted. "You had your chance at the pass, but you chose to make a statement."

The courtyard was silent for too long a moment. Even Lewa was still. She sat beside Azikiwe, her arm resting on his shoulder. Obaseki shook his head angrily at her. She looked back and smiled but did not remove her arm.

"Let everyone hear my words," Noncemba announced. "I decree that my son, Azikiwe, disgraced his family and his people by his actions in battle. For this he will be punished."

Noncemba walked over to his son. Azikiwe prostrated and Noncemba put his left foot on his head.

"Although you have failed me, you are still my son. You will take a regiment of your choosing to the eastern borders. Once there you will build a fort and enforce the boundaries between Mawenaland

and the Kossi. You shall not return from this duty until the Kossi have been defeated or offer terms. If you cannot follow my orders, maybe you will do better by following your own."

Noncemba removed his foot from Azikiwe.

"I will not fail you, baba," Azikiwe promised.

"You already have," Noncemba replied. The oba trudged back to his golden stool and sat heavily on the silk cushions. Lewa stepped back as Azikiwe came to his feet, backing away until he was outside the courtyard. His face remained expressionless as he turned away and disappeared into the streets. Lewa came to Obaseki's side and sat.

"You almost got me in trouble!" he whispered.

"They cannot see me," she replied sweetly. "I am for your eyes only."

"You must behave," he said. "We must respect my grandfather."

"He's not my Oba," Lewa protested.

"Shhh!" His cousins were looking at him and whispering.

The royal family waited as the other noble families left the courtyard in an ordered procession by rank. The royal family dispersed soon afterward, everyone heading for their part of the compound. Obaseki stood with his cousins to leave when he heard his name called.

"Obaseki, come," Noncemba said.

Obaseki clinched his teeth and approached his grandfather, prostrating before him.

"Get up, boy. There are no formalities between you and me."

Obaseki rose with a grin.

"It is because of your mother that I am so lenient with you," Noncemba explained, patting Obaseki on his head. "You are also my eldest heir."

"What about uncle?"

"Apparently you did not understand what happened here today. Your uncle will never be my heir. Even if I wanted to select him it would not be possible now. He has disgraced himself too many times. The elders and the noble families would protest his selection. That brings us to you."

Obaseki's mouth became so dry his response resembled a croak. "Me?"

"Yes, you. Your condition has disturbed me for some time now. When you were a boy your oddities could be explained and ignored. But you are a man now and this problem must be addressed."

Salako stepped forward and Obaseki stepped back. The old man steadied himself with a short walking stick crowned with a ball of gold carved in the shape of a sleeping crocodile. He wore a white robe barely visible under the talismans and gris-gris hanging from his waist and charms dangling from gold chains around his narrow neck. Salako shuffled up to Obaseki and circled him as he always did, shaking his head and waving his horsetail swatter.

"I cannot help him," Salako announced. "His gift is well beyond my understanding. You must seek Fuluke, the Man of the Woods. He will know what to do."

"You must go to this man, Seki," Noncemba said gently. "Maybe he can give us understanding so we can see the benefit of this…talent."

"I don't want to go," Obaseki said. "I can make them go away on my own."

Noncemba rested his chin in his hand. "You have no choice. You will leave in the morning. I suggest you say your goodbyes. I don't know how long this will take, but you may be gone for a long time"

"Grandfather, please."

Noncemba called Obaseki closer. "I don't want to send you to this Fuluke, but I must try to solve this puzzle. This "sight" of yours may be a gift or it may be a curse. I must trust Salako's suggestion. He has served our family for many years and has never led us wrong."

Obaseki dropped his head. His grandfather had been kind to him, kinder than with his own. He would not make a decision that would harm him.

"I will pack my things for the journey," Obaseki said.

"Your servants will do that for you," Noncemba replied.

Obaseki bowed to his grandfather and trudged away. Lewa followed behind him.

"He is sending you away!"

Obaseki shrugged. "There is nothing I can do about it."

"Who is this Fuluke?"

"I don't know. Grandfather thinks he will be able to help me."

Lewa stopped, placing her hands on her hips. "There is nothing wrong with you."

"Let's not talk about it." Obaseki felt queasy. He put his hand on his stomach and rubbed it.

"You are afraid," Lewa said.

He could not deny how he felt. She had been his friend for as long as he had memory, his constant companion for all his years. She had even walked with him during his initiation rites despite his protests.

Obaseki was quiet the rest of the day, wandering about the palace with Lewa tagging along, responding to her questions with short angry answers. Sometimes he wished she would go away and let him have some time to think alone. But she never left unless she chose to, which was when he made her angry. He tried his best to upset her, but she persisted, staying at his side until he went to sleep later that night.

He awoke with the morning drums, his possessions resting at the foot of his bed in a neat pack. Lewa sat at the foot of his bed as always.

"You were very noisy last night," she said.

"I was dreaming.""

"About what?"

"Will you leave me alone?" Obaseki shouted.

"No."

He flung his headrest at her and watched it pass through her, slamming against the wall and breaking.

"See what you made me do? Why don't you just go away?"

Lewa eyes glistened. "Why are you so mad at me?"

"If I didn't see you, I wouldn't have to go away!"

Lewa said nothing, her head sagging. Obaseki's anger trickled away.

"If you didn't see me, I would have to go away." She dropped to her knees, looking at Obaseki with pleading eyes.

"I don't want to go there. I want to stay here with you."

Obaseki looked into Lewa's pleading eyes and sighed. The Spirits talked about there often, most of them afraid to leave the familiarity of Mawenaland for this place that waited for them. Salako told him that all spirits must eventually move closer to Oyo, returning from where they came. But it was Mawena nature to be afraid of the unknown in death, even though they swore their belief in life. So they would linger, living their lives as they had when alive until even that existence no longer satisfied them. That's when they became trouble and had to be driving away.

A bodyguard stuck his head into Obaseki's room. He looked at him oddly, and then quickly formed his expression to one of respect.

"My prince, we are ready to depart," he said. "Oba Noncemba wishes to speak to you before you leave.

Obaseki nodded and the bodyguard left.

"Come on, Lewa. My grandfather waits."

They walked down the bleached white corridor into the central courtyard. His grandfather sat alone under the acacia, fanning himself with his swatter, a kola nut lodged firmly in his jaw. He motioned for Obaseki to sit beside him.

"Your mother was my favorite," he said. "I know a father shouldn't cherish one child over another, but I could not help myself. She was a bright girl, with a smile that shamed the sun and eyes that glittered like stars in the dry season sky. She was strong, too. Not physically strong, but strong of mind and spirit.

"The worst day of my life was when she married Dingane. It was necessary for the Sesu were becoming a nuisance and I did not have the strength or the resources to fight them. I invited Dingane to meet and form an alliance. He suggested a marriage to seal our agreement and he chose Shani to be his wife. I had no choice; they were married and I have not seen her since."

"At least you know what she looks like," Obaseki said.

Noncemba smiled and patted Obaseki's head. "Yes, I do. You have her eyes and her smile, Obaseki. When I look at you I have my daughter back."

A shadow of sadness hung over his grandfather and Obaseki could sense its weight. He continued to sit motionless, watching his grandfather look into the distance with painful eyes.

"Your mother sent you to me to save you," Noncemba finally said. "I tried to raise you as she would, but this sight of yours seems to be getting in the way."

Obaseki felt brave enough to speak. "What I see is real, baba. The Spirits are like you and me.

"I know they are real," Noncemba replied. "But it is not your place to see them. You are of royal blood. Even the Sesu blood that runs in you speaks of a noble past. Leave the Spirits to the medicine-priests. That is why I'm sending you to Fuluke. It is my hope that he will be able to free you of this handicap and send you back in full strength to receive your birthright."

Obaseki could do nothing but drop his head. Lewa was close by, her touch colder than usual. His grandfather's words had frightened her.

"Do whatever this Fuluke tells you, Obaseki. He will not harm you because he knows that if he does he'll have to deal with the fury of the Mawena. There is not enough herbs and spells in the world that could stop me taking my revenge. The more you obey, the faster he will be able to bring you back from the valley of ghosts."

Obaseki resisted the urge to look at Lewa. "I will do as you say, grandfather."

Noncemba signaled one of his servants to step forward. The woman held a rectangle of gold, the bull leopard icon impressed on its surface. The servant hung the necklace around Obaseki's neck and stepped away.

"You wear my symbol," Noncemba said. "This will guarantee you safe passage throughout Mawenaland. Be safe, Obaseki."

"Thank you, grandfather." Obaseki bowed to his grandfather and stood. A rush of sadness overwhelmed him and he lunged, throwing his arms around Noncemba's neck and hugging him tight. Noncemba's eyes widened then closed as he smiled.

"I'll miss you, too," he said. "Come, now. You are a prince."

Obaseki was sure to wipe his eyes before letting his grandfather go. He turned and marched away, Lewa trailing behind him.

"I'm sorry," Lewa said.

"It's not your fault," Obaseki replied. "The ancestors have given me this ability for some reason. I hope Fuluke can show me why."

His escort waited for him beyond the wall. Ten Atuegbu waited, each covered in royal kapok, their swords dangling from their leather shoulder sheaths. Each man held double blade lances. They snapped to attention when they noticed Obaseki, clearing away to reveal a final surprise. A pure white stallion waited, draped in a royal red kapok outfit matching the pattern of the Atuegbu. The saddle straddling the stallion's back was a beautiful object obviously from the saddle smiths of Bosede, polished black leather studded with gold and a horn crowned with cowry shells. Obaseki ran to his mount and clamored onto the horse before his servants could assist him. Lewa approached the beast warily. The horses turned in her direction and snorted, pounding their feet into the dirt nervously. His escorts looked about for the source of their mounts agitation, but they could not see the girl. Lewa backed away, turned and ran, disappearing into crowded street.

Obaseki looked for her as they rode down the broad avenue leading to the western gate, ignoring the praise calls and bows of the people surrounding him. The gate masters manning the ramparts beat their drums in a solemn rhythm that barely covered the shrieking joints of the massive metal gate as it swung open. Obaseki raised in his saddle, scanned the throng for Lewa, his heart beating faster the further they galloped away from the central city. His nervousness increased when he realized Lewa was not the only one missing. They were all gone, every one of them. The Spirits that had shown themselves to him entire life were nowhere to been seen.

"I must go back," Obaseki whispered. "I must go back to the palace."

The leader of the escort, a serious man with deep eyes and a stern face, rode up to his side.

"My prince, what is the matter?"

Obaseki reached out to the escort, almost falling off his horse.

"Dapo, I have to go back."

Dapo's expression softened. "I'm sorry, prince. Oba Noncemba gave me specific orders to deliver you to Fuluke. I cannot let you go back."

Obaseki pushed Dapo away and grabbed the reins of his mount. Dapo signaled his men and they crowded around Obaseki, hemming him in.

"Let me go! I order you to let me pass."

"I am sorry, my prince. I cannot."

Dapo nodded his head and Obaseki was swept off his horse by a strong arm. He tried to struggle but the man was too strong. He was in the grasp of Malomo, a hulking figure known throughout Mawenaland for his strength. He tied Obaseki's hands quickly then placed him back on his horse. Dapo grabbed the reins.

The fight left him as suddenly as it came. Obaseki slumped forward, his head resting on his mount's neck. He kept his eyes closed as they rode, not knowing when they left the city behind and entered the countryside. The despair he felt in the city subsided the further they traveled until he felt strong enough to lift his head. The sun descended behind the trees, leaving a familiar void that darkness rushed to fill. Abo had disappeared beyond the western horizon. Obaseki was lethargic, swaying with the rhythm of his stallion, his mouth dry. He tried to speak but only croaked.

Dapo heard him and slowed his mount to fall in step with Obaseki.

"It is good to see you awake, my prince," he said. "We will camp soon. There is a village up ahead that will give us shelter for the night."

Dapo extended his water calabash and Obaseki drank greedily, almost choking himself on the cool liquid. No sooner had his thirst been quenched did he regret the decision. As his energy returned the emptiness inside him reappeared, not as intense as it was leaving Abo, but painful just the same. If this was the way his life would be without the Spirits he wanted no part of it. He would rather die than live the rest of his life feeling so bad.

They found the village at dusk. It was small; a cluster of a dozen huts circling a wide clearing. Obaseki and his protectors entered through the dilapidated gate dangling from a ragged thorn fence. The ditch behind the fence was filled with debris. It was a poor attempt at security, more a bluff than anything else.

No one came out to greet them. Dapo ordered one of his men to check the huts. The man went from hut to hut, exiting each one alone. Dapo frowned and climbed from his horse.

"We will camp here tonight," he said.

The men had no problem finding firewood and built a huge fire in the center of the village. They located iron pots for boiling sorghum and a clay oven sturdy enough to bake bread. Malomo helped Obaseki from his horse and guided him to the fire. He spread a blanket and motioned for Obaseki to sit. Once he was seated Malomo freed his hands.

Obaseki rubbed his wrists as he watched the others cook and set up camp. The void inside was not as severe as earlier. Obaseki thought it was because he was far away from Abo, but the answer became obvious as he peered into the darkness persisting around the huts. Something moved beyond the flickering firelight, something strange yet familiar. The people might have left the village, but the Spirits had remained.

Dapo noticed his stare and an uncomfortable look came to his face.

He stood before Obaseki and handed him a bowl of porridge.

"Thank you," Obaseki said.

Dapo nodded. He squatted before Obaseki and bowed his head.

"My prince, I know it is not my place, but I wish you would not look in such a way into the darkness. Although my men are brave and would fight any foe on my command, they are wary of spirits, especially being so far away from the city. If they see you with that look in your eyes they will be unnerved."

"I will try my best to control my strangeness," Obaseki replied.

"I did not mean to insult you."

"Of course you didn't." Obaseki turned his back to Dapo and ate his porridge. He listened to Dapo and Malomo walk away to join their comrades opposite the fire. The big man kept his eye on Obaseki while speaking and laughing with his brethren. Food made him sleepy; he lay down on his kapok blanket and quickly gave into the night.

The village came alive in his dreams, the huts transforming into brightly colored buildings with newly thatched roofs. Handsome people sauntered back and forth across the clearing, the men bare-chested with red kilts tied around their waists and heavy necklaces dangling from their necks. The women were dressed the same, their beaded kilts shorter to display their elegant legs. Children darted about, singing in a strange yet familiar language. They stopped suddenly, looking about as if something had intruded upon their peace. One man turned to face him, then another. Soon the entire village walked towards him, their curious stares changing to anger. Obaseki felt their indignation and realized he was not dreaming.

"Seki! Seki!"

Obaseki turned to the voice calling his name. Lewa stood outside the thorn fence jumping up and down and waving her hands furiously.

"Get out of the village!" she yelled.

Obaseki jumped to his feet. The spirits of his dreams milled about his escorts, their pleasant looks replaced by glares. He ran to Lewa, stopping only when he felt her cold arms wrap around him.

"Come on! Let's get away!" he cried.

"No," Lewa replied. "They cannot get out. The thorn fence is gris-gris to keep them in."

Obaseki understood. "And it kept you out."

Lewa nodded.

The spirits looked at him a moment longer then turned their full attention to the sleeping Atuegbu. Lewa pulled him away.

"Come, Seki. You don't want to see this."

Obaseki snatched away. "We have to help them."

"We can't. "

"What will they do to them?"

"They will feed the spirits."

The spirits hovered close to the sleeping men, their spectral mouths expelling a chant in an ancient tongue. Obaseki felt the words seep into him, summoning him toward the spirits. Lewa held onto him.

"Don't listen to them, Seki. Listen to me."

Lewa's voice grounded him. He backed away as white shadows formed about the Atuegbu. The chants grew louder as the auras lifted from the men and passed into the spirits. Each warrior took a final exaggerated breath then fell still.

Obaseki looked helplessly at his men then turned away, following Lewa into the forest. She led him through the darkness as if the sun shone; following a trail he could barely see.

"Where are we going?"

Lewa turned to look at him. "Back to Abo."

Obaseki snatched his hand away from her. "I can't. I promised my grandfather I would find Fuluke."

"You're so stupid!" Lewa snapped. "You almost died in that village and you don't know how to find Fuluke. You have no choice but to go back."

Obaseki sat down in a pile of wet leaves. He understood his grandfather now, making him even more determined to find Fuluke.

"Take me to a dry spot," Obaseki said. "I need to sleep. In the morning we will find Fuluke."

"No!" Lewa shouted. She let go of him and disappeared into the trees.

"Lewa! Come back!" Obaseki waited for a reply that never came. He slumped against a tree, knocked down by waves of despair, fear and desperation. He was lost, his men dead and Lewa had abandoned him. He closed his eyes and with no other alternative, he slept.

The morning came with humming. Obaseki listened, his eyes closed. He stayed motionless as the humming increased. The humming was replaced a foul odor.

"You can open your eyes if you wish," the voice said.

Obaseki eyes flew open despite his fear. A man squatted before him clothed in a tattered, oversize animal hide pulled tight around his waist with a grass cord. Gris-gris covered the hide, some Obaseki recognized but many other unrecognizable. He had the face of a grandfather but moved with the dexterity of one much younger. Every hair on his face was grey, from his thick eyebrows to his beard.

"Who are you, uncle?" Obaseki asked.

"Fuluke," the man replied, "and you are Obaseki."

Obaseki was pleased and dismayed by the sight of the ancient medicine-priest. Though his face projected the image of a wise and learned man, his ragged clothing and his smell made the young prince wary.

"How do I know you're him?" Obaseki asked.

"You don't," Fuluke answered. "Come, I have food and medicine at my hut. By the look of things, you need it."

Obaseki sat frozen. This man could be Fuluke or some bandit attempting light banter until his cohorts arrived.

Fuluke peered over Obaseki's shoulder. "Who is she?"

Obaseki turned his head. Lewa stood behind him glaring at the old man, her small fists shaking.

"You can see her?"

Fuluke smiled. "I cannot see her, but can feel her. That makes all the difference."

The faint sun streaming through the gaps in the leaves weakened as clouds moved in.

"Her name is Lewa. She wants to stay with me so she won't get killed. She is afraid that if I forget her, she will fade away and be nothing."

Fuluke stood. "Come. We have much work to do in a short time."

Obaseki stood and gathered what little he was able to bring the night before. Lewa grabbed him by his arm.

"Don't go with him Seki. He is evil like the spirits in the village."

Fuluke turned, his face concerned. "You went into the village?"

Lewa's hand covered her mouth and she backed away. Obaseki gazed at the old man, a smile forming on his face.

"Yes, we went into the village," he replied.

"That is what happened to your men. I am sorry. The spirits of Okuthe are vengeful. They carry a grudge that time has not healed, and they despise the living.

"Why didn't they attack me?"

"That's a good question. That's why your grandfather sent you to me."

Fuluke leaned on his walking stick as he sat. "You are a strange one, Obaseki. You live among the living, yet you exist among the dead. This is not a natural state."

Lewa had regained her strength and moved beside him. "Do not listen to him, Seki."

"Mawena were not meant to exist in two worlds. We must choose one or the other. To move in body and spirit is to disrupt the world that Oyo created."

Fuluke stared at Lewa and she grasped Obaseki's arm again.

"I did not ask to be different," Obaseki argued.

"No, you did not," Fuluke agreed. "But we cannot ask for the life we want to lead. We must accept Oyo's gift with humility and live the life that has been woven by the threads of time. But you can make one choice, Obaseki. You can choose to live among the living and separate yourself from the spirits. If you can do this, you will have the life the ancestors have chosen for you."

Obaseki stood, pulling his arm away from Lewa.

"No, Seki," she cried. "Don't go. Don't leave me."

Obaseki turned and looked at his life long friend, her glistening eyes almost making him turn back.

"I have to try, Lewa. I promised grandfather."

"Then you will lose me," she whispered.

Obaseki gazed at Lewa, concentrating on every part of her. No matter what Fuluke taught him, he wanted to remember her always. He managed to smile, and then turned away.

"I love you," she whispered "I will wait for you, Seki. I promise."

Obaseki turned back. Lewa was gone. He couldn't see her, but worst of all, he could not feel her.

Fuluke grasped his shoulder and squeezed it gently.

"Come, son," he said. "You have much to learn."

Obaseki tore his eyes away from where Lewa had stood. Fuluke patted his shoulder then turned and headed into the forest. Obaseki followed and they disappeared into a wall of leaves and darkness.

6

Shange kaVilakaze strode the perimeter of the royal kraal in search of Shani's hut. He was a walking legend, one of Sesuland's greatest warriors second only to Dingane. He moved with exaggerated arrogance, his muscled shoulders swinging back and forth in time with the stride of his thick legs. His golden headring gripped his head so tight wrinkles creased his brow. Facial and body scars made him appear older than his thirty-five years but to him they were symbols of bravery far beyond a mere simba mane or ostrich feather. It was rare to see him in the city, let alone stalking the huts of Dingane's wives. A lesser man would be dead, struck down by Dingane's guards without question. But he was Shange, with certain privileges associated with his rank.

Shange reached the last hut, the home of Shani. Shange felt sadness upon seeing the dingy abode, a sign of Shani's fall from Great Wife status. She had been spared physical death, but in some ways exile was just as final. Her disobedience could not go unpunished, though even in this Dingane displayed his usual leniency towards his former Great Wife. He stripped her of her status, moving her to the smallest wife hut. She was denied the use of the household servants and required to make her own way while raising Ndoro. She was allowed the company of Jelani and Themba, but she could never return to Mawenaland. Any other wife would have faced shunning or death for such an act. While others criticized Dingane for his decision, Shange saw no wrong in it. He had always favored Shani. She was beautiful and strong, the type of woman normally frowned upon among the Sesu but admired by the Mawena. Shange wore the headring signifying his eligibility for marriage, but he had taken no bride. Shange lived for battle; he had no time for family and idleness. Glory was earned on the battlefield, not the yam field. If he ever was to take a wife, it would be a woman like Shani.

She emerged from her hut, radiant despite her worn clothes and faded beads. Shange surprised her and she jumped back into her hut with a squeal.

"Forgive me inkosa," he said, honoring her despite her diminished status. "I should have announced my approach."

Shani emerged from the hut with a welcoming smile. "No, Shange, don't apologize. It's rare that we get visitors."

Shange felt uncomfortable looking into Shani's desperate eyes. She should have been allowed to return to her people. She was unworthy of this torment.

"I am looking for Ndoro," he finally said.

Shani's expression moved from desperate to wary.

"What do you want with him?"

Shange raised his head regally. "Has Ndoro completed his initiation rites?"

"Yes," Shani confirmed. "The elders did not perform them. Jelani did."

That was disappointing. Shange respected the Mawena, but no matter what the stigma, Ndoro was Sesu and should have been initiated properly into manhood.

"Is he part of an induna?"

"Yes, but they do not accept him as they should."

Shange began to doubt his decision. Ndoro was clearly the outcast he had heard he'd be. If he was not accustomed to the camaraderie of an induna he might be more of a hindrance than a help.

"Where is he?"

Shani pointed to the river. "He is with Jelani."

She stepped closer to Shange, her face hard like a lioness.

"You will not harm my son, Shange."

Shange smiled at her boldness.

"I bring no harm to the son of Dingane," he replied. "I offer him a chance for honor. I have planned a cattle raid and I have picked Ndoro to join my party."

Shani's hand jerked to her face to hide her shock. "Dingane is allowing this?"

"This is not the inkosi's decision," Shange replied. "Every man must be blooded before he can wear the headring and claim a wife. You know this."

"Sesu rights have not applied to Ndoro."

Shange shrugged his shoulders, his first slip of respect before the inkosa.

"He shall have his chance. Maybe the ancestors will favor him and drive the demon from his body."

Shani's anger was obvious. "Like I said, he's at the river. Goodbye, Shange."

Shange followed the twisting road down into a steep drift. At the bottom of the narrow valley the Mfululo flowed, lined by small trees and wavering shrubs. A familiar sound came to his ears, the ringing of metal meeting metal and the clash of cowhide shields. Jelani and Ndoro sparred near the river's edge, their only spectators a mixed herd of zebra and wildebeests more interested in the spring grass than fighting men. Shange found a comfortable clump of grass and sat. Ndoro's stature impressed him. At twelve he was as tall as Jelani, although still not filled out with the muscles his Sesu bloodline required. His face was a perfect blend of Dingane and Shani, his eyes a strange light brown. They locked on Jelani like the stare of a lion on the hunt as they circled each other, vainly probing for the opening the experienced Mawena would never reveal.

Jelani's shield dropped slowly, a feint Shange spotted easily. Ndoro sprang at the trap, his assegai flashing forward with a speed as surprising as his strength. Despite the set-up Jelani barely dodged the strike. With a flick of his wrist he struck Ndoro's elbow with his shield. Ndoro winced, dropping his assegai as the burning pain ran up his arm to his shoulder. Before Jelani could strike Ndoro spun away, throwing his shield at Jelani in frustration. Shange shook his head; the boy was acting his age now.

Shange stood noisily and Ndoro reacted. He snatched his

assegai from the ground and threw it directly at the warrior. Shange was so impressed he almost lost his life, raising his shield at the last minute and knocking the spear aside. Ndoro recognized the warrior, his mouth wide with shock. He dropped to the ground, touching his head to the dirt. Jelani remained standing, his face filled with suspicion.

"Get up, boy," Shange said. "I am no inkosi."

"Forgive me," Ndoro said. "You startled me."

"I would hate to see your reaction if you knew I was coming." Shange stood before Jelani and nodded. The Mawena nodded in return, still not speaking.

"I am leading a raid on the Jamburu tomorrow. You will accompany me as my attendant."

"By whose authority?" Jelani challenged.

"I need no authority," Shange replied. "The boy is of age and I am his elder. My status allows me to choose who I wish and I have chosen him."

"What does the inkosa say of this?"

"Don't make me speak of Shani in front of the boy," Shange warned. "He needn't be reminded."

"I will go," Ndoro said.

Jelani cut his eyes at Ndoro. "You are not ready."

"That is my decision, Mawena. From what I have just seen he's more ready than most. You've done a good job, Jelani, but it's time Ndoro learned the ways of battle from a Sesu warrior."

Shange saw Jelani's forearm tense, the tip of his assegai rising. He smiled, hoping the Mawena would lose his composure and attack. It would be a good death for either of them. Unfortunately Jelani relaxed, the spear tip dropping towards the ground.

"Meet me here tomorrow," Shange finished. "The Jamburu village is three days away. Make sure we have enough provisions for the journey."

Shange marched away to his kraal in the hills beyond Selike.

"What are you thinking?" Jelani growled.

"It is time, Jelani," Ndoro replied. "I am of age and it is time

I began to build my herd. I know Shange will get most of what we take, but if I do well I will get something. It won't be much, but it's a beginning."

"This has nothing to do with your skills or your wealth," Jelani shot back. "This is about your life. Did it occur to you that Shange might have been sent by Mulugo?"

Hatred flashed across Ndoro's young face. "Shange would not answer to that baboon. He is a honored warrior. His magic is strong. He does not need Mulugo's tricks."

"You never know what a man owes another man," Jelani replied. "If Shange is with Mulugo, he may attack you away from Selike. You can't stand against him alone and you know your induna won't help you."

"So be it. I am tired of living in disgrace. If Shange decides to kill me at least it will be said that Sesuland's greatest warrior had to do the deed. Moma will be free of this prison and allowed to return to the Mawena."

"I can't stop you," Jelani admitted. "If you're intent on going, let's get back to our practice. There are some things I must show you that may keep you alive long enough to see a second raid."

Darkness had long cast its shadow on the kraal when they returned to Shani's hut, firelight beckoning them through the door slats. Jelani retired to his hut outside the thorn fence. Ndoro moved the door aside and ducked into Shani's hut.

"Hi, momma." His voice was soft, his way of apologizing for being late.

Shani kept her back turned to her son to hide her joy. She was afraid Shange might have taken him or worse still, decided to kill him without the excuse of a cattle raid. She stirred the iron pot full of goat stew slowly, well aware of how famished Ndoro might be.

"Where have you been?" she snapped. "I had to take the cattle to the high grass myself."

"I'm sorry, momma," Ndoro said. "Jelani decided I should practice longer since..."

"Since what?" Shani turned to face her son.

"Momma, Shange came to me today. I have been chosen to go on the cattle raid with him."

"What does Jelani think about this?"

"He thinks Mulugo is behind this. He thinks Shange will try to kill me once I am away from Selike."

"What do you think?"

Ndoro sat on the floor. "I don't care."

Shani rushed Ndoro, grabbing his shoulders and shaking him with all her might.

"Do you want to die? You would leave me alone?"

Ndoro hugged her. "I don't want to leave you, mama. You know I don't. But I am tired of this way of life. If I return people will respect us and leave us alone. Maybe baba will come see us."

Shani stroked his hair. He was so big now, a man by years but still a boy.

"Don't risk your life for something that will never happen," she whispered. "You are a man and must make your own decisions. I will not make you weak with my worries. If you wish to go on the cattle raid, go. I will pray that Shango watches over you and bring you back to me."

Shani let Ndoro go and went back to her pot. She filled a bowl with stew and handed it to him.

"How long will you be gone?"

Ndoro slurped down the stew and wiped his chin. "Three days."

Shani's eyebrows rose. "Three days? I don't have enough time to gather food for three days. I can barely keep food in our bowls day to day."

Ndoro lowered his bowl, anger evident in his eyes. "I am the son of Dingane. I should not have to scrounge for food."

"You must learn to accept your place," Shani said, barely able to keep the anger from her voice. "I will gather the food with Jelani's help."

Ndoro slammed his bowl down. "I'm not hungry anymore." He crawled to his sleeping cot and lay down with his back to his mother.

Shani's mind swirled with a mixture of anger and sympathy. She picked up the bowl and went outside to scrap it clean. Jelani sat before the hut, his dagga pipe hanging from the corner of his mouth.

"He shouldn't go!" she blurted. "You know that."

Jelani nodded his head and removed the pipe from his mouth. "I can't stop him. He is a man now, inkosa."

Shani grasped Jelani's wrists. "He should not suffer for my discretion. If he was in Abo he would be a great warrior, a noble among men. Instead he is an outcast."

"He is also a meji," Jelani replied. "He will rise above his adversity. He has the fighting skills of men twice his age and the wisdom of his grandfather. The ancestors have blessed him despite his circumstances."

Shani kissed Jelani's wrists. "Thank you for your words."

"I wish I could offer more."

Shani smiled. "I am still Dingane's wife. Now is not the time for us." She pushed him away. "Take care of my son. He may need your words to soothe his disappointment."

When Ndoro awoke the next morning Jelani waited for him outside the hut. He held a hunting bow in his right hand and a throwing knife in his left. A quiver stuffed with arrows and throwing spears rested on his back.

"Wake up, little monkey. The day is short and we have much to do."

Ndoro ran into the hut, emerging with bow, arrows and spears. They crossed the river and travelled well beyond the city into the thick of the savannah. Below them thousands of herd animals wandered the grasses, barely noticing the two men staring down on them from the rise. Zebra bachelor stallions jousted among themselves as the luckier ones kept a careful eye on their mares and colts. Springboks and gazelles grazed nervously, always on the lookout for the simbas and leopards that lurked in the high grasses. The two hunted until nightfall.

Jelani and Ndoro sat before the fire, the succulent smell of the springbok spreading with the smoke. Shani came out to sit with them. It was a clear, warm night with a slight breeze that played about them. Ndoro gazed into the fire, watching the flames dance.

"There are some that can read fire," Jelani said. "They say that fire is the spirit of the ancestors. The story of every man lives in the flames. If a man could read the fire, he would already know his life."

"Don't tell him such things," Shani scolded. "He has enough to worry about."

Ndoro turned his head to Shani. "Jelani did not have to tell me, momma. I have watched the flames all my life."

"What do they say, Ndoro?" Jelani asked.

"They say I will be a great warrior one day. They say the Sesu will bow before me as they do my father, and I will have thousands of huts surrounding my kraal. My thorn fence will bulge with white cattle, and my wives will be the most beautiful daughters of my allies and enemies."

"So much from such a little fire," Shani commented. "Come, you must sleep. If you are to travel with Shange, your journey will be fast and hard. He takes only the best warriors with him and raids the strongest villages."

Ndoro looked at Jelani and the warrior nodded his head. He kissed his mother and went inside to his cot by the clay chimney. Momma made fun of his words, but he had seen it in the flames. He was destined to be inkosi. But first, he must be a warrior.

The morning came too soon for Ndoro. He was stirred from his dreams by Shani, shaking him by his shoulders.

"Wake up, warrior," she whispered. "Shange will punish you if you are late."

Ndoro jumped from his cot and almost knocked Shani down. He grabbed her before she hit the dirt, pulling her up with his left arm.

"I've got to go momma. Pray for me."

Ndoro ran out of the hut and into Jelani. This time he wasn't fast enough and they both tumbled into the grass.

"Slow down, boy!" Jelani admonished. "Shange won't leave without you."

Ndoro whistled in frustration. He found his hatchet and shoved it back into his belt then gathered his throwing spears. His iklwa was by his shield and he crawled over to them, snatched them up and sped away.

Shange and the others waited by the river. Ndoro recognized faces in the group, went cold. There were twenty Sesu, ten warriors and their attendants. As soon as the warriors saw him they confronted Shange, yelling and gesturing towards him.

He knew the warriors Shange had gathered and he knew their attendants. Dabule, Hamu, Thuka, Amanzi, Senzan and Sitefu; all were members of his intanga. This would not be a good journey.

He finally drew close enough to hear the warriors' argument.

"He cannot go!" shouted the tall man with a massive plume sticking from his headring. "He is bad luck!"

"Are you afraid of Mulugo, Zidewu?" Shange asked calmly. "If you are, then maybe you should take off your headring and wear your wife's dress."

Tantashi laughed. Ndoro knew Tantashi; he was a lean, handsome man with bright eyes and a generous smile. He wore a simple leopard headdress and a necklace of leopard claws.

"The boy is harmless," he said. "If he is cursed then the ancestors will deal with him, not us."

Big Bekuza shook his head. "These are Jamburu cattle we're talking about. They will be watching their herd carefully, so it is likely we'll get in a fight. If we do, I want the spirits with me, not against me."

"You should stay home, Bekuza. You are too fat to run from the Jamburu."

Shange gave the rest of the warriors a mean look. "You are wasting my time. Ndoro is going. If you have a problem, leave now. I'll be sure to have the maidens share their skirts with you when I return."

Ndoro stood beside Shange, his smile disappearing when he saw the snarl on the warrior's face.

"You're not worth the trouble, but it's too late for me to change my mind. Pick up my things and let's go."

Shange jumped into the river and waded across. The other warriors looked at each other, waiting for someone to leave. Tantashi laughed and followed Shange, as did Bekuza. Ziwedu rubbed this gris-gris strung around his neck and walked into the river. The others, not wanting to be labeled cowards, finally followed.

The pace was brisk but tolerable. Ndoro ran awkwardly at first, struggling to handle Shange's gear with his own. By the time they reached the first rest spot he was comfortable. Shange halted under the shade of a large acacia tree, dropping his shield and assegai.

"Why are we stopping here?" Ziwedu asked. "This is a simba tree. Look at the bones."

"If they return our cattle hunt becomes a simba hunt," Shange replied. "Ndoro, set up my sleep roll and get me some water. There is a waterhole in that direction. Be careful of the crocodiles. I don't want to have to sleep on the ground."

Ndoroset off before Shange's last words escaped his mouth. The other boys followed him, and the task soon became a race. Ndoro climbed the hill well before the others and froze at the crest. A pride of simbas languished at the edge of the waterhole. Five females and two males slept by a zebra carcass while the cubs gnawed on the remains.

"Let's go back," Sitefu said from behind him. "It is too dangerous."

"My father will beat me if I come back with no water," Dabule said. He was the smallest of their age group, smaller than his brother Pukane who was only eight.

Ndoro crouched, staring at the simbas. If he worked his way to the right, he could reach the closest edge of the waterhole without disturbing the simbas. Sitefu looked at him, his face bunched in anger.

"No, Ndoro!" he barked. "If you go we all must go!"

Sitefu grabbed his shoulder and Ndoro shrugged him off. "Don't touch me again, goat." Ndoro crept down the hill until the dingy water shimmered before him. He dipped his water bag into the water, letting it set as it filled, then made room for the other boys. They each took turns, watching the simbas and the frolicking cubs.

Amanzi was filling his back when the fly bit his cheek. He yelped and the cubs froze, looking in their direction.

"Run!" Ndoro shouted. The boys streaked up the hill while the cubs ran to the females, their weak cries loud enough to stir their slumbering parents. Ndoro looked as he reached the hilltop and saw the simbas on their paws, their narrow pupils looking into his. He ran for the warriors as the simbas roared.

Shange was on his feet, assegai in hand. The other warriors scrambled for their weapons as boys ran past, all of them except Ndoro. He dropped his water bag and took up his assegai with the warriors as the simbas approached.

"Everyone to me!" Shange shouted. The warriors came together forming a wall of cowhide shields, the points of the assegais sticking out from the gaps. The simbas milled about, roaring at the formation but experienced enough to know this would be no easy kill. They trotted away, the males the last to leave after a half-hearted charge at the warriors. Ndoro held his fear down as he stood with the warriors, fighting the tremor that threatened to shake his assegai from his hand.

Once the simbas disappeared over the hill the formation broke and Shange ran to the edge, peering down the hill to make sure the beasts were no longer a threat. He spun about and charged Ndoro, slamming his shield into the boy and knocking him into the dirt.

"I ask you to bring me water and you bring a pride as well!"

Ndoro was more embarrassed than hurt. He could stand Shange's punishment alone, but he would not tolerate it before the eyes of his age-group.

"I did what you asked. If I had come back with no water you

would have beat me just the same."

Shange glared at him. "That is true, but in trying to avoid punishment you almost killed us all."

Shange backed away. "Set up my camp and prepare my meal. When you are done take your sleeping roll and set it at the hill over the waterhole. You will protect us from your friends tonight."

Ndoro felt the eyes on him as he did as he was told. He set up his cooking pots and prepared izikobe with strips of dried rabbit. After the izikobe was done, Ndoro prepared himself a bowl, grabbed his sleeping mat and headrest then went to the hilltop.

Shange had done him a favor. Ndoro wanted to come with Shange because of the honor, but he was not prepared for the loneliness he felt among the raiding party. All his life he'd dealt with the alienation, the stigma of being born a twin and the accusations of Mulugo. But Momma and Jelani were always there at the end of the day, giving him words of encouragement and strength. Now he was alone, staring at the others as they ate. There would be no words of encouragement or soothing hand. If he was lucky the punishment would not last beyond the night.

Ndoro was not lucky. After a restless night watching the waterhole for signs of the simba's return he was awakened by a sharp kick in the ribs by Shange.

"Today you will apologize to your brothers by carrying their load. They are waiting for you."

Ndoro rose slowly. He looked into Shange's eyes and for a moment he thought he saw a glint of uncertainty in the warrior's face. The emotion fled as quickly as it appeared and Shange strode away. His brothers came single file, Sitefu leading them. Sitefu lifted the shoulder strap of his bundle and dropped it over Ndoro's head and onto his shoulder, the narrow leather strip digging into his bare skin.

"Look my brothers," he shouted. "An ass wandered into our camp last night. Let's load it up quickly before it runs away!"

The boys' laughter was forced. Ndoro stared at each one as they put their bundles on his shoulders. Hamu, Thuka and

Dabule were enjoying themselves, but Shapi and Zibe were clearly uncomfortable. Amanzi was afraid, his hands shaking as he eased his bundle over Ndoro's head.

"I'm sorry," he whispered. "My father said he would beat me if I did not join the others. I fear him more than I fear you."

"I will do my best to change that," Ndoro whispered back.

Amanzi's eyes widened and he stumbled back, turned and ran away. Senzan dodged his flight, walking up to Ndoro with neither fear nor pleasure in his eyes.

"Do you have any sheepskin or cloth with you?" he asked.

"Yes."

"Put it between your shoulders and the straps. It will ease the pain."

Senzan sat his bundle at Ndoro's feet. "I will help you."

"No," Ndoro replied. "Don't get in trouble for my sake."

Senzan nodded and walked away. His older brother Dabaze ran up to him and shoved him. Senzan shoved him back. He would do anything to aggravate his older brother, even helping the outcast. Dabaze trailed behind Senzan, yelling at him the entire walk back to the group.

Ndoro took Senzan's advice. He took the sleeping rolls off his shoulder and tore a piece of cowhide from his loincloth. He laid the skin on his right shoulder and put the rolls back in place. By the time he was done the raiding party had moved on. He could barely see them on the horizon, their shimmering shadows obscured by rising heat and dust. There was no way he could catch up with them so he walked, the sleeping rolls slapping against his ribs with every step. Ndoro finally lost sight of the group and followed them by tracking. Trotting alone through the grass and shrubs he felt relieved and afraid. He was happy to be away from the tension of the raiding party, but he knew being alone made him vulnerable to attack by a pride of simbas or hyenas. As the sun descended behind a clump of low hills to the west, Ndoro picked up his pace. He was a good hunter but the night would hide their trail. He had no intention of spending the night in the wild alone.

He spotted the flicker of their fire as the sun carried the last shreds of daylight behind the hills. The stare of his companions ranged from surprised to indifferent, but the look in Shange's eyes was best described as impressed anger.

"That demon inside you must be a luck charm," Shange said as he took his sleeping mat. "You made it in spite of yourself."

Ndoro handed everyone their mats then set about preparing a meal for Shange and himself. He was famished from the long walk and extra burden, but he knew Shange would not let him eat more than his allotted share. If he could get away from the group for only a moment, he could chew on the dried strips of springbok that lay hidden in his pouch. He was lucky, for after their meal Tantashi revealed his dagga pipe, which brought wide smiles to all the warriors. The attendant boys would not be able to share, but they moved closed to the circle in hopes they would be able to feel the effect of the burning dagga. He waited until the voices were loud and distracted before he made his way into the darkness, stealing a thick burning stick from the fire to use as a torch. He settled under a low tree and propped his torch against a thick granite rock resting far enough from the tree as to not cause a fire and to prevent drawing any night hunters to his sleeping area. The meat was tough but welcomed; Ndoro rested his back on the tree and closed his eyes, letting the sounds of the night take him away from the struggles of the day. Sleep captured him like an unseen trap and he dreamed of a life that could never be, a life as the favored son of Dingane, leader of his intanga and eventually inkosi of the Sesu. Warriors from the farthest ends of Sesuland would dance in his kraal and sing his praises as he handed them their shields to march and subdue their enemies. His wives' huts would be as numerous as the grass and his cattle countless. By the time Shange jostled him awake the sun was high on the horizon. He had overslept, but so had Shange. The sour smell of dagga clung to the warrior's skin like sweat.

"Damn Tantashi!" Shange snapped. "I should have made him leave his pipe. Now we are late!"

He lifted Ndoro to his feet by his right arm. "You were smart not to smoke."

Ndoro rolled his sleeping mat. "I'm am sorry, Shange. I will make breakfast quickly."

"We don't have time. The Jamburu will arrive at the high pastures tonight. We must be in place before they arrive or we will never be able to get the cattle."

He placed his hand on Ndoro's shoulder and smiled. It was the first sign of friendliness the boy had received since leaving his mother and Jelani.

"Everyone will carry their own weight today. We will run until we reach the Old Men."

Shange waited until Ndoro was packed and they ran to meet the others. They followed Shange, the warriors in single file from highest to lowest rank. The boys followed, arranged in the same pecking order. Ndoro was last, but he didn't mind. It was the closest he had felt to the group during the entire trip. For the moment, he was Sesu.

It was the hardest day of the trek. Shange set a fast pace that never slowed. They ran across the short grass, through the welcomed shade of scattered acacias and around the enormous herds of zebras, wildebeests, elephants and the host of other creatures that filled the lands of the Sesu. They stopped briefly for water along the river, only to see Sitefu almost lose his head to a hungry crocodile. Azani spotted the creature moving in and saved Sitefu by screaming and running away from the banks. The crocodile lunged just as Sitefu lifted his head. The warriors drove the beast away as they did the simbas, but Sitefu's nerve fled with the beast. He refused to approach a waterhole afterwards.

By dusk the tops of the Old Men appeared on the horizon, their grey ice caps a jarring contrast to the heat swirling around the weary runners. Ndoro's heart banged against his chest like a war drum; his left side felt as if someone had driven an assegai into him and left it to rot away. He was sure he would never make it to the ambush spot; he was more tired than he could imagine anyone could be without dying. As the sun crept closer to the top of the Old Men the pace increased. Ndoro's eyes went wide. How could he keep this up?

"We're not far," Shange shouted. "Stop hobbling like monkeys and run like Sesu!"

They chased Shange into the valley of the Old Men. Throughout their run the river had never been far away, meandering between the grasslands and hills like an indecisive lover, teasing each one relentlessly for over a thousand strides. The river led them into a narrow valley, only a few strides of rock between them and the grey stone walls. The slice of land became so narrow that Ndoro thought they would surely have to swim the rest of the way to the pastures. He was not a good swimmer and the river between the walls of the Old Men was swift and angry, careening off huge boulders and swirling around unseen barriers. The path finally broadened and steepened; soon the river ran below them. The land beneath his feet began to level when Shange finally stopped running.

Everyone fell where they stopped except Shange and Ndoro. Ndoro doubled over, his hands grasping his knees as he heaved. The other sprawled about on the rocky crest, moaning, cursing or a combination of both.

Shange looked at them all and spat. "I have brought women with me to do a warriors' work."

He walked up to Ndoro and shoved him. "Where is my food?"

Ndoro looked at Shange bewildered. "Your food?"

"You are my servant, are you not?"

Ndoro straightened and went to his pack. He removed his cooking pot.

"Come," Shange said. "I will show you where to find wood and water."

Shange led Ndoro into the bush. The side of the mountain sloped gently into a vast grassland ringed by low shrubs and sparse trees. The grasses teemed with large herds more numerous and larger than anything he had seen in Sesuland. Directly opposite them a range of low hills rose from the plains. The river flowed to his right, resuming its broad and laconic nature.

"An alert scout would see us enter the pastureland no matter what we do," Shange said. "We will camp in the trees below and wait for the Jamburu to arrive."

"How will we see them through the trees?" Ndoro asked.

Shange smirked. "We won't have to see the Jamburu. Their cattle wear huge bells around their necks that wake the ancestors and their warriors sing as bad as they sing loud. We will wait until night fall and then strike."

Ndoro looked at Shange with grudging admiration. "Why are you telling me this?"

"Because you will lead your intanga into the valley to gather the cattle once we drive off the Jamburu."

For a brief moment Ndoro felt pride, but his reality was always near. "They won't follow me."

"They will if I tell them. Now go fetch water and cook my food. There is a stream in the bush about five strides away."

The others came down into the brush and set up camp. The boys began cooking and serving food, each one glancing at Ndoro as they passed but saying nothing. Each one except Sitefu.

"The others are afraid of you," he said. "Shange leads this party, but he is not inkosi. No matter what he says, in Selike I am the elder."

"We are not in Selike," Ndoro replied. "In Selike I cracked your head like a melon and helped you heal. Here I won't be as generous."

"You are a demon," Sitefu spat. "I hope Mulugo kills you soon."

Ndoro sat awake while the others slept, peering through the trees onto the grasslands below. Sitefu's words had bothered him more than they should. He had not thought about Mulugo since their journey began and he was glad of it. The medicine-priest lurked about his life like a hyena, waiting for the chance to kill him. When he was young he was afraid of the old man, but now he just wanted to be rid of him. Maybe he could convince Shange in taking him in to live at his kraal. He could attend him on his adventures and learn the Sesu ways from a true legend. He decided he would ask Shange when they returned.

Ndoro was awakened by jangling bells and singing voices.

"Jamburu," he whispered.

He scrambled over to wake Shange but the warrior shoved him away.

"I hear them!" he growled.

Shange came to his feet and kicked everyone awake. He had especially hard words for the other warriors.

"The pride of the Sesu and a boy had to tell us the Jamburu are coming."

Everyone worked to the edge of the thicket. The cattle descended the hill in single file, flanked by Jamburu herders. They were tall, lithe men draped in red robes that hung from one shoulder. Their shaved heads glistened with sweat and they walked down the trail using their tall spears like walking sticks. They were terrible singers, at least to Ndoro, but their songs scattered the other beasts and warned the predators of their coming. The Jamburu herded their cattle to the choicest grass then drove off a skittish herd of zebra. Ndoro counted fifteen. There were no boys among them, just herders and warriors. While five of the men stood watch over the cattle, the others set about gathering sticks and straw. Some of them wandered to the tree line, close to where the Sesu were hiding. The warriors grabbed their assegais as the Jamburu moved closer to their position. The foragers were satisfied before they reached the Sesu and returned to their brothers. They build grass huts in a circle around their cattle and settled in for a few weeks of grazing, or so they thought.

The Sesu warriors watched the Jamburu all day, never moving from their spots. Ndoro and the other boys scampered about silently, making food for the warriors and attending to their weapons. The immediacy of action pushed all differences aside as the party prepared for the raid. The day seemed to stretch on forever, the sun taking its time across the sky, descending into the horizon with aggravating patience.

No sooner had the sun disappeared Shange stood. Without a word the other warriors grabbed their weapons and followed him through the thicket and down into the grassland. Ndoro and the boys ran to the higher ground to watch the men work their way to the Jamburu.

"Can you see them?"

"Barely," Ndoro answered. "They are crouching low and using their shields to hide."

"If we can see them the Jamburu can," Sitefu said.

"The Jamburu are busy watching their cattle."

"Everyone be quiet!" Ndoro snapped.

They watched the warriors work closer and closer to the Jamburu kraal. As the sun slipped completely below the horizon the warriors disappeared, swallowed by the valley darkness. The only light came from the Jamburu campfires that flickered like stars on the valley floor. There was a commotion in the camp, shapes flashing by the fire.

"Something is wrong," Ndoro said.

"I can't see anything," Sitefu said.

"The Jamburu are moving."

Ndoro eyes went wide and he ran from the others to his sleeping mat. He grabbed his assegai and shield.

"What are you doing?" Sitefu demanded. "Shange told us to stay here!"

"It's an ambush!" Ndoro replied.

Ndoro burst through the bush as the Jamburu camp came alive with torches. The Jamburu warriors ran into the grasses shouting and waving their assegais. Shange stood and waved his shield. The other warriors emerged and charged with him. Before they could clash the Jamburu archers let loose their poison arrows, taking down half the Sesu. The archers had no time for a second volley; Shange was among them, his assegai flashing like lightening.

Ndoro was close enough to see the battle was not going well

for the Sesu. Shange held his ground but the other warriors were overwhelmed by the Jamburu. He ran faster, fueled by anger as his comrades fell one by one. In moments only Shange remained. The master warrior stood surrounded, his shield held high, blood running down his arm and onto his assegai. Three dead Jamburu lay at his feet; the others taunted Shange, jabbing their assegais at him but none daring to move close. Shange yelled back, challenging the warriors to come closer. Behind them an archer crept closer, his bow loaded and drawn.

"Shange!" Ndoro shouted, but it was too late. The arrow pierced Shange's thigh, knocking him to one knee. One Jamburu warrior leapt at the wounded Sesu and discovered his mistake too late. Shange sprang back to both feet, slapped the man's shield aside and stabbed him, driving his assegai through the man's chest and out his back. He kicked the man off his spear. The others stepped back, waiting for the poison to take effect.

The Jamburu warriors never saw Ndoro. Ndoro slipped between them and stood beside Shange.

"What are you doing here?" Shange hissed. "I told you to stay with the other boys."

"You are the only warrior left alive," Ndoro answered.

Shange smiled. "Then it will be a good death."

He stumbled and Ndoro leaned against him to keep him from falling.

"This is a good poison," Shange said. "I will be dead soon, though there is no honor in killing a man like a springbok."

"You will die honorably, Sesu."

The speaker broke from the circle, tall and thin like the others with muscles more defined. He wore no headdress, but a necklace of leopard claws rested around his neck. He smiled as he stepped forward, his eyes on Shange.

"Your taste for Jamburu cattle has finally caught up with you, Shange," he said.

Shange managed to laugh despite his obvious pain. "Bamuthi, I should have killed you when I took your herd."

"It looks like I will sing the praise song tonight," Bamuthi said. He jumped at Shange and Ndoro stepped between them, his leaf shield covering him from ankles to chin, his assegai hidden. He charged Bamuthi Sesu style, ramming his shield into the Jamburu's and pushing him back. Ndoro hooked his shield under Bamuthi's and with a yell, jerked his arm back and opened the Jamburu to his thrust. Bamuthi turned sideways and Ndoro missed, his blade grazing the Jamburu's ribs.

Bamuthi brought his shield back, striking Ndoro on the head. Ndoro hit the ground hard, but he felt no pain. The blow broke the calabash that held his rage and it spilled over him like a flooding river. He rolled back onto his feet and attacked Bamuthi again, beating the man relentlessly with his shield, jabbing with his assegai. Flashes of other faces jumped between him and Bamuthi but he swept them aside, determined to strike down the arrogant Jamburu. Everyone and everything that ever stood against him walked with the legs of Bamuthi and Ndoro was determined to crush it once and for all. Fear shaped the Jamburu's face and he fought without skill but with desperation. Ndoro saw a small opening, a glimpse of flesh open to his assegai. He stabbed, opening the vein of Jamburu's neck. The warrior yelled and dropped his shield, grabbing his neck, blood seeping through his fingers. He fell to his knees, his wide eyes staring at Ndoro then fell dead onto his face.

Ndoro stood over Bamuthi, his shoulders heaving with each breath. The rage subsided and fatigue dropped on him like stone. He crumbled onto his hands and knees, retching until there was nothing left. He fell back onto his backside and looked about. They were all dead; every last Jamburu sprawled about him in a circle.

"You killed them all," he heard Shange said. "You killed them all."

Ndoro turned to see the warrior sitting on the ground with him, holding his wounded leg.

"You must have helped me," Ndoro replied. "I could not have done this."

"I did nothing." The confidence was gone from his voice,

replaced by a tone of bewilderment. Ndoro stood. The moon was high above, its weak light forming small shadows about the Jamburu herd. He staggered to Shange and grabbed his arm.

"What are you doing?" the warrior asked.

"We must go before more Jamburu come," Ndoro said. There was no rage to protect him, only the fear of a boy too far from home.

Shange gathered his feet under himself and assisted Ndoro in lifting him. He winced as he put weight on his leg.

"I won't make it," Shange admitted. "The poison is slow but sure. Take the herd; you deserve it. Let me die here with honor."

Ndoro leaned against Shange. "I am you attendant. I will take you to your kraal. Your medicine priest will know what to do."

He carried Shange across the grasslands, through the trees and up into the bush. He hoped the other boys would be waiting for them but he was disappointed. They were gone, every one. The boys had fled, leaving sleeping mats, pots and headrests behind. Ndoro eased Shange down against a small tree and built a fire. He made uputhu for the both of them, adding his last strips of springbok.

"Here." He gave Shange a bowl. "You must eat to stay strong."

Shange snatched the bowl and attacked the porridge, finishing it before Ndoro could sit.

Ndoro refilled Shange's bowl then made his own. He said nothing to Shange, afraid of what words might come from his mouth. Something was inside him; he was certain. There was no way he could have defeated so many men by himself, seasoned Jamburu warriors equal to the best Sesu. He had killed his first men as if it was nothing. He sat eating porridge with the same hands that had just slain men. A smile came to his face. He was a Sesu now, a blooded warrior. His father could deny him many things, but he could not deny him that.

Shange groaned. Ndoro dropped his bowl and went to him.

"Get away!" Shange scolded him. "I don't need a nursemaid. Let me die in peace."

"I can't," Ndoro replied.

Shange chuckled. "By the morning I won't be able to walk. Are you going to carry me for three days? Even you don't have the strength. Bring me Tantashi's dagga pipe and let me smoke myself to oblivion. By the time the hyenas come I will be dead and blissful."

Ndoro set out Shange's sleeping mat and headrest. "We will leave in the morning."

Shange laughed. "Your demon is strong, but not smart."

Shange fell asleep so quickly Ndoro thought he'd died. Ndoro remained awake, watching the camp until daylight struggled over the shoulders of the Old Men. He grabbed his assegai and shield and proceeded down the hill to the neglected Jamburu herd. Using the skills taught to every Sesu boy from birth, he went to each bovine and removed the cumbersome bells dangling from their necks. He then herded the cattle, driving them up the hill, through the thicket to the camp. Shange was awake when he returned, propped up on his elbows.

"So you have decided to claim your prize?"

Ndoro did not smile. "The cattle will help me take you home."

Shange looked puzzled but did not argue. The cattle grazed on the short grass under the trees, ignoring Ndoro as he gathered branches and the blankets abandoned by the others. By the afternoon he had fashioned a respectable litter which he attached to the most docile of the cattle. He led the young bull to Shange.

"Can you get in?" he asked.

Shange looked at the litter with disdain. "I will not return to Sesuland like a child!"

"You don't have the strength to walk and I am not going to leave you here for the hyenas," Ndoro said. "When we get to Sesuland you can use your strength to walk into your kraal in pride. For now, you need to get on."

Shange dragged himself onto the litter. "Why am I listening to a boy? I am a grown man with wives and cattle, yet I listen to a boy with the soul of a demon."

Shange's words stung. "I am no demon!"

Shange nestled into the litter and closed his eyes. "That is the thing about demons. A Sesu does not know if he has one inside him. I think all men do. It is what makes us brave and gives us strength. But just like Unkulunkulu made simbas different in size and strength, so it is with men. Until I met you, I did not know a single man with a demon stronger than mine, and you are still a boy."

"You don't think I am a curse to the Sesu?"

Shange laughed. "I wish I possessed such a curse! Dingane is a fool. He will never have another son with your strength."

Ndoro squatted near the warrior. Shange's encouraging words were the first he'd ever heard from someone other than Momma and Jelani.

"Mulugo says I am cursed because I was born meji."

"Mulugo is a fool as well. He is a medicine priest because he was afraid to answer Dabulamanzi's call to war.

Dabulamanzi's call to war. In the early days the Sesu marched every dry season. Many Sesu became healers and diviners to avoid the inkosi's call to the kraal.

"Dingane believes him."

"I said Mulugo was a fool, I did not say he was without power. I have seen him do amazing things, but I have also witnessed him condemn good Sesu for his own ends. Everything he has done has benefited Dingane until you. For him to go against the inkosi means you are a greater threat to him than Dingane's anger."

Ndoro did not understand Shange's words. What could he do to Mulugo? An assegai was no match against a medicine priest's charms and spells.

"Well, boy, what are you waiting for?" Shange complained. "If you're determined for me to die in shame then get on with it!"

Ndoro drove the herd up the Old Men and down into the river valley. He lost many along the narrow pass to the swift river currents and the occasional crocodile lurking in the slow eddies and pools. As they passed from the rocky riverbanks to the shrub lands, the dangers turned from water and reptiles to simbas and hyenas. Although his priority was to get Shange home safe, he cursed with every cow or bull lost.

Shange's health diminished with every passing day. By the third day he no longer spoke, swaying back and forth in the litter, his eyes half-closed and his mouth locked in a delirious grin. He was dying; Ndoro had no doubt. Keeping the herd was slowing him down. By the sixth day he abandoned them to the wilds, keeping only the bull pulling Shange's litter. They rested only when the bull would go no farther, the stubborn bovine halting to graze and loll about at one waterhole or another. Ndoro took no rest, keeping a constant eye out for any predator and trying to get Shange to eat.

Eight days later they reached Sesuland. Ndoro trudged behind Shange and the bull, too weary to celebrate his return home. Shange's kraal was another day's walk away and his legs burned, but he would not stop. He was too close.

"Master Shange, we are home," he whispered. "Soon you will hear the songs of your village. They will welcome their warrior home with a great celebration."

Shange said nothing. His eyes were closed and the smile had long left his face. Ndoro refused to think he was dead although he knew it was possible. He prodded the bull on, determined to reach the kraal before the end of the day.

He spotted the impi a half a day away from his destination. There were ten men total, their head plumes bouncing against the undulating hills from where they came. Their broad chests were hidden by the brushed white cow tails hanging down from their necks to their waists. They ran hard, their chant drifting on the breeze to Ndoro's ears. He stopped, pulling back on the rope around the bull's neck and waited for the warriors to come to him.

The first to reach him was a broad man as tall as Shange with a large chest and larger stomach.

"You are the one called Ndoro," he said.

Ndoro nodded.

"The boys said you were dead, that you died with Shange and the others."

"You can see they lied. They were too busy running away to know what happened."

Another warrior stepped forward as the other ran to Shange's side. This man was much younger, a leopard cap ringing his bald head, a plume of ostrich feathers rising out of the back.

"The boys said the warriors were dead and Shange was struck by an arrow. How did you rescue him?"

Ndoro lowered his head. "I killed the Jamburu."

The warriors looked at each other then back at Ndoro.

"We thank you for bringing our inkosi back. Come with us. We have food and a good medicine priest to tend to you and Shange."

"I think Shange is dead."

The old warrior laughed. "Shange is not dead. He would not dare die away from his kraal. Come, everyone is waiting for us."

Ndoro hesitated. He could go with these men and become part of Shange's kraal. Shange wouldn't dare deny him after saving his life but he would give up any claim as Dingane's heir if he did.

"Thank you, but I must return to Selike."

The warriors raised their shield in respect and headed back to the kraal with Shange and the bull. Ndoro watched them until they disappeared over the rise before heading to Selike. He set a warriors pace, reaching the Mfululo by nightfall. Ndoro took his time crossing the shallow river, savoring the sight of home and his mother's hut. He was halfway up the hill when the door of the hut swung open and Jelani emerged. Ndoro cleared his throat and Jelani jumped with his sword ready.

"Ndoro? Ndoro!"

Jelani charged down the hill and ran into Ndoro so hard they fell. He heard a shriek and in moments his momma was with them, the three of them rolling in the dust. The pain and fatigue was gone, replaced by joy he thought he could never feel.

Jelani lifted him from the ground and Shani squeezed him as tight as she could.

"You are not dead!" she exclaimed. "You are not dead!"

"No, momma, not yet."

"I told you those boys were lying," Jelani said. "I could see it in their eyes, especially Sitefu."

Shani looked him over, running her hand over his body. "You are hurt. Here, come inside."

Shani dragged him into the hut and pushed him down on his cot. She ran over to a small box by the chimney and returned with an armload of calabashes. She went to work on his wounds as he lay down and fell asleep, lulled by the sing-song rhythm of his mother's voice.

The next day was strange in its normalness. No one came to the kraal even thought Ndoro was sure the word had spread of his return. Shani tried to persuade him to remain in the hut, but Ndoro refused. He took the cattle out into the grazing fields. Sitefu and the other boys tended their family herds, but they would not look at him. One boy broke away from the others, driving his herd towards Ndoro. Ndoro recognized Senzan and grinned.

"So you are alive," he said.

Ndoro nodded.

They walked side by side not saying a word, tending their cattle together. Ndoro could stand the silence no longer.

"Why did you run?"

Senzan continued walking, staring at the ground. "Sitefu told us to run. He said we would be killed once the Jamburu finished with the warriors. They all ran, but I didn't, at least not at first."

"You stayed?"

Senzan stopped and looked at Ndoro. "I wanted to be sure my brother was dead. I wanted to tell my baba that he was dead, that I saw him killed. I saw you reach Shange and I saw you fight. Then I ran."

"I don't remember killing anyone, Senzan. I remember attacking Bamuthi, but I don't remember the others. I thought Shange was helping me."

"No, it was you. You were a storm and the Jamburu were sticks in your path."

Ndoro looked away from Senzan and saw him. Mulugo stood at the edge of the grass, his eyes set back deep in his head, his mouth trembling. His lips strained to form silent words. Ndoro had stood watching the priest curse him before, but the anger coming from him seemed deeper this time. Then he saw it, and he understood. He knew why the Jamburu waited for them; he knew why they brought archers with poison arrows. Mulugo's eyes went wide and a surprised look came over his face. Fear came with realization; the medicine priest turned and ran back to the village.

"I must go, Senzan," Ndoro said. "Do yourself a favor and stay away from me. You are lucky only your brother died."

Ndoro rounded up his cattle and led them back to the kraal. He could tell no one, because no one would believe him. It was a feeling confirmed by an expression. Everyone believed Mulugo wished him dead; no one would believe he would kill one of the Sesu's greatest warriors to do so, not even his momma and Jelani.

Ndoro drove the cattle into the enclosure, securing the thorn fence behind them. Shani met him on his way to the hut.

"You are back early," she said. "Are you feeling well?"

"I am a little tired."

"I told you to rest. You just came back yesterday. Go inside. Jelani and I will tend to things."

Ndoro went to his cot and fell into a deep, dreamless sleep. When he finally awoke, Shani stood above him.

"You must come outside now," she said.

Ndoro scrambled off his cot and ran outside. The hut was

surrounded by Sesu warriors dressed in full ceremonial garb, hundreds of men covered in braided cow tail necklaces and leggings, with feather plumes protruding high over their heads from leopards and otter skin caps. They carried the battle shields of Shange, black cowhide with three white spots in the center. They saw him and dropped to one knee in unison.

"Ushange!" they barked.

One warrior stepped forward bearing a white shield with a black circle on top and bottom. He stood a head taller than Ndoro without the spectacular eagle feather headdress towering above him. The face was familiar; the man was definitely related to Shange. He scrutinized Ndoro for a moment then smiled.

"Ndoro kaDingane, I am Mayinga kaShange, nephew of Shange kaVilikaze. I have come to inform you that inkosi Shange is dead."

The words hit Ndoro like a war club. He wanted to fall to his knees and curse Mulugo, but he had to show dignity.

"The ancestors have chosen a strong bull," he said.

Mayinga nodded. "The elders of our kraal have honored me with their choice as inkosi. I would have rather served beside my father than in his place, but I do not try to understand the wisdom of the ancestors."

Mayinga turned and raised his shield. "Shingwa! Dabaze!"

Two warriors sprinted forward to Mayinga's side.

"My father told us of what you did. We are thankful that you brought him back to us so he could die with honor among his own. He asked that we give you his shield and assegai as thanks. May his magic add to your strength and protect you from your enemies. We also gathered what was left of the cattle you brought from Jamburuland."

The warriors placed the shield and assegai at Ndoro's feet. Mayinga grasped Ndoro's shoulders, looking him in the eye as an equal.

"Whatever is your fate, Ndoro kaDingane, the warriors of kaShange will always be with you."

Another commotion drew his attention. Dingane's warriors marched across the royal kraal led by Dingane's senior induna, Qethuka. He was simply dressed, apparently not expecting the visit of Shange's warriors. The grey-haired man was plainly out of breath as he stood beside Ndoro. He glanced at Ndoro, clearly angry, and then smiled at Mayinga.

"Inkosi Dingane has heard of Shange's death and his sorrow is larger that the sun," he said. "We hope that his son will follow his father in respecting the rule of the Inkosi over the Land between the Mountains."

"My allegiances are those of my father's," Mayinga replied. "The kaShange remain the friends of Dingane…and his son."

Mayinga raised his assegai and his warriors stood. He spun and ran, his warriors making a path as he passed through them. As he crossed the river they turned and followed. The kaShange left the way they came, running and chanting until they disappeared over the rolling hills in the eastern horizon.

Quethuka glared at Ndoro.

"Inkosi Dingane knows the story of the cattle raid. You may have deceived the kaShange, but the inkosi is no fool. Still, Mayinga is a valuable ally and he seems to favor you. You and your mother will have access to the royal kraal and your food will be provided by the royal household."

"Will my father come see us?" Ndoro asked.

"Of course not," Qethuka snapped. "He is still Sesu, and you are still a meji."

Qethuka walked away, Dingane's guardsmen close behind. Ndoro wanted to be angry, but he could not muster the energy. The words of Mayinga stayed in his head, bringing with them hope. He would see his father one day, he was sure now. Shange's honor would one day make it come to pass. He knelt, picking up the assegai and shield of Shange and walked back to his mother's hut amid the murmurs of the curious. He looked at them all, smiled and closed the door behind him.

7

War season was over. The monsoons had come, the sky a perpetual gray, the rain continuous. Roads that once made way for warhorses and wagons became rivers of mud and water, virtually impassable. It was a time to rest, heal and plan.

Azikiwe watched the torrential rain from the window of his main palace and cursed the ancestors. It was his luck to be so close to crushing the Kossi army only to have the rains arrive early. He had no choice but to pull back or be trapped deep in Kossiland with no clear road to receive provisions from Baba-Ile, his main fortress. The few bridges spanning the Kalu River were overwhelmed, the lazy river transformed into a muddy torrent by the endless downpour.

Isala sat up, letting the white cotton sheets fall away from her naked form.

"Come back to bed, Azikiwe," she whispered.

Azikiwe turned and grinned, his large eyes growing even wider as he admired her. Her dark skin was flawless like porcelain, her full lips parted slightly as her brown eyes stared back at him. Perfect, beautiful, passionate Isala made his exile bearable. Five years had passed since he was banished from Abo by his father but the anger burned in him as if the punishment had occurred moments ago. The first four years were a jumble of battles won and lost, but gradually he and his Tijuku elite gained the upper hand against the tenacious Kossi. In the last year he had finally been able to accomplish what his father sent him north to do, and he had done it on his own.

Azikiwe sauntered back to the bed, dropping his robe along the way. War and leadership had hardened his body and mind since his days in Abo. Anyone who knew him then would hardly recognize him. He climbed back into the bed and wrapped Isala with his arms, kissing her fiercely. The made love furiously, their grunts and cries rising above the rumbling clouds and drumming rain. When they were done Azikiwe threw the sheets on the floor and jumped out of the bed, breathing heavily.

"You're a lioness," he said.

Isala sighed as she rolled onto her stomach. "Only for you, my lion."

Azikiwe picked up his robe and put it back on. "I have a meeting with Chimela in a few moments. Call for a servant to draw my bath."

Isala rose from the bed reluctantly and dressed. "Shall I accompany you?"

"No, you may not accompany me," he replied. "I need some strength left."

Isala left the room. Azikiwe found himself back at the window staring into the rain. It was time to bring this war to an end. Despite his success, the new prosperity in the North and the company of Isala, Azikiwe wanted to go home. Nothing he accomplished in the north would never equal the prestige of Abo and the comfort of being among his family. He could not return until he defeated the Kossi and he was determined that the next dry season would mark the beginning of his return to Abo.

A servant entered the room and immediately fell to the floor, flattening himself in complete submission.

"Oba, your bath is ready," he announced.

Azikiwe stepped over the man, walking to the end of the granite hallway and down the ironwood stairs to the baths. The granite tub was filled with warm water and fragrant oils which soothed his mind as he entered. He sat against the back of the tub, letting his head fall back on the cushioned headrest and closed his eyes, dreaming of Abo. His musing was interrupted by a deep growl.

"And how long was I supposed to wait while you took your beauty bath?"

Azikiwe opened his eyes to the great bulk that was Chimela. The commander of his army stood with his legs spread, his massive hands balled into fists pressed against his hips. Muddy leather riding boots covered his huge feet, climbing his calves to his knees, the tops draped by dark brown pantaloons. A thick belt circled his wide waist supporting his sword and scabbard. His shirt was covered with fetishes and talismans.

The huge man standing in his bath was his best and most loyal friend, choosing to leave in exile with him despite the protests of his family and his mentor, Kumba. Azikiwe was the first to admit he would not have survived in the north without Chimela's abilities and council.

"You know as well as I how important it is to keep the customs of civilization in the frontier," Azikiwe replied. "You smell like you need a bath."

Chimela began to remove his shirt. "I guess now is as good a time as any."

Azikiwe jumped out of the bath laughing. "Wait your turn!" He dried himself and dressed as Chimela waited.

"I'm surprised to find you alone," Chimela said. "Where is your woman?"

"She is in the bedchambers."

Chimela frowned. "You spend too much time with that girl. She will not be accepted in Abo."

"Who says she will ever see Abo?"

"You must have faith. We will return to Abo as heroes, my brother."

Azikiwe reached up and patted his friend on the shoulder. "Come, let's get this over with."

Azikiwe followed Chimela down the hall to the conference room. Rich woven carpets draped the walls, each representing the various villages, cities and tribes of the Mawena borderlands. Each corner of the room held abstract soapstone carvings of leopards, the royal symbol of Noncemba's clan. A large ebony wood table filled the center of the room, standing on a massive rug woven in the kente pattern of his family. A map of Mawenaland and Kossiland was carved into the surface of the table. Wooden pegs carved in the shape of Mawena and Kossi warriors lined the edge of the table.

"Don't you ever stop planning?" Azikiwe asked his friend.

"The Kossi outnumber us," Chimela replied matter-of-factly. "You know this as well as I. The only way we can keep them at bay is to stay ahead of them."

"I am tired of keeping them at bay. It is time we ended this game."

Chimela leaned against the table and stared. "And how do propose we do this? We have just enough warriors to patrol the border. Our advance into Kossiland was pure luck. The rainy season benefited us just as much as the Kossi."

"What if we concentrated our forces into a massive, decisive strike?"

Chimela frowned. "Where do we strike? If we attack any of the Kossi cities near the border we accomplish nothing. The only way an attack you suggest could work is if we…"

"…struck the heart of Kossiland," Azikiwe finished.

Chimela's expression was not complimentary. "You have finally lost your mind."

"Have I? Let's see. To strike the heart of Kossiland, we must break every rule of war as we know it."

Azikiwe walked to the war table and set up the warrior pieces. Each piece represented a Mawena or Kossi regiment, depending on the shape. Azikiwe placed the pieces on the board according to his latest briefing from Chimela. Chimela studied the placement and nodded in approval.

"This was the position of the Kossi army before the rainy season. We pulled back because our position in Kossiland was unsustainable," Azikiwe said. "The Kossi army pulled back as well. As a matter of fact, the majority of their army has gone home to their villages to plant their fields."

"As has ours," Chimela said.

Azikiwe smiled. "That leaves us with a standing army of four regiments, three warriors and one cavalry. If we include my Tijuku the total increases by one regiment."

A gleam came to Chimela's eyes. "The Kossi has no standing army, though their oba's guard totals three thousand, four thousand counting the city guard."

Chimela rubbed his chin. "This is an interesting exercise, but by the coming dry season Kossiland would be back to full strength."

"Who said anything about waiting until next dry season?"

Chimela stepped back from Azikiwe. "You can't serious! The roads are impassable, the men are tired and still healing and the priests are still pouring libations to the Kossi dead."

Azikiwe was undaunted. "We can use the forests instead of the roads if we divide our army into small units. The men are tired and hurt, but gold, salt and loot brings out the best in a warrior. The priests are always pouring libations. But most of all, the Kossi won't be expecting it."

Chimela went to the table and began shuffling the figurines about, pausing to study each scenario before shuffling them again. Azikiwe sat on his stool and waited patiently while his friend searched for a flaw in his plan. After an hour the big man stepped away from the table, sweat beading on his forehead, his massive hands gripping his waist belt.

"This could work," he finally said.

Azikiwe smiled. "Do you really think so?"

Chimela's smile was all the answer he needed. "There are a few issues that need to be worked out, but they're minor."

"So my friend, who will buy the beer when we return to Abo?"

"I will!" Chimela bellowed. "And I will buy it with Kossi gold!"

Chimela rushed Azikiwe and lifted him in the air in one of his familiar but painful hugs. "You are truly Oba Noncemba's son!"

Azikiwe regained his breath as Chimela put him down.

"There was a time I would have considered that a compliment," he said. "I'm going back to my bedchamber. I think you have a few details to take care of, my friend. I wish to be ready to proceed in two weeks. Can I trust you?"

"Of course!" Chimela charged out of the conference room. Azikiwe strolled down the hallway and returned to the bedchamber. Isala waited for him.

"What do you wish, my Lion?"

"I wish to take you to Abo and proclaim you my Great Wife," he said, pulling her and spinning her around.

"I wish to give you gold dust to sprinkle in your hair and amber to wear around you lovely neck. But instead, I will have to give you Povo."

Isala broke away from their dance and gave Azikiwe a serious look. "My oba, what are you talking about?"

"Don't worry about it, little bird," he answered. "These sorts of things need not concern you. Come, let us walk."

"But it is raining, my oba."

Azikiwe smiled. "Only on the outside, Isala; only on the outside."

* * *

The days passed and the rains continued. Chimela worked relentlessly on Azikiwe's plan, concentrating his forces at Baba-Ile. The fort had been evacuated of everyone except the Tijuku and the royal court. Secrecy was the rule; anyone looking the slightest suspicious of the activities surrounding the main fort was killed. As for Azikiwe, he continued his daily routine, unconcerned about the details of the coming campaign. He had ultimate trust in Chimela; his friend would let him know the details at the right time.

That time came during a Monday morning meeting with the village elders of a Kossi vassal village. Azikiwe struggled to stay awake as the tattered old men complained about the occupying Mawena. Chimela appeared behind the men, an angry look on his face. Azikiwe sat up on his stool.

"I will deal with your concerns later," he said to the elders. The old men bowed and left the chambers, glancing at Chimela in obvious fear.

"Well my friend, are we ready?"

Chimela said nothing until he was face to face with Azikiwe. "Why do you want to march on Povo?" he asked.

"I think I explained that to you," Azikiwe replied.

Chimela folded his arms across his chest. "You told me what I wanted to hear. What is your reason to want Povo?"

Azikiwe smiled. "You're losing your touch, my friend. It took you longer than I expected."

Chimela waited for an answer.

Azikiwe stood and began to pace. "The Kossi raid Mawena not for loot but for slaves. Their Oba possesses vast plantations surrounding the city that supply his merchant fleet with goods to trade across the ocean. If I can defeat the Kossi, I can establish a power base independent of Abo. Instead of Mawena working the plantations it will be Kossi men and women bearing the yoke."

"And when was I to be told of this?"

"When it was necessary."

Chimela found a stool and dragged it before Azikiwe. He dropped his bulk down hard and the stool cracked.

"This doesn't feel right, Azikiwe. This is beginning to resemble a rebellion."

This was no time for his sarcasm, Azikiwe thought. He sensed the struggle in his friend and had to choose his words carefully. Chimela was many things, but he was no traitor. He went to Chimela and sat on the ground before him, noting his surprise in the slight raise of his eyebrows.

"I thought you knew me better to think I would ever challenge my father's right to rule," he began. "He was chosen by the Queen Mother and confirmed by the elders. It is his right to rule."

Chimela nodded his head in agreement.

"You also know what my father thinks of me." Azikiwe dropped his head.

Chimela shifted on his stool. "Sometimes fathers are so busy correcting our faults they fail to see our attributes."

Azikiwe knew Chimela would understand this path of argument. His own father had admonished him for choosing the life of a soldier to that of a priest, the profession of his lineage. Chimela's family disowned him for his decision. Kumba's clan adopted him and raised Chimela as one of their own.

"When he feels his time is near, he will not select me as a candidate for oba."

"You do not know this, Azikiwe. Defeating the Kossi may change his opinion of you."

"I wish it were so, but I know better. I gave up on that dream long ago. He fancies my nephew Obaseki now."

Chimela chuckled. "The one who sees ghosts? I seriously doubt that."

"I may be wrong, but I'm sure I am not being considered. What I fear is what will happen afterwards. Whoever is selected may fear my claim. He may decide to simplify matters. If that happens I must have a refuge and a position of strength to protect myself and those who follow me."

"So this is your plan for Kossiland?"

"Yes it is."

Chimela moved from his stool to sit beside Azikiwe. "You plan to pledge your loyalty to your father?"

"Of course."

Chimela rubbed his chin. "This changes things. I envisioned a plan that would lay ruin to Povo and the surrounding villages. We would burn Diallo's plantations and destroy his docks. As we marched back to the river we would let the warriors plunder whatever stood between us and home as a reward for their victory."

"We need to keep as much intact as possible," Azikiwe said.

"I know." Chimela stood and extended his hand. Azikiwe let his friend pull him to his feet and they hugged.

"You are my best friend, Chimela. Thank you."

"Keep your thanks. We are outcasts together. You will have

your foundations before the rains cease. Kossiland will be ours."

Chimela walked to the door. "We will be ready to move in a week."

"I will be ready as well."

Chimela scowled and Azikiwe read his thoughts.

"I have to go," he said. "It is my place. The men will expect it."

Chimela strode back to Azikiwe with such force the prince was not sure of his intentions.

"This will not be a dainty march down a wide avenue," Chimela said. "The forest will be wet and miserable. We will have nothing to eat but cold hardcake and what we can steal from the local farmers. I can't allow anyone on this march that is not a fighting man, which means you must leave your servants behind unless they can wield a sword and a shield."

"I know the trials of the march, my friend. I was a soldier once."

"Excuse me Azikiwe, but your status shielded you from what most warriors endure. I'm not sure are prepared for this march."

"I am going, Chimela. I say this as your Oba, not as your friend."

Chimela flinched and Azikiwe immediately regretted what he had said. It was seldom when he had to use the power of his lineage on his friend, but he knew Chimela would not allow him to come on the march otherwise.

"As you wish...oba. You will be part of my group and dress as a common warrior. You will do as I order until I am sure the battle is won. We will reveal you to our men as if you had arrived at the moment of glory."

His friend always managed to find a way to be defiant.

Azikiwe bowed slightly. "As you wish, my commander."

"This is not a game, Azikiwe," Chimela warned. "Please take this seriously."

"I do, Chimela. Believe me, I do."

They parted ways, Chimela to his warriors and Azikiwe to the courtyard. The rain has stopped for a moment, the clouds thinning to tease those below with the promise of sunshine. Isala would take advantage of the respite for a walk and he was not surprised to find her stepping gingerly across the muddy expanse. Her servants walked beside her, their arms flying out to catch her at the slightest hint of a fall.

"You walk through the mud like you were born to it," he shouted.

Isala turned and smiled. "Are you calling me a buffalo?"

Azikiwe stomped through the mud to her side. He dismissed her servants and wrapped his arms around her.

"I must tell you something of great importance. I trust you with this knowledge as a pledge of my desire for you to be my Great Wife."

Isala eyes were wide and glistening. "What is it?"

"In one week we march against Povo."

Isala's hand flew to her mouth. "Attack…Provo? How can you do this? This is the rainy season. The warriors won't be ready."

"'The Kossi warrior won't, but the Tijuku will."

Azikiwe shared his plan with Isala who looked at him in disbelief. By time he was done the clouds bulged above them, robbing the sky of its hope. Drizzle covered her tight curls with a sensual sheen, but her beauty could not hide her emotions. She was very upset.

"What is wrong, sweet one?"

"I am honored to be by your side, my Oba, and I feel you plan is a good one. Despite my feelings for you I am still Kossi, and the thought of my people subject to the whims of Oba Noncemba sickens me."

"You will never answer to Abo," he assured her. "Kossiland will be in my charge."

"You will defy your father for my people?"

"No, I will defy my father for you."

Isala threw her arms around his neck and kissed him hard. "You will be a kind Oba."

"Only if you promise to be by my side, Isala. I will have only one wife, and it will be you."

Isala placed her head on his chest and Azikiwe hugged her.

"I am already yours," she whispered.

They kissed again as the rain fell heavier. Isala grasped his hand and pulled him toward the palace.

"Come, we must get out of the rain," she urged.

"You go on," Azikiwe said.

Azikiwe watched her run into the palace before continuing across the courtyard to the stables. The servants immediately fell to the ground, burying their faces into the mud. Three Tijuku appeared before him and bowed.

"Bring me my horse," he ordered.

The Tijuku rushed into the stable and returned with Azikiwe's stallion. The four of them mounted and galloped through the mud and the iron gate. Azikiwe led the men down the Oba's Highway towards Abo. They rode at a constant gallop until they reached a small road that intersected the highway. Azikiwe reined his horse and dismounted into the ankle deep mud. He ignored the filth on his boot, proceeding down the road without his bodyguards. He would need no protection in this place, for it was the Oba's woods, home of the Oba's priest.

The narrow path widened into a broad highway flanked by massive ironwood trees. They were in straight order, too perfect to have grown naturally. Azikiwe looked to either side, almost expecting to see the ancestors that dwelt among them watching one of their own perform the same ritual many of them had performed when a part of the living world. He was not a priest, nor was he Obaseki, so the spirits remained invisible to him, the occasional rustle of leaves the only sign of their presence

When he reached the ceremonial grounds the priests were waiting. They sat in a semi-circle around an ancient baobab so wide a village could live inside its hollow trunk. The mammoth tree towered over its brethren, its dense roots and dense canopy sucking the life from them. The priests sat as silent as the tree, unmoved by the constant drizzle.

Azikiwe dropped to his knees before them. He reached into his robes, extracting a bundle wrapped in an elaborate kente blanket. He bowed and extended the bundle.

"Uncles, I come to you for your favors," he said. "This is a symbol of my respect for you and the spirits of these woods."

Azikiwe kept his eyes closed as the bundle was taken from his hand. He knew its contents; there was more gold dust in the calabash than in the entire city of Abo. He didn't come to the sacred woods to ask the ancestors favor; he came to buy it.

"This is a generous gift," they said in unison. "But what is gold to those beyond? Your offering will afford us much, but what do you bring for those who have gone before you?"

"I have nothing, my uncles, that will sway my fathers before me," Azikiwe admitted. "But if they grant me this victory over Kossiland, their rewards will be unlimited."

The grove shook with hysterical laughter. "You wish to bargain with the ancestors? That is like holding smoke in your hand. Bring us something you value more than gold and victory will be yours."

Azikiwe thought on the request. There was little in this world that meant more to him than gold. The power he possessed was nothing to the ancestors. He could think of only one thing, and she was not negotiable.

"I will not give you Isala," he said

"Then you have nothing for us. Go and win your war alone."

Azikiwe jerked his head up angrily but the priests were gone. He ran to the hollow baobab tree and charged inside. The plant was like the inside of a large hut. Stools sat around a smoldering fire, sleeping cots braced against the inside trunk. He tore the hovel apart but found neither the priests nor his gold. He left the tree and the grove with a bitter taste in his mouth. Chimela warned him long ago never to go into battle without the blessing of the ancestors, but he was not about to give up the only person he truly loved. Nothing was worth that price.

The Tijuku were waiting as he exited the grove. He climbed

on his horse, looking one more time at the grove, angry that he wasted his time.

"I want this place burned to the ground when the dry season comes," he said. "It is useless to me."

He reined his horse and galloped back to Baba-Ile.

Chimela adjusted Azikiwe's chain mail, pulling each buckle tight. He stood back to observe his work then handed the prince a black kapok tunic.

"The cloth is treated to repel the rain and the kapok will stop poison arrows," he said.

"Do you expect us to encounter archers?"

"Not during the attack," Chimela replied. "Our scouts tell us there are First Men in the Kossi forest, and they hate the Kossi the same as Mawena. The will not attack us in force, but if one of the bastards thinks he can kill one of us and escape he will try."

"We should have cleared the forests of them before the attack," Azikiwe said.

"It would be easier to eat every leaf in the forest," Chimela said. "It's a minor risk, but we must be prepared. Our group will be the largest and the most likely to draw attention."

Azikiwe knew why. The group had been doubled in size to protect him. The plan was to separate the army into ten man units, each unit with a Kossi scout to lead them to rendezvous point on the banks of the Kossi River. There they would form into a complete unit and quick march to Povo. Mawena merchant spies had informed them there were no walls surrounding the outer city; only the royal grounds with its prosperous plantations were walled. The docks were unprotected as well. The Kossi were apparently very confident in their ability to protect their capital city.

Chimela began to wrap his turban when Isala entered the stables.

"I would like to wrap my Oba's turban," she said.

Chimela glared at the woman. "She should not be here," he hissed.

"I know how you feel about protocol. It's okay, my friend."

He motioned for her to come forward. Isala went to Chimela and took the black cloth from him. She turned to Azikiwe and pulled him to her with the cloth.

"Don't go," she whispered.

"We had that discussion and I won. Now wrap my turban."

Isala draped the cloth over his shoulders. She reached into her dress and revealed a piece of amber strung on a simple leather cord which she hung on Azikiwe's neck.

"Wear this for me," she said. "It will bring you back to me."

"Chimela will bring me back to you," Azikiwe said. "My turban, please."

Isala wrapped the cloth around his head into a perfect turban. She kissed on his check then left the room, glancing back with a smile.

Chimela handed him a standard issue sword, a plain steel blade with an iron hilt and wooden scabbard.

"We are ready now," Chimela said.

"May the ancestors protect us," Azikiwe replied.

They slipped from the fort at dusk under the cover of shadows and rain, following their scouts until they were well beyond the Kossi-Mawenaland border. Once they were deep in the forest they built huts for the night, Azikiwe sharing shelter with Chimela. They broke camp before dawn and continued their march, fighting the dense woods and brush for every step forward. Azikiwe struggled more than the others; too many years had passed since he took part in a hard march. His legs felt as if the bone had disappeared as they wavered with every step. His men offered their hands but he refused, determined make his own way. When the night came he helped build his hut then collapsed onto his cot exhausted.

They had estimated a twelve day march to the rendezvous point but the heavy rain and dense forest slowed them. Azikiwe worried that the others had arrived and were waiting anxiously for them. The longer they gathered, the more likely they would be discovered. Every group had been instructed to remain secluded until he and Chimela arrived, but is would be nearly impossible to hide such a large force for any extended period of time. Chimela tried to increase the pace but the forest fought back, tangling their arms and legs with vines, striking their faces with sharp branches and wounding them with thorns and stinging insects. When they finally stumbled out of the woods to the clearing they were totally drained.

Azikiwe fell to his knees gasping for breath. He lurched forward and found himself staring into the face of a dead Mawena warrior.

"Chimela!"

Azikiwe jumped to his feet and yanked his sword free. Kossi warriors rushed from the woods on the other side the clearing, their white robes and turbans in contrast to the Mawena dark disguises. The Mawena charged, Chimela well in front of the others, his massive sword gripped with both hands. He slammed into the enemy and scattered their line with one massive swing, decapitating a hapless warrior in front of him while slicing another man's arm off with the same stroke. Azikiwe and the other fell in beside him and the struggle began in the downpour. As he fought with all his strength he realized his dream was at an end. The Kossi had discovered his plan; how, he did not know. At least he would die fighting and be spared the humiliation of his father's admonishment.

The Kossi pulled back. Azikiwe and the others gave chase, led by the unstoppable Chimela. The massive warrior turned the tide of battle single-handedly, his speed and fury unmatched. Azikiwe found a reason for hope. Maybe they would not march on Povo, but they might just survive this attack and make their way back to Baba-Ile. Strength flooded his legs as he chased the remaining Kossi back into the woods. He was about to let out a victory cry when the Kossi archers emerged from the brush.

The Mawena halted. Chimela turned to Azikiwe, his eyes sorrowful.

"Go back, Azikiwe. The ancestors are not with us today."

He turned and charged the archers, his men following in

silent determination. Azikiwe ran to the other side of the clearing surrounded by his Atuegbu. He stopped at the woods' edge and turned back.

"Oba, we must go now before they catch us!" one of his guards urged.

Azikiwe glared at the man and turned back. Chimela and his men were close when the archers let loose their first volley. Half of the men went down, Chimela taking an arrow in the shoulder. He broke the shaft with his free hand and continued charging, swinging his sword over his head. The second volley fell more men but the Mawena continued their assault. Chimela broke another arrow from his chest. He slowed but he continued forward, curses flying like spittle from his mouth. The Kossi archers fumbled with their arrows as huge bleeding Chimela ran down upon them. They broke and ran, throwing their bows into the mud and fleeing into the trees. Chimela was alone, charging forward, yelling and waving his sword. The Kossi warriors reappeared like hyena pouncing on their wounded prey. Like a cornered lion Chimela fought, slashing and hacking the growing number of Kossi warriors. The objective was no longer to defeat the Mawena; it was to kill this unstoppable warrior decimating their ranks.

The Kossi surged again and Chimela went down. Azikiwe had seen enough; he would tell the story of his friend's final stand, holding him up to the highest honor.

"We can go now," he said. He turned away just as a volley of Kossi arrows fell down on them. A sharp pain pierced his back and Azikiwe fell to his knees. The blow took whatever energy remained in him. He slumped to his knees, easing himself down into the wet underbrush. There was no use fighting any longer. He hoped the ancestors would be kinder to him that he was to them. He placed his face against the wet grass, closed his eyes and let the darkness take him.

He awoke in darkness, a damp stench heavy in the stale air. The pain in his back had diminished to a dull throb. He lay still, waiting for his eyes to adjust but they refused. He realized he was no longer outside; he was inside some chamber that blocked the light.

He tried to rise but he was too weak. How long had he been in this room? Where was he? The realization that he had been captured made him even weaker. He had failed to conquer Povo and he had failed to escape. The best that could happen to him was that he would die in this prison, saving himself and his father the disgrace.

That grim hope was taken away with the rattling of metal and squealing hinges. A vertical seam appeared and light seeped into the room. A Kossi warrior stepped into the chamber followed by two men dressed in grey tunics and black shorts. They held short metal studded clubs in their hands as they advanced toward him.

"Is this the one?" the warrior asked.

One of the grey men nodded his bald head. The men rushed forward, pinning Azikiwe to the rotted straw. The warrior bent over him and reached into his shirt, extracting the amber necklace."

"It's him. Bring him."

The grey men lifted him to his feet and carried him out of the chamber. The dim light hurt his eyes so he kept them closed as they took him to another chamber and stripped of his clothes. Azikiwe yelled as they dropped him into a tub of hot water and scrubbed him with coarse brushes. His eyes were wide open now.

He was lifted from the tub and dried with soft towels. The warrior stepped forward and bowed, extending a bundle of clothes to him.

"Oba Azikiwe, Askia Diallo wishes you to join him at the palace as soon as you are able. He sends these garments with his apologies and hopes you will join him soon."

The robes were Mawena constructed with the finest cotton cloth and trimmed in royal kente. Azikiwe dressed as the trio watched, his mind working furiously to figure out what was happening. Once he was dressed the Kossi warrior smiled and bowed again.

"Please follow me," he requested.

Azikiwe followed the warrior through the plain building

and out into the brilliant sunlight. He stopped, shielding his eyes from the intense brightness. The light dimmed quickly; he turned to his right to see another man standing beside him holding an elaborate royal umbrella over him. The large man was dressed only in a loincloth with an iron slave band encircling his right bicep. The man was Mawena, one of the many captured by Kossi slave raiders. He did not recognized Azikiwe but he turned away in respect.

He was in Povo. The smell of the sea burned his nostrils, the sharp blue sky dotted with high white clouds and seagulls. White washed stone homes with blue roofs lined the broad stone avenues leading to the royal wall protecting the Askia's palace. Kossi crowded the streets, moving with their characteristic saunter, no one in any hurry to reach their destination. Their sing song dialect was pleasant to the ears, making the city seem like a continuous celebration to his unfamiliar ears. No one seemed to notice him; Azikiwe assumed they saw him as just another noble visiting the Askia. Only the warrior and the prison guards seem to know his true identity.

He followed the warrior to the wall gates. The gate entrance was a towering door of metal inlaid with golden threads that wove abstract images of the Askias past and their military triumphs. Mawena images were just as numerous as Kossi, although his people were almost always shown in chains or in poses of death. Two warriors holding tall assegais flanked the gate. They bowed and stepped away as the gate was raised.

Azikiwe hesitated. He was being set up; he was sure, but for what he did not know. His escort stood beside him.

"Please continue, Oba. The Askia is waiting."

Azikiwe entered the palace compound of Askia Diallo. The wealth of the Kossi was immediately evident everywhere he looked. The common tabby stone of the highway was replaced by elaborate mosaic tile of blue and white which led to the gilded palace gate. Towering bleached white walls punctuated with narrow towers at each corner enclosed the palace. The palace gate stood as high as the wall, thick planks of wood bolted together by wide straps of iron and inlaid with gold and cowry shells. A golden octopus filled the center of the gate, the clan totem of Kossi's royal family. The broad building wore a dome blue as the sea. Although their kingdom extended deep into the interior, the Kossi were and would always be a people of the sea.

Askia Diallo sat on a gilded throne before the entrance of his palace, flanked by the Kossi elders and backed by his personal guard. He was dressed simply in the traditional Kossi white pants and robe, a simple golden ring with milky white pearls encircling his head. His dark brown complexion reminded Azikiwe of Isala. He seemed young, but there was hardness in his smile that betrayed his age.

Askia Diallo rose as Azikiwe approached and bowed. The others did the same, remaining in the submissive pose until the Mawena sat on the cushioned stool before Diallo's throne. Diallo sat and smiled.

"I am honored. I apologize for your terrible treatment. My men did not know you."

A dull pain appeared in Azikiwe's stomach. "How did you know who I was? How did you discover our plans?"

Diallo's face became sad. "I must apologize again. We are a proud people, but not as numerous or brave as you Mawena. We must fight our wars in ways which require our people to make personal sacrifices for the good of us all. Isala is one of those people. She is one of our best."

Nausea swept over him and he swayed, weak from the word of his betrayal. She had marked him with the amber necklace so they would be sure to find him.

"She said she loved me," he stammered.

"I'm sure she does," Diallo replied. "You are a handsome man and you offer much to a woman of her status. But that is the beauty of Isala. She does her duty for her Askia despite her feelings. She is a true treasure."

Diallo leaned forward and placed his hand on Azikiwe's shoulder.

"I did not bring you here to embarrass you, my friend. Your

plan was brilliant and would have succeeded if not for Isala. Your men fought valiantly, especially your friend Chimela. He will always be remembered by my warriors with great respect. Many sons in Kossiland will bear his name."

Diallo leaned back into his throne, his face distraught. "I am troubled, Azikiwe. I see before me a brave man, a hero of Mawena who deserves to be respected by his people and more importantly, honored by his father."

"Do not speak of him," Azikiwe spat.

"We must," Diallo replied. "Your father is the scourge of both of us. It is said that a common enemy forges unlikely friendships."

Azikiwe resisted Diallo's logic. "My father is not my enemy."

"He is certainly not your friend. He banished you to the outskirts of his kingdom and forced you to take a risk to regain his favor. Word of your defeat has surely reached Abo yet no delegation has come to ransom your freedom. He has left you here to die, Azikiwe. Your fate is in my hands."

"Then be done with it," Azikiwe retorted. "My skull is ready to take its place in your collection."

"I have no intentions of executing you. I see us both as victims, Azikiwe, victims of the rivalries of our fathers. But my father is dead and yours has disowned you. This is our opportunity to end the fighting between our people and come together for the prosperity of us all."

Azikiwe's head began to throb. "What are you asking me?"

"I wish to see peace between the Kossi and the Mawena. With your father in power that is not possible."

Azikiwe fought to stay upright in his stool. "Forgive my inattention, Askia. It has been days since I've eaten, I think."

"I understand. You need rest. We will talk again after you have had time to rest."

Diallo signaled his bodyguards and they came forward. Azikiwe's escort helped him to his feet and led him to a small house beside the palace. He stepped through the wooden door and was relieved. A small bed rested against the wall; beside it was a table covered with fruit and a simmering pot of stew. He stumbled to the table and attacked the stew, almost spilling it as he devoured it. With his stomach settled and his headache gone he collapsed onto the bed and fell into a dreamless sleep. He had no idea how long he slept when a woman's voice stirred him awake.

"My Oba?"

Azikiwe sat up to see Isala at the foot of his bed. She rushed him before he could speak, kissing him and pushing him back onto the bed. He wanted to hate her but his body responded hungrily to her touch. He held her tight in his arms, kissing her everywhere. Her love for him was a lie, as was everything Diallo said to him, but he didn't care. The lie in Povo was better that the truth waiting for him in Abo. Diallo was true about one thing; in order for him to be his own man, he had to rid himself of his father.

When they were done Isala tried to lie beside him but he pushed her away. She seemed shocked, her eyes wide and glistening.

"What is wrong?" she asked. "Have I offended you?"

Azikiwe rose from the bed and dressed.

"I need you to take a message to Diallo," he said. Pain and confusion had fled his mind, leaving him free to make a clear decision unfettered by the opinion of his father and his people.

"Tell the Askia I wished to meet with him," he continued. "Not as Kossi and Mawena, but as brothers."

8

Dingane and Inaamdura sat side by side under the solitary baobab dominating the Royal Courtyard. A messenger knelt before them, resplendent in his white robe and cap, the royal insignia of Shamfa dangling from his neck on a thick gold chain. He extended his arms, handing a message scroll to the inkosi. Dingane, covered in brushed cowtails from neck to ankles, sneered at the messenger and looked to his wife. Inaamdura took the scroll from the Shamfa messenger's trembling hands and nimbly untied the cords binding in together. She took her time, unraveling the leather strips with a delicacy they did not deserve. She was splendid as always, her head shaven and adorned with a simple golden cord. She'd shed her admiration beads the day she wed Dingane, replacing them with a single necklace of amber and gold. She still wore her Bonga robes, refusing to adopt the drab cloaks of married Sesu women. She did succumb to their intricate beadwork, wearing a belt of white and red beads; a clear symbol of her supreme status among Dingane's other wives.

She hesitated unraveling the scroll. She knew what it contained; it was a message as inevitable as the coming and going of the rains. It had come sooner that expected, which meant her plans were more transparent than she hoped. Still, the wheel was in motion. No one could stop it now.

She unrolled the scroll and handed it back to the messenger.

"Read it," she commanded.

"Inkosa, I thought…"

Inaamdura's smile calmed the worried herald. "Of course I can read. I would prefer you to read it, my brother. It has been a long time since I heard the words of my homeland spoken by someone other than myself."

The messenger bowed and unraveled the scroll.

"My dearest daughter," he read. "It has been five dry seasons since you left us and my heart still aches when I visit my garden. The days are colder without your company and council. It is time you visited your mother. We have much to discuss."

Dingane shrugged his shoulders. "Is that all? That was a waste of good paper. The damn messenger could have memorized it."

"Please, Dingane. This is a letter from my mother. She deserves your respect."

Dingane laughed. "She is not my wife or my mother. She deserves nothing from me."

He lifted his bulk and left. Inaamdura watched him, admiring his firm form. She had been right when she advised her mother on the Sesu Inkosi years ago. Her sister could not have controlled this man. But she was also wrong that day as well. Inaamdura, her mother's greatest pupil, could not control him, either.

She took the scroll and read it silently. The words forming in her head were different from those she read. It was the hidden meaning behind the obvious, the true intent of the message far from innocuous.

"I know what you are up to," the words said to Inaamdura. "Meet me immediately if you wish to avoid a war."

She rolled the scroll and handed it back to the messenger.

"Thank you for your loyalty to my father and mother. I will give you a message to return to them and I pray for your safe return.

"When shall I leave with your reply, Great Mother?"

"The rainy season will be over soon," Inaamdura mused. "I insist you remain as our guest until then."

The messenger didn't try to hide his disappointment.

"Inkosa, the journey from Shamfa was long and dangerous. It's been months since I've seen my family. If it is not too much to ask, I wish to leave as soon as possible. I have performed my duty. I wish only to return home."

Inaamdura kept her smile despite the anger seething beneath her flawless brown skin. This fool was probably some noble's son, someone who thought his rank gave him the privilege to speak to her in such a way.

"I am aware of your discomfort, but my decision is final. You will remain with us until the dry season, and then you will accompany us to Shamfa. You can, of course, disregard my command and leave on your own accord. I must warn you that although the Sesu are not well versed in Shamfa protocol, they know an insult when they see it. You may not survive the trip home."

The messenger's eyes narrowed. "I am a messenger! My position grants me immunity."

Inaamdura frowned, allowing her true emotions to the surface. "This is not Shamfa. This is Sesuland."

Her guards grasped the messenger under his arms, lifted him from the ground and carried him from the courtyard. Inaamdura remained composed until he disappeared then slumped into the soft kapok cushions of her throne. The messenger was right; he did have immunity. Among the cities of the north protocol was important, a necessity that always allowed an opportunity for rival kingdoms to converse in times of peace and war. But she was also right when she stated the obvious. The Sesu had no need of protocol. Dingane once told her that negotiations were for the weak. The strong made demands and the weak acquiesced. The Sesu way had seeped into her pores, molding her way of thinking and way of living. Though she exerted great influence over the inkosi, she did not control him. He remained his own man, listening to her council but not always following her advice. Every decision she made had to be confirmed by him. He made it obvious to her; she was his Great Wife, but she was not his equal.

Still, she could bask in her accomplishments. Under her guidance the Sesu had transformed from a powerful clan depended on plundering their weaker neighbors to a kingdom that controlled the ebb and flow of life in the grasslands. The constant raids acquiring tribute had been replaced by a series of fortified towns positioned strategically by major trade routes to collected tariffs for safe passage. The accumulated wealth allowed Dingane to form a standing army, one that was well fed, well armed and well trained. A farming class developed, focusing its energy on the rich soil along the Kojo. Selike became a permanent city, grass huts replaced by wood and stone homes, weak thorn fences replaced by stone enclosures holding each clan's cattle.

Sesuland's prosperity sparked the message from her mother. There was no way it would go unnoticed in the north, since most of the merchants taxed by the Sesu were headed to Shamfa. The caravans arriving in the northern reaches carried less goods, driving up the prices of the little they were allowed to keep. The caravans were also less frequent as the southern merchants realized they could seek their fortunes among the Sesu and take advantage of the relative peace Sesu domination had imposed upon the grasslands. Shamfa would not sit by and watch its wealth be siphoned away by a people they considered beneath them.

She left in search of her husband, recalling the first time she saw Dingane. She was overwhelmed by his vitality and seduced by his presence. He was a man born to lead, a warrior who gained his position by proving his fitness to his people and his ancestors by bringing victory long before their marriage. The Sesu were not a people that valued politics; their way was straightforward and brutal. If an induna wished to challenge Dingane's authority he would gather his warriors and attack him. There was never a doubt in Dingane's intentions.

She found him in the Royal Kraal, standing under the acacia wearing only his loincloth and headring. Inaamdura frowned; the years had not softened her feelings on Sesu attire. Nakedness was tolerated among common folk, but nobles must display their rank.

"So you will go visit your mother?" he asked.

Inaamdura knelt at his feet. "If you allow it, my husband."

Dingane laughed and lifted her to her feet. "I couldn't stop you if I tried. Your attempt at being a good Sesu wife is admirable, but

I know you suffer. Bonga men are weak. They need their women to give them counsel. We Sesu are a different breed."

"You are, indeed."

Dingane studied her face then smiled. "I don't think you meant that as a compliment. Of course you can visit your mother. It has been a long time since you've seen your family."

"She expects gifts," Inaamdura warned.

"And she shall have them," her husband replied. "Take what you think will make her happy."

Inaamdura looked up at her husband. Was he agreeing with her? She expected an argument or at least a lively exchange. Her eyes focused on him, studying his expressions, his body movements, his breathing, all the signs a Bonga wife was taught to understand the mood of her husband as so to manipulate him. She jumped as she realized what Dingane was doing.

"You know, don't you?" she said.

Dingane smiled. "I can't read that mountain scribble, but the words spoken by your messenger carried many meanings. Go to your mother with her tribute. But let her know it is only a gift from a daughter to a mother, not a tribute from the Sesu to the Shamfa."

"She won't accept anything but tribute. We are strong, Dingane, but we are not ready for war with Shamfa. The tribes we defeated in the grasslands are ants compared to the northern nations. They will not balk at the sight of your warriors. They are well-armed and their walls are made of stone, not branches. If we don't offer tribute their armies will come the moment the rainy season ends."

"Walls are only as strong as their weakest gate," Dingane answered. "As I said, take you mother her gifts. You decide what you will need. I will organize your escort."

"My escort?"

"Of course," Dingane said smiling. "You are my Great Wife. I cannot let you go into the wilderness with such a treasure alone."

Inaamdura felt coldness in her throat. "It is not necessary, my husband. Who would dare threaten the wife of Inkosi Dingane?"

In a sudden motion he lifted her off her feet, cradling her in his massive arms like a child. "Come inkosa, let us talk of other things. His fierce kiss doused her protest and she wrapped her arms around his shoulders. As he carried her to their bedchamber she realized she would never control this man. She never wanted to.

Small hands played with Inaamdura's face, dragging her from pleasant slumber to muted daylight. She grabbed the culprit's little wrists and lifted him above her as she opened her eyes. Ligongo stared down at her, a clever smile on his face.

"What are you up to, little zebra?" Ligongo squirmed but Inaamdura's grip was sure.

"You're not as strong as your baba, at least not yet." He squealed when she dropped him, catching him before he hit her chest then holding him tight. Four years ago the ancestors had finally given her a child. A boy, a true blessing compare to the abomination born to Shani twelve years before. Though she loved her son, she knew he was not the boy Dingane hoped for. There was no trace of Sesu in his face. He resembled her father, the fat cheeks and narrow nose a clear sign of Shamfa blood. Some whispered that he was not Dingane's son, but the child of some long lost love from her past, some noble who had managed to slip into the royal kraal and sleep with her, leaving his seed to be raised as the son of Dingane, much like the cuckoo leaves its egg in the nests of others. The words attacked her virtue but she ignored them. Ligongo was her pride; she loved him as she loved Bikita, unrestrained and uninhibited.

"Momma, are we going on a trip?" he asked.

"Yes we are. We are going to see your grandmamma."

Ligongo looked puzzled.

"Your grandmamma is my mother. She is a great queen."

"Is she a greater queen than you?"

Inaamdura laughed as she played with his hair. "Much greater. Come now, we must get ready for our journey."

"I'm ready!" he proclaimed, throwing his arms into the air.

"Not quite, little zebra. Let's go to your room and find you some decent garments."

Ligongo broke free and ran ahead. Inaamdura watched him go, fighting the fear that crept into her heart. In Shamfa he would be celebrated; gifts piled at the foot of his cradle, hordes of people lined outside the inner walls to catch a glimpse of their new prince. In Sesuland a shadow loomed over him, an obstruction named Ndoro. By Sesu law his ascension to the stool was impossible due to the shunning imposed on him by Mulugo. The ancestors seemed to have ignored their own curse, for Ndoro was growing up to be more than anyone could have imagined. At sixteen he was an accomplished warrior, tall and broad of shoulder with agility none could match. People still told the story of Shange's honor, whispering among themselves that maybe Mulugo was wrong. Ndoro was Dingane's son in every way; the elders must surely see the obvious.

Such talk had not bothered Inaamdura until Ligongo was born. He deserved to be Dingane's heir. Everything the Sesu had become was because of her tireless work. She would not let the son of a disgraced wife claim what her son deserved. Mulugo had done a fair job keeping Ndoro down, but his influence was wavering. Dingane was noticing the boy more of late, giving him long glances and an occasional smile when he thought no one looked. Inaamdura always looked and she always saw.

Ligongo broke her trance, pulling on her hem.

"Look, mamma. I'm ready to go!"

Inaamdura looked at her boy and tried to keep a smile on her face. Ligongo was dressed in Sesu regalia, a leopard headring round his head, a necklace of brushed cowtails cascading over his chest and back. Another ring of cowtails encircled his waist, the ends brushing the tops of more cowtails around his ankles. He held a white shield in his left hand, a small assegai in his right. Dingane's youngest wife, Ntozake stood behind him, a smug smile on her face.

"You look wonderful," she said. "Now go outside and wait for me. I must speak to Ntozake. Ligongo skipped out into the courtyard, jabbing his assegai at imaginary opponents.

Inaamdura waited until her son was at the opposite side of the courtyard before slapping Ntozake, knocking her to the ground. She dropped her knee into the young wife's stomach and grabbed her hair, pushing her head into the ground.

"Who do you think you are?" Inaamdura hissed. "You wish to play games with my son?"

Ntozake tried to answer but Inaamdura slapped her again.

"I am tired of you Sesu and your damned insults. You can attack me, but you will not use my son against me."

Inaamdura pushed Ntozake's head into the floor as she stood. "If I killed you today Dingane wouldn't care. If you wish to live long enough to bear him sons, you will do well not to cross me."

Inaamdura fled the room full of anger and shock. What had she done? Whatever possessed her rushed through her like a wildfire. Ligongo's innocent face triggered her rage, the boy oblivious to the insult his outfit represented. This emotion was new to her; she would have to learn to recognize it and control it. Control was essential for a Bonga wife. If she could not restrain her own emotion she stood no chance manipulating the emotions of others. She repeated the incident over and over in her mind as she went to the stables, analyzing each moment for signs of weakness.

Her porters waited with wagons filled with precious objects and provisions for the journey. Each wagon was hitched to a team of oxen, a driver assigned to every one. A small man with a muscular build and a speckled beard approached, falling to his knees and touching his head to the ground.

"Inkosa Inaamdura, we are ready," he announced.

"Good, Ramosa. Where is my escort?"

"I do not know inkosa."

"Didn't the inkosi send them?"

"I have seen no one, inkosa."

Inaamdura sighed. "I will not wait for them. Prepare my wagon. I will get Ligongo."

Inaamdura found Ligongo chasing his younger brothers with his shield and spear. She grabbed him and dragged him away, her patience growing shorter and shorter as her departure neared.

Dingane's escort had not arrived when she returned. She pushed Ligongo into the wagon then signaled Ramosa.

"We leave now," she shouted.

Ramosa's worried face angered her more.

"Inkosa, we must wait for the escort."

"Ramosa, get these wagons moving now!"

Warrior chants spilled into the stable yard. The escort arrived, fifty warriors dressed similar to Ligongo, their cowtails bouncing as they ran to surround the escort. Induna Kotsi approached her wagon, bowing with exaggerated motions.

"Inkosa, I apologize for my lateness. Inkosi Dingane insisted we visit Mulugo for his blessings before we came. We wished the ancestors' sanction for this special journey."

Inaamdura looked at the escort and was disappointed. They were Dingane's best, she was sure, but there were so few of them. Her mother would not be impressed.

"Is this all?"

Kotsi bowed again. "I am sorry, inkosi. Mulugo is slow. The others will catch up to us later."

Inaamdura looked at the man, letting her rage trickle away. She was weary of reacting to every situation without thought. A fly landed on Kotsi's head and she focused on it, watching the insect attempt to burrow into his dense hair. The fly wandered to his head ring, crawling and buzzing around the warrior's dome. The humor drenched her rage; she now stood before him trying not to laugh.

"You are here now, Kotsi," she said with a grim. "There is no need to discuss your tardiness. Take your place. We leave now."

Ramosa cracked his whip and the journey was underway. Ligongo slept, his lean body stretched across two pillows at the head of the wagon. Inaamdura went to the rear, reclining on rugs of leopard and lion, an ivory head rest covered with a navy silk pillow placed at the edge of the rugs. She went to the rugs and collapsed, her head throbbing. The wagon lurched and they were on their way, the oxen keeping time with the cadence chant of the escort. Inaamdura closed her eyes and let the chanting and rocking coax her to sleep.

She chose to meet her mother close to Nontuluzelo, the lush valley that served as a boundary between Shamfa and Sesuland. It was once the home of the Shamfa before frequent Sesu raids pushed them north into the foothills of the Urowo Mountains, homeland of the Bonga. The Sesu chose not to settle the area because of its lack of good grazing, but attacked the Shamfa when ever they attempted to reclaim it. Eventually both tribes abandoned the valley, accepting it as an unofficial buffer zone. The journey would take ten days, too long a time for Inaamdura to worry herself over the meeting with her mother. Instead she immersed herself in the amusement of Ligongo, playing countless games of oware and naming the endless procession of animals they saw along the way. The warriors insisted on taking the prince with them on their daily hunts, but Inaamdura permitted him to go every other day. He needed to develop a kinship with the men he would one day lead, but he also needed to keep a respectful distance. This was her advantage over Ndoro and his mother. They could admire the ostracized boy, but they would never bond to him like they would Ligongo. She would see to that.

One night away from the rendezvous Inaamdura awoke to darkness. The day had long passed, the sky sparkling with constellations, the full moon casting a strong light across the fields. She climbed out of the wagon, pulling her cloak close as a chilly wind swirled about her. She smiled as the familiar breath from the distant mountains danced about the camp, teasing the withering fires and agitating the smoldering embers of earlier flames gone dead. The air was sweet, tinged with the moisture of the nearby river and seasoned with the musky fragrance of constantly blooming shrubs. The image of her mother's garden appeared in her thoughts and the wind suddenly became cold, shaking her limbs and raising bumps on her soft skin. She pulled her cloak tighter, protecting herself from the fear that drifted on the wind and touched her soul. Was this some sort of spell? Was her mother making sure she would not be ready to face her? Inaamdura turned to run back into her wagon when she saw the silhouette of a warrior against the horizon, a chagga pipe dangling from his lips as he leaned on his assegai. His shield lay at his feet, serving as a makeshift bed while on the march. He displayed no fear, though he was miles away from home near the land of his enemy. He was a Sesu; no man could defeat him. Death could only claim him if he allowed. She calmed, the wind's frigid grip subsiding. She looked at the warrior a moment longer before retiring to her wagon, a decision clear in her head.

Morning had long passed when the Shamfa party came into view. It was a grand spectacle, an arrival designed to impress and awe. Inaamdura stood before her tribute wagon, a smirk marring her perfect countenance. The Imperial Wagon lumbered forward, pulled by ten oxen and five drivers. Two hundred Shamfa cavalrymen flanked the wagon, covered in yellow kapok quilts, red cylindrical caps rising high from their heads. Each rider carried a lance flying the yellow banner of the royal family. Their mounts were decorated as well in yellow kapok quilts with red piping. Drummers played and dancers performed, singing a song that Inaamdura knew by heart but for some reason struck her as unfamiliar.

Lingongo clapped to the rhythm, a joyous smile on his face.

"You were right, mama," he squealed. "Grandma is a greater queen than you!"

Inaamdura ignored the naïve enthusiasm of her son. Kotsi, standing on her right, was not as forgiving.

"It is a dance of fools," he said. "Only the weak would be impressed. A man still bleeds when he is stabbed by an assegai, no matter how pretty his clothes."

"Whenever you are ready," Inaamdura said to Kotsi.

Kotsi barked and a young warrior ran forward, a throwing spear gripped in his hand. The induna nodded and the man took a running start and let the spear fly. It soared in a perfect arc, landing over a hundred paces from where they stood.

The Shamfa stopped. One of the riders dismounted, pulling a spear from his quiver. He ran and threw as well, his spear landing a good fifteen paces away.

"It will be a long walk, inkosi," Kotsi commented. "You should ride on the wagon."

"I'll walk," Inaamdura replied. She grasped the nose ring of the ox harnessed to the tribute wagon and led him away, her firm grip quickly subduing the protests of the beast. She watched as the door opened to the Imperial Wagon and her mother emerged. From a distance she looked the same, but Inaamdura had readied herself for the changes time may have visited on her. Another woman emerged from the wagon and stood beside her mother. She was too tall to be Amadika; it was possible her mother had acquired a servant. The duo came forward, walking with the graceful dignity of Bonga women. Halfway across the field the woman with her mother broke away and ran towards her, her arms outstretched.

"Rah-rah!" she shouted.

"Bikita?" Inaamdura focused on the woman's face as he came closer. It was her; the woman running to her was Bikita. She succumbed to a rush of joy, releasing the ox and running to her little sister. They hugged, Inaamdura comforted by the willowy arms of her sister.

"I missed you so much," Bikita confessed. "I wanted to visit, but momma said it wouldn't be proper."

Inaamdura forced her arms to let go of Bikita, her hands sliding down into her sister's.

"You have been to the garden, I see."

Bikita's face became solemn. "Yes I have."

Inaamdura nodded in understanding. Her little sister was gone, her innocence lost once she ventured beyond the wooden gate of Azana's garden.

"She's headstrong just like you," Azana said. Inaamdura had not noticed her mother's approach. She looked older but still beautiful, the lines on her face adding wisdom to her presence. Inaamdura knelt at her mother's feet.

"Forgive me if my time with Bikita poisoned her with my bad habits."

Azana touched her shoulder, giving her permission to rise.

"Bikita was destined to behave the way she does. You have no fault here."

Inaamdura stepped aside, displaying the wagon. "I can never hope to repay you for all you have given me, mamma. I hope you accept my offering in the spirit in which it is given."

Azana glanced at the wagon and stared at Inaamdura. "My love knows no price, daughter. The Shamfa require something more."

Inaamdura pushed the emotions stirred by Bikita's presence aside. Her mother was ready to talk. There would be no more indirect banter.

"Inkosi Dingane respects my wish to honor my mother. He does not understand why he should send tribute to the Shamfa."

"The Shamfa have allowed the Sesu to establish themselves as protectors of the trade routes leading north," Azana replied. "This has caused some discomfort among our people which can be reconciled by the proper tribute for our generosity."

"Sesu warriors subdued the tribes of the grasslands. Sesu servants built the roads that cross the grasslands. Sesu elders administer the peace impartially, allowing the trade north to prosper more than anyone has seen. We see no Shamfa hand in this."

Azana's eyebrows rose when Inaamdura used the term "we". She came at Inaamdura quickly, stopping so close their noses almost met.

"Is this the best you could accomplish?" she demanded. "Your husband careens around the grasslands like a drunken child, claiming to be the master of it all. I knew Amadika would fail as soon as I saw him, but I thought you had a chance. No, I knew you could do it. Instead you stand before me insulting me with this nonsense of Sesu control."

"You have underestimated them," Inaamdura argued. "You did then and you still do now. My council has played a part in this, but Dingane is more than just an ambitious barbarian. He leads a people that believe the world belongs to them and they will not stop until they claim it all. They don't bog themselves down with the intrigues of politics. Their actions are simple, direct and effective."

Azana seemed to listen to Inaamdura's words. She stood silent, her face emotionless. It was Bikita that warned her something was wrong. Her younger sister's expression was one of puzzlement and fear. The inkosa turned to see Kotsi running towards her, shield and assegai in his hands.

Go back, she said silently. Go back or the Shamfa riders will attack.

"Inkosa! Inkosa! The rest of your escort has arrived!"

Bikita was terrified. "Rah-rah, what is he talking about? What is happening?"

Inaamdura couldn't answer. She could hear the chanting, the beating of thousands of assegais against thousands of shields, the thumping of countless of feet against the ground. The Sesu warriors emerged from the horizon running full speed toward the inkosa and her family. Inaamdura feigned shock, but she knew something was about to happen. Her surprise came from the number of warriors Dingane sent and how quickly they covered the distance. Dingane had planned this march the moment Inaamdura received the Shamfa messenger, she was sure. He had no intentions of offering any tributes to the Bonga. War with the Shamfa was inevitable.

Bikita staggered away, her hand over her mouth.

"Come to me, Kita," Inaamdura urged. "They will not harm you if you are close to me."

Bikita's terror could not overcome her fear.

Inaamdura looked to her mother for help and found an expression no child should see. Her eyes seethed with hatred, her teeth bared like a cornered wolf.

"This is your doing!" she hissed. "You have violated every law I taught you. You have taken all that I have and smashed it into the mud."

Inaamdura ignored her mother's insult. Her attention was drawn to the Shamfa cavalry. They charged, obviously not to confront the approaching Sesu horde but to protect Azana and Bikita. The Sesu wave surged past the women, surrounding the horsemen and bringing them down under a barrage of assegais and orinkas. Moments later the slayers danced among the dead, draped in blood stained kapok armor.

Azana's rant penetrated her trance. She looked at her mother, a solemn smile on her face.

"You have betrayed your family, your honor and your heritage! You've done it for this…this horde!"

Inaamdura reached out to her little sister and pulled her close, burying her head into her shoulder to comfort her. Her words for her mother were far from kind.

"Look at them, mother. This is the future. This is the Shamfa's future."

A group of warriors approached, leading the royal wagon. Inaamdura flinched as she recognized Ndoro, his bloody assegai dangling from his hand, his shield blocking his left side. His grim face was in contrast to the warriors surrounding him, each one smiling with pride, their eyes on the ostracized son of Dingane. He was their leader, not by title but by deeds. She felt a nudge at her hip and looked down to see Ligongo, his young face locked in admiration of his courageous half-brother.

Ndoro and the warriors dropped at her feet. "Great Mother, what do you wish?" he asked.

Though his words were respectful, Inaamdura felt the scorn in his voice. Her tone was no less threatening.

"I have no use for you," she replied. "Take your place among the warriors."

Ndoro turned away and led his warriors back to the ranks.

"Kotsi!" The induna came to her side.

"Escort my mother and sister back to Shamfa. Take them close enough to the walls to be seen, but don't endanger the lives of your men."

She turned to Ndoro.

"Your ibuthu will escort me back to Selike."

Ndoro's eyes narrowed. "As you wish, Great Mother."

It was a petty gesture but it made her feel better. She could not stop all of Ndoro's efforts to raise his status among the warriors, but she would at least squelch this legend unraveling before her eyes.

Bikita clutched her tighter. "I want to stay with you, Rah."

Inaamdura's hardness melted away. She patted her sister's head and pressed her lips close to her ear.

"You must go with momma," she whispered. "She has lost me; she wouldn't be able to go on if she loses you. She needs you more than you know."

Bikita pulled away, her glistening eyes bewildered. Inaamdura smiled as her heart broke to pieces.

"Go, Kita. Take momma back to Shamfa."

Bikita walked to Azana, placing her hands on her mother's wet cheeks. Inaamdura watched her gestures and smiled. She learned that from me, she thought. I taught her to be kind.

"Come, momma," Bikita whispered. "It's time to go home."

Azana looked up at Inaamdura. Age had conquered her face in those brief moments. Her face seems drawn, like all the energy had seeped away into the grass. Inaamdura realized the words she spoke to Bikita were true. Her mother's spirit was broken. She saw it in her tired eyes.

"You have killed me," she whispered. "You have stabbed my soul."

Inaamdura took her mother's cheeks between her hands and kissed her.

"I am what you made me, momma. Farewell."

Bikita guided her mother to the wagon and helped her inside. She climbed in behind her, stopping long enough to take one last look at Inaamdura then disappeared. Kotsi took control of the oxen, guiding them around and leading them away, his ibuthu chanting as they headed for Shamfa. Inaamdura watched until they disappeared into undulating horizon. It was done; she was free. She gave Ndoro the order and the Sesu party set a brisk pace across the grasses to their home, no, her home. She was no longer Shamfa. From this day on she was Sesu. She was the Great Wife of Dingane and her son, not Ndoro, would be his heir. She would make sure of it.

(9)

Ndoro placed the antelope carcass downwind of the pride, careful that he was not seen. He smeared himself with the animal's blood to cover his scent and made certain the females were hunting before approaching the ancient baobab tree under which the males and young ones rested. They were all there, the three immature males, their manes barely visible from his distance, still young enough to cavort under the tangled tree branches. Ndoro was not concerned with the young simbas. He watched the old one, the full, dark mane beast languishing near the tree trunk, the other simbas keeping a respectful distance. The pride belonged to him, and he ruled with quiet strength.

Old Simba raised his head, his nostrils flaring as he caught the scent of the antelope. He was an opportunist; Ndoro had watched him chase hyenas and jackals from their kills and indulge himself on their hard earned rewards. He knew Old Simba would come for the kill. He had no doubt in this part of his plan.

Old Simba yawned, stretched, and then came to his paws. Looking at his magnificence, Ndoro began to have second thoughts. This massive beast could break a bull's neck with one bite; one swipe of his paw would break Ndoro's limbs. Maybe there was something else he could do to prove his bravery, some other task that would break the silence between him and Dingane. Ndoro bit his lip until blood came, the anger welling up in his chest. He was the best, the smartest, the strongest and the fastest of all the young men in his induna. But he was disowned. No bravery he committed thus far dispelled this condition. He and his mother existed in the last hut of the royal kraal, their lives a pale reflection of that of the Great Wife Inaamdura, a position his mother once held. Ndoro was tired of being an outcast. No longer would he suffer the taunts and insults of the villagers, people less than cattle in his eyes. That time would come to an end this day.

Old Simba looked his way. He sauntered to the kill, his stride confident and deliberate. The younger ones attempted to follow; Old Simba turned and roared, swiping at the closest of the three. They roared back feebly then sulked back to the shade. Old Simba turned and continued to follow the scent. Ndoro's hands clenched about his mouth spike, his chest pounding. His plan was simple. He would take the simba the old way, the way the elders talked about in their stories of the first Sesu. Then he would cut the simba's throat with his knife. He practiced the maneuver on lesser animals, but now as his true target came closer Ndoro was in awe. He did not realize Old Simba was so big. His plan would not work. He wanted to run away in shame, but it was too late. Old Simba was almost upon him.

Old Simba halted before the antelope and tilted its head to the side, his eyes distant. Ndoro stumbled back and Old Simba focused on him, a low growl escaping between his bared teeth. Ndoro could not run now even if he wished. He crouched and waited.

Old Simba sprang. Ndoro waited until the simba was almost upon him, then shoved a mouth spike into its open maw. The simba's head slammed into Ndoro's chest, knocking the wind from him. He crashed into the grass, gasping for breath, sightless with pain, waiting for Old Simba's bite. Moments passed and nothing happened. When his sight returned he saw Old Simba hovering over him, his mouth locked open by the spike. The simba stood frozen, just as the elders said. Ndoro seized his knife and slashed across the simba's throat. A roar of pain came from its gaped mouth and it swung its paws in reflex, raking its claws across Ndoro's chest and tearing at his flesh. Before he could scream, Old Simba collapsed on him, again knocking him breathless.

Ndoro lay trapped under the dead simba, blood oozing over him. Slowly and painfully, he brought his legs up one at a time until he could press the bottom of his calloused feet against the simba's torso. He stopped, his breath heavy, his entire body throbbing. He looked into the sky, the vultures already beginning to circle. The sight fueled his limbs and he pushed the dead simba up and dropped it to the side, his exhausted body turning in the same direction. Old Simba lay on its side, the blood still flowing from his neck, his mouth open in a silent roar. The young males were halfway between the baobab and Ndoro, looking at the warrior with penetrating eyes. Ndoro crawled over and jerked the mouth spike from Old Simba's throat. He stood and spun in the direction of the young simbas, crouching low. The young males turned away. This beast had done something they could not do, and they were in no mood to challenge him.

Seeing the simbas retreat, Ndoro set about his next task. He staggered to where he'd hidden the harness and dragged it back to the body. Securing the carcass, he positioned the yoke across his shoulders. The wood bit into his neck, but it was a good pain, a trophy he relished as he did the wounds Old Simba had inflicted on him. There would be no denying him his place any longer.

* * *

The celebration began the night before with the return of the ibuthu. The raid went well, securing many cattle, slaves and the assurance that the Komo would never again be a threat to the Sesu. The southern grasslands were now open to Sesu expansion, giving Dingane a kingdom larger than any inkosi before him.

Morning brought the celebration to full scale. The Sesu awoke to the sound of the royal drummers, their jubilant rumbling echoing throughout the city. Dingane had done well imitating the grandeur of Abo; his city of Selike was the greatest known to the grasslands. Stone huts, gaily painted, lined the wide avenues of pounded mud. Each road led to the center of the city, terminating at the Royal Kraal. Here the Sesu inkosi concentrated most of his work, building a palace unlike any other. The main palace loomed over the city, constructed of stone carved in the Kijaru Mountains and transported by oxen and slaves to Sesuland. The palace rested in the center of a wide pasture surrounded by the royal cattle, magnificent white bovines marked with the brand of Dingane family. A road lined with cowry shells and filled with ivory brick descended from the palace and merged into the mud-packed wheel that encircled the Kraal. Bordering the wheel was the white wall, and within these walls were the homes of Dingane wives. They numbered twelve, from the grand residence of Inaambura, his Great wife, to the plain brick hut of Shani, the once great wife now fallen from grace.

Drummers stood upon the royal wall, their muscular arms beating a triumphant rhythm. Down the avenues came the celebrants following brightly-dressed dancers. They all sang the same song, a song which had become common in the city, a song of triumph and greatness.

The dancers converged in the royal courtyard, a wide area outside the royal wall where the gilded stools had been placed that morning. Dingane's wives sat in their places of honor, each dressed in the cloth of Dingane clan, the Imbubesi. Flanking the Royal Stool were Inaamdura and Mulugo. The medicine-priest seemed as ageless as ever, a permanent scowl on his face, his frail body wrapped in his own print. He held his staff as always, his herb bag hung loose about his waist. The look on his face made it obvious he was in no mood for celebration; he'd spent all night performing the necessary spells to ward off the spirits of enemy slain by the Sesu in addition to his ever constant vigil against the evil inspired by the presence of Ndoro.

Inaamdura was in a more festive mood. Her precious son Ligongo stood at her side pretending to be as serious as his father. She stroked his head and he turn and smiled, his smile brighter that the sun above drenching them with its heat. The inkosa wore her hair in the style of her people, the Shamfa, long braids tipped with brightly colored beads. She wore the yellow cloth of her tribe, a symbol of the strength of the alliance between the tribes. She smiled as the dancers approached the courtyard, her ivory smile like a crescent moon against a night sky.

Shani sat on the stool at the end, her face a picture of worry, her eyes searching frantically among the children sitting before them. Where was Ndoro? He left the hut before she woke days ago. She did not know where he had gone, nor did anyone else in the city. Not that anyone cared. There were many who agreed with Mulugo, wishing both she and her son would disappear. Inaamdura only made matters worse. Although Inaamdura had succeeded in pushing Shani to the lowest wife status, she failed in banishing her altogether. Dingane would not go that far. For reasons of his own, Shani remained with the Sesu, which for her and Ndoro was no great favor.

"Jelani," she called. "Where is Ndoro?"

"I don't know," Jelani replied. "I haven't seen him in two days."

"Did he tell you where he was going?"

"No. He seemed preoccupied when we last spoke."

Jelani was cut off by the rumble of the elephant drums. Everyone's attention turned upward to the royal palace. The ebony wood doors swung wide and the procession began. First to appear were the indumas, each bearing a staff topped with the symbol of his impi. Behind them came the tribal council, men and women representing the royal families. They wore the cloth robe, a pure white garment clinched at the waist by a broad beaded belt. The belts were meticulously crafted in the pattern of each honored family. The elders carried staffs as well, but unlike the indumas, the staffs were made of gold and ivory, a symbol of each family's wealth.

The Blood Men came next. They were Dingane's bodyguard, each a member of the Imbubesi clan. They marched with cold precision, garbed in traditional Sesu warrior clothing, bare-chested with a leather loincloth wrapped around the waist, a single black stork feather extending from their headbands. In their left hands they carried white shields made from the hides of the royal herd, each shield scribed with symbols to ward off evil spirits and to make them invulnerable in battle. The Blood Men carried no assegais;

their weapons were the sword, the wrist knife and the orinka. They chanted as they ran, their deep voices reverberating like elephant drums. The crowd took the chant as the litter of Dingane emerged from the palace. He sat cross-legged, his gray head embraced by a bejeweled head ring. Braided cowtails encircled his neck, a leopard robe draped over his broad shoulders. The excess of rule showed, his once lean face rounded, his paunch clearly visible beneath his clothing. Dingane held a gilded orinka carved with intricate hieroglyphics, each symbol a chronicle of his reign. When the celebration was complete its symbol would be added to the long list of his accomplishments. What had begun as a dream of an ambitious chief had become the reality of a king.

The procession made its way down the hill to the courtyard. The marchers took their places as Dingane litter was placed between Mulugo and Inaamdura. Dingane nodded to Mulugo, and then turned his full attention to his beautiful wife.

"Unkulunkulu smiles on us," she said. "Once again we celebrate victory."

"Victory is not new to me," Dingane replied. "It is you who are the true prize."

Inaamdura gave Dingane a coy smile. "I await your attention," she answered.

Fire blazed in Dingane's eyes. Inaamdura was his jewel, the best thing to happen to him since Shani. The thought of his former Great Wife doused his passionate musing and he turned his attention back to the celebration.

The dancers began again, their vigorous movements repeating the victories of the impi. The drummers picked up the pace and soon the entire city danced. Dingane was filled with pride; he'd taken a village and built it into a city on the verge of becoming an empire.

Something was happening in the distance. The throng parted and the din of celebration subsided as that something moved closer, dividing the Sesu like an invisible knife. Without thinking Shani stood. Dingane and Inaamdura remained on their stools, stretching their necks as much as they could toward the approaching commotion. The dancers stopped, they too caught in the curiosity of the crowd. The palace drummers played on, too far away to see or hear the strange interruption to the celebration.

The crowd pulled away to the edges of the avenue. Ndoro staggered up the road, wooden yoke on his shoulders, blood running from his arm and splattered on his chest and stomach. Behind him was the body of Old Simba. Shani went for him, but Jelani grabbed her arm.

"No, Shani," Jelani advised. "This is his moment."

Ndoro dragged Old Simba a few more steps then stopped. He dropped the yoke, untied the carcass and knelt before it. He worked his hand slowly under the body and lifted the hind quarters. He ducked his head under the body, supporting the lion on his shoulders. Drawing his legs close, he struggled to push himself erect.

Jelani's grip tightened around Shani's arm. "Stand boy, stand!" he whispered.

Ndoro let out a deep grunt and stood. He wavered, his legs shaking from the effort of lifting such an enormous burden. The strength was leaving his body, seeping away like his blood. But he saw his father and anger rushed in his limbs. He steadied, and began to walk.

Jelani let go of Shani's arm. He took up his shield and assegai, leaped from the platform and ran to the courtyard, halting in plain sight of Ndoro. His face stern, he hit his shield with his spear, again and again, setting a steady pace for the boy.

"Show them your Mawena blood, Ndoro!" he shouted. "Show them a true warrior!"

Others joined in with Jelani, beating against their breasts, stomping their feet, whatever they could do. The same people who had once shunned Ndoro now encouraged him. Even the Blood Men were overwhelmed. They stood in unison, beating their gilded clubs against their shields.

Ndoro's world was silent. His father's face filled his vision, the bewildered countenance growing larger with each step. Flashes of fatigue ripped the image away and replaced it with blackness, but the image always returned. Finally, he could walk no longer. Anger could push the body only so far. Each beat of his heart stabbed him; each breath burned. With his last effort Ndoro lifted the simba's body over his head. The crowd fell silent.

"I...am...your... son!" Ndoro boomed. He dropped the simba at his father's feet. Dingane looked down at the slain beast, then to Ndoro. Inaamdura leaned toward the inkosi with Mulugo, anxious to hear Dingane's response. But before he could respond, Ndoro collapsed.

Dingane looked at Shani with a kindness she had not seen in many years. "Go to him," he said. "Your face is the first he should see when he revives."

Shani smiled brightly. "Thank you, my husband." Jelani and members of the Blood Men lifted Ndoro onto their shoulders and carried him away. A chant began somewhere in the crowd and raced throughout like wildfire. The chant was for Ndoro, and the drummers and dancers joined in. The Sesu continued to sing until Ndoro and his bearers disappeared behind the gates of the Royal Kraal.

* * *

Inaamdura waited patiently beside the trickling stream alone. She sat on the ground, her legs folded to the side, her hands resting in her lap. In such a pose she resembled a sculpture carved from ebony wood, her features artistic perfection. Her eyes looked westward, toward Shamfa.

She longed for her mother's council but Azana had separated herself from the world, locked away in her precious garden refusing all visitors. The task of advisor had fallen on Bikita's callow shoulders. Her first act was to establish an alliance between Shamfa and Sesuland, a decision that split the kingdom. Shamfa and Bonga became enemies, dividing the royal family as well.

Amadika fled to Bongaland and married Twaambo. Twaambo then claimed himself ruler of both lands by marriage, which her father quickly denounced. Both sides declared war, but not a sword was unsheathed nor a spear thrown before the factions fell into a tangle of procedure and protocol. Bikita, overwhelmed by the responsibility, sent word to Inaamdura for help. Her answer came in the form of twenty thousand Sesu warriors who swept through Bongaland like a dry season grass fire. They drove the Bonga out of the foothills and over the mountains into the Barrens. Dingane declared Shamfa under his protection, annexing the kingdom and doubling the size of his empire in one swift stroke. Muchese became a vassal of the man he once called a savage and Bikita remained his advisor. Azana remained in her garden.

She heard shuffling in the grass and stood. The person approaching took his time, stopping once to curse the darkness and the thorn lodged in his calf. Although she knew who he was, waiting in the darkness made her nervous and wary.

"Mulugo?" she called out.

The medicine priest responded with a grunt as he stepped into the torchlight.

"Are you alone?" she asked.

"I am," Mulugo replied. He sat, laying his staff beside him. "Why have I been summoned here?"

"What I wish to discuss is of the utmost privacy," Inaamdura replied.

Mulugo laughed. "You are full of secrets, Great Wife of Dingane. Which one will you share with me tonight?

Inaamdura ignored Mulugo's disrespect. "I wish to discuss Ndoro."

Mulugo's face turned grim. "I will not speak about it."

"It?"

"Yes, it. The demon you call Ndoro"

Inaamdura was surprised by Mulugo's response. "I see no demon, only a troublesome man-child."

"You see with normal eyes," Mulugo replied. "Ndoro was

one of twins, an abomination. His twin was killed according to tradition, but he was spared to satisfy Dingane's lust for a son. Since then I have spent my time appeasing the ancestors and driving off evil omens summoned by that demon's presence. I have good reason to hate this thing."

Inaamdura smiled. This would be easier than she thought. "I understand. It would be best that Ndoro was driven away."

Mulugo let out a dry cackle. "Ndoro will stay, Great Wife. Even you cannot change that fact."

"Why?" Inaamdura asked.

"Because Dingane loves the thing. Oh yes, he shuns it, never speaks to it or acknowledges it, but he loves it and has ever since it was born."

Mulugo was not telling Inaamdura anything she did not already know, but it was in her own interest to act otherwise.

"If that is true, yesterday's display might overcome Dingane's shunning," she said. "For the sake of the Sesu we must not let this happen."

Mulugo took on a venomous look. "Do not mock me with your false concerns for the Sesu, Great Wife."

"You take your liberties too far, medicine-priest," Inaamdura retorted.

"It was you who asked for this meeting," Mulugo shot back. "I detest Dingane's habit of marrying outside the tribe. There are Sesu women of strong lineage more suited for Great Wife than you or Shani. You care only for yourself and your son, and Ndoro stands in your way. The only thing you and I need to discuss is why you think I should listen to your plan."

Inaamdura grinned. She had underestimated Mulugo. "We both have our reasons to be rid of Ndoro. The servants say the day Ndoro was born was the day Mulugo lost his magic. They say the longer he lives the weaker you become. That is why you cannot get rid of him. Some even say you see your death in his eyes."

"They are all fools!" he exclaimed. "I have lost nothing! They forget who drives the spirits from their homes and who keeps the ancestors placated. They run to the warrens now, spending their cowries on that fool from east."

Inaamdura's eyes widened. This was something new.

"What fool?"

"Cacanja," Mulugo spat. "He's a blind man who lives in a hovel spouting nonsense and selling poison."

Inaamdura stood. She needed nothing else from Mulugo.

"We are finished. I will contact you when we need to speak again."

Mulugo struggled to his feet. "Cacanja cannot help you and neither can I. I doubt you'll send for me again."

"We'll see, Mulugo. We will see."

She hurried back to the royal kraal, changing from her royal clothes to a plain sand colored robe and hood similar to the desert nomads. There was only a few hours of darkness left and she had to make the best of her time alone. Dingane was amusing himself with one of his younger wives, giving her all the time she needed. The guards flanking the doorway to her house recognized the disguise and followed, careful to keep a respectful distance but close enough to respond to any threat. The Great Wife was on an adventure; they would follow and obey.

She had no idea where to find this Cacanja. Mulugo mentioned the warrens so she made her way there. The Warrens was a jumble of makeshift buildings and cluttered streets, a part of the city as unpredictable as its inhabitants, home of those people not numerous enough to petition Dingane for a city compound. Inaamdura wandered about, hoping to find someone who could tell her where to find the sorcerer. To her dismay the streets were empty. She was about to turn back when some force held her in place then guided her down a winding, muddy street. She let herself heed the pull until she stood before a small mud shack embellished with an intricately carved door incongruous for the dilapidated structure. Smoke seeped from gaps at the bottom and sides. Inaamdura looked turned and looked into the darkness. Her bodyguards were still with her though she sensed their uneasiness. She took a deep breath and knocked on the door.

The door creaked open and blinding smoked billowed out, swallowing her in pungent confusion. A pair of calloused hands grabbed her wrists and pulled her inside, the door slamming shut behind her. Inaamdura rubbed her eyes frantically as her bodyguards pounded the door. Someone laughed before her and dread coursed through her. She had made a mistake.

"No, inkosa, you have made no mistake," Cacanja cackled. "You are where you wished to be."

The sorcerer emerged from the smoke, a tall, thin man with deep brown skin. A wide grin creased his gaunt face as he stared at Inaamdura with white dead eyes. A leather cloak covered with gris-gris hid his body, heavy with the smell of smoke and decay.

Inaamdura did her best to stay composed despite her fear.

"Let my men in," she insisted.

"You need no protection here," Cacanja replied. "You are in the safest place in Selike."

Cacanja shuffled to the iron pot in the center of his home, the source of the enveloping smoke.

"You are just in time," he said. "It is ready."

"Just in time for what?"

Cacanja pulled a pouch from his cloak and opened it. He dipped the pouch into the pot then closed it.

"There are no secrets to me. I see with eyes not of this world."

He extended the pouch to Inaamdura. As she reached for it he pulled it away.

"Consider what you are about to do, inkosa. The spirits will grant your desire, but they demand a price."

"If this will rid me of Ndoro it is worth any price."

Inaamdura took the pouch.

Cacanja returned to his pot. "Take it to the hill overlooking the Royal Herd. Raise it over your head and open it. The wind shall do the rest."

"Is that all?"

Cacanja grinned. "Sleep with Dingane tonight. He should be with you when it happens."

Inaamdura's throat tightened. "What will happen?"

"You shouldn't know. You must be just as surprised."

Inaamdura nodded. It was sound advice. "What do I owe you?"

Cacanja looked away. "You have already paid a great price."

The door swung open and her bodyguards tumbled inside. They made their way to Cacanja, assegais lowered. Inaamdura stopped them.

"Let him be. We're done here."

She led them back into the streets, the pouch clutched tightly in her hand. She loosened the strings and opened it, revealing an innocuous looking white powder. She closed it quickly and tucked it away in her robe. She had no idea what Cacanja had given her or why she accepted it, but she sensed she had crossed a river where there was no turning back. As she followed the winding roads back to the Royal Compound, the last words of Cacanja echoed in her mind.

"You have already paid a great price."

* * *

Ndoro awoke in an unfamiliar place. The roof above him showed no gaps like those of his home, the thatch woven by expert hands. The bed he rested upon was soft and comfortable, entirely different from the cot he slept upon each night. He ached, but there was no deep pain. A bandage covered his wrist; he felt wet poultice against his skin. The walls of the room were covered with mud cloth and expertly carved masks. Ndoro was overwhelmed by the room's opulence.

"Well, well, the simba is not dead after all." Jelani strode into the room, a wide smile splitting his grizzled face. "I have something for you."

He handed Ndoro a small leather pouch. Ndoro opened it,

revealing hair balls from the old simba's stomach.

"The elders asked me to give these to you," Jelani said. "They are a symbol of the courage you showed by taking the simba the old way."

Ndoro was honored, but his mind was on more pressing matters.

"Jelani, where am I?"

"You are in Dingane's kraal." Ndoro jumped at the sound of his mother's voice. She sat beside the bed, her tired eyes emitting a mother's joy.

"Unkulunkulu brought you back to me," she said. They hugged for a moment; Ndoro felt awkward showing such emotion before Jelani and gently pushed his mother away.

"This is my father's house, mama," Ndoro said, "your husband's house."

"You should know better by now. Dingane stopped being my husband the day you were born," Shani snapped. "He was never your father. You wouldn't be alive if not..."

"Shani," Jelani interjected, "this is not the time."

Shani's eyes went wide. She plunged her face into the palms of her open hands and sobbed.

Ndoro was driven by curiosity. "It is not for what, mama?"

"If it was not for your grandfather," Dingane replied. He stood in the entryway, draped in his royal robe, his hair braided Shamfa fashion. Shani's head jerked up, a poisonous look aimed at her husband. Ndoro stood to face his father. It was the first time Dingane spoke to him directly.

"I see you are well," Dingane continued. "I am happy." He looked at Shani and smiled, oblivious to the tension he created.

"You did a good job, Shani. Maybe you should be a healer."

"Don't tell him, Dingane," Shani demanded.

"It's time he knew," Dingane answered.

"I am his mother. I decide what he should or should not know."

"I want to know, mama," Ndoro interjected. "I want to know

why we are shunned. I want to know why my own father rules Sesuland but can't speak to his son. I want to know why I have been denied my place beside him."

Dingane stared at Ndoro for a moment, and then motioned to him. "Come with me," he said.

Ndoro followed his father out of the room, through the palace and outside to the kraal. The sunset painted the rolling grasslands evening red as the sounds of a city preparing for rest breached the kraal walls. Dingane walked to the meeting tree and sat, motioning Ndoro to sit beside him.

"Do not be fooled by my appearance of power," Dingane said. "It is not truly mine. The power belongs to those you see below you, the Sesu. It was our elders who selected me to serve as inkosi, and that power can be taken away just as easily."

"But they would not do such a thing," Ndoro replied. "You have a made us a great people."

Dingane gave Ndoro a weary smile. "That's not important. What's important is I rule without violating Sesu traditions. I have done so only once, when I let you live."

Ndoro was puzzled. "Let me live?"

Dingane told Ndoro the story of his birth. The young warrior was stunned, his mind a tempest. Tradition said he should be dead, but since that had not been allowed, a living death had been imposed. In Ndoro's mind his brother suffered a kinder fate. But nothing changed his right to claim what was his.

"Can you break the rules again?" Ndoro asked.

"I may not have to," Dingane replied. "Yesterday's show was enough to change the minds of many, although there were those who saw what you did normal for an athakathi."

Ndoro's blood burned. "I am no demon!"

"Of course you aren't," Dingane replied calmly. "On the day you were born I vowed my son would be inkosi. Shani's mistake put an end to that dream for a time, but you have given it to me again."

"But what of my brothers?" Ndoro asked. "What of Inaamdura's son?"

"Inaamdura's son is not Sesu," Dingane replied. "As for your other brothers, none of them can hold a shield to you. It is what hurt me so, seeing you grow into a proud warrior and not being able to say one thing to you. You are a son that any man would be proud."

Dingane grasped Ndoro's shoulders, his eyes intense. "The next few days are crucial to your future, Ndoro. You must avoid doing anything that would offend the elders and the spirits. Be humble and obey your mother, and above all, avoid Mulugo. Anything you do around him will be used as judgment against you."

"What will this change?" Ndoro asked skeptically.

"It will give me time to talk to the elders and convince them it is time you took your rightful place at my side," Dingane replied.

"No matter what the elders decide, I will still be shunned. I will still be thought of as a demon."

"I can do nothing to change the minds of people," Dingane said. "That will be up to you."

"I will do as you say," Ndoro said. "Must we leave the Royal Kraal?"

"You must, for now." Dingane took off his cowry necklace and placed it around Ndoro's neck.

"My promise to you," he said. He smiled, stood, and then walked away, leaving Ndoro alone among the royal herd.

Ndoro stood. If he were the sun, Sesuland would burn under his brilliance. The time had come for him to take his rightful place beside his father as heir to the stool. There would be many to oppose him, but he knew what the outcome would be. It was his destiny, and he would accept nothing less.

* * *

The wail echoed throughout the royal kraal. Dingane jumped from his bed, knocking Inaamdura to the floor. He ran to the window, snatching aside the cowhide and looked across the grounds. Kefi, his royal herdsman, dashed up the hill, his heavy arms spread wide.

Inaamdura gathered the cotton sheets about her nude body. "What is it?" she asked.

"I don't know." The inkosi dressed quickly and left the room.

The Blood Men waited for him, armed and ready. Dingane trotted through the gauntlet and down to the ground level where Kefi waited, his head buried in the grass.

Get up, man," Dingane ordered. "What is the matter?"

Kefi struggled to his feet but could say nothing. He grabbed Dingane's arm; the Blood Men jumped toward him, but Dingane waved them back. A sense of dread gripped him. He'd never seen Kefi so distraught. Something terrible must have happened; something more than the loss of a calf to a hyena or simba.

Kefi towed him to the edge of the hill. Strewn across the fields of green grass were the white bodies of the royal herd. There was no bovine standing, just white humps of flesh motionless in the verdant grass.

"What...," Dingane said.

"I don't know, my inkosi, I don't know!" Kefi replied. "Nothing was done wrong, nothing!"

Dingane stared at his wealth scattered across the hillside. Something more foreboding was growing in his mind, something which the evidence was too powerful to deny. He turned slowly, eventually facing the Blood Men.

"Bring Mulugo here," he ordered.

The medicine priest came to the royal kraal immediately. Upon seeing the dead cattle he fell into a fit. For what seemed like hours he was unintelligible, running and rolling about the field touching each of the corpses with his staff. He finally ended his gesticulations at Dingane's feet, spread eagle on his back, his eyes staring into the cloudless sky.

"A powerful evil is among us," Mulugo moaned, "an evil that has festered among us for many seasons."

Dingane took on a harsh look. "What are you leading to, Mulugo? Are you saying Ndoro caused this?"

Mulugo came to his feet. "I am not accusing anyone. There is a demon wearing the skin of a man in this city, and it has demonstrated its power. We must have a smelling out."

Dingane felt the hairs on the nape of his neck raise. No one knew if they were possessed; only Mulugo could determine so. The demon could be in anyone; only impalement could drive it away. But death was a small price to pay to rid the Sesu of a demon powerful enough to cause such carnage.

The darkness that filled Sesuland that night seemed alive, touching every man and woman with an evil cold. The moon fled the night sky, giving up the heavens to the palpable blackness. The only visible light came from the royal kraal, its source a huge bonfire made from selected branches of the meeting tree. A ring circled the fire, a ring made of the inhabitants of Selike. The firelight danced across their faces, revealing glimpses of the fear that gripped everyone. Ndoro was part of the ring, his rigid face hiding his turmoil inside. He remembered his father's words and fought to keep from shuddering. Mulugo thought he was a demon. What if he was? It was said a man did not know if a demon rode his back. Only a smelling out can reveal the spirit and only impalement of the host could drive the vile creature away. Ndoro clinched his hands, his nails cutting into his palms. No, he convinced himself. The demon was not in him.

Mulugo occupied the center of the circle. He sat cross-legged, his small chest bare, his groin covered with a loincloth. In his hand he held his staff, his face covered with the demon mask. The mask was decorated with inhuman perfection, its fierce expression fitting for a smelling out. Mulugo sat stiff, his gaze unsettling to those brave enough to look directly into his burning eyes.

Mulugo jumped to his feet, yelling into the night sky. He fell into an energetic, foreboding dance that attracted as much as it repelled. The medicine priest chanted a litany Ndoro knew well. It was a prayer of protection every Sesu learned as a child.

> *Unkulunkulu! We are your children!*
> *We pray for your protection!*
> *Give us your shield!*
> *Drive the evil away!*

The Sesu took up the chant, falling into the rhythm of Mulugo's steps. The medicine priest's dancing became more vigorous, the chanting stronger. Suddenly the chant changed. Mulugo ranted, his words streaming from his mouth so rapidly they were unintelligible. His dance transformed into a struggle against an unseen foe, his arms reaching and grasping the night. He fell to the ground, writhing in the dust and grass, the Sesu falling into a deadly silence as they watched the spiritual struggle.

Mulugo sprang to his feet, running as fast as his old legs could manage towards Ndoro. Ndoro tried to back away but the ring held him firm. He looked to either side and was met with hateful eyes. Mulugo finally confirmed what many Sesu suspected. He was possessed with a demon.

"No!" Ndoro protested. He broke away from the ring, backing away from the babbling Mulugo. He searched desperately for his father but he was nowhere to be seen. The realization transformed Ndoro's shock into anger. He stopped, his eyes narrowing as he looked into Mulugo's crazed face.

"I am not a demon, medicine priest!" Ndoro shouted. Mulugo fell silent, and then with a shriek raised his staff over his head with both hands. Ndoro grabbed the staff, wrenching it from the old man's hands, and, as if continuing Mulugo's motion, smashed the staff down on the priest's head. There was a sickening crack and Mulugo fell to a heap at Ndoro's feet. The circle was silent, stunned by what had occurred. Ndoro took advantage of the inaction, breaking away and running down the hill, back to the city. He was almost among the buildings when he heard a deafening roar. The spell was broken; the Sesu rushed down the hill, each one determined to rid their city of the demon.

Ndoro ran on, his mind a jumble of anger and fear. He became lost, scampering back and forth through the streets, the din of his pursuers growing louder with each moment. He stumbled deeper into the city, despair beginning to settle into his mind. He should stop and let them take him, he thought. This torture which had passed for his life for eighteen years was no longer worth the struggle. He had been cursed at birth, and Mulugo sealed his fate. If he was to die, then so be it.

"Ndoro!"

He jerked his head in the direction of voice and saw Jelani running towards him, spear and shield in hand.

"You've got to get out of here now," Jelani said.

"Why?" Ndoro asked. "Mulugo wants me dead, so here I am."

Jelani threw down his spear and shield. "That old crow will never see that day. You killed him."

Ndoro smiled, but it was like closing his eyes before the gods.

Jelani stripped down to his loincloth. "Give me the simba hide."

Ndoro removed the hide and gave it to Jelani.

"Take my clothes and put them on now," Jelani instructed.

"You don't have to do this," Ndoro said.

"You don't have much time," Jelani replied. "They will find us soon."

Ndoro donned Jelani's garments. Jelani gave him a quick inspection and smiled approvingly.

"You'll make a fine Mawena warrior," he said. "Now chase me out into the open. Once they see us, you stop and point them to me."

"This is my fight, Jelani," Ndoro said.

"But you cannot win it now," Jelani replied. "Go to the Mawena, to your grandfather. They will welcome you, and you will meet your...."

The pair heard voices and saw flickering torch lights in the distance. Jelani turned and ran towards the light. Ndoro went after him, shield and spear in hand. Jelani disappeared down a side alley; before Ndoro could follow he found himself standing before the Blood Men. Ndoro raised the shield to obscure his face.

One of the Blood Men stepped forward. "Was that him? Answer me, Mawena!"

Ndoro nodded and the Blood Men took flight, yelling for the others to follow them. Ndoro watched and waited until the crowd disappeared. But still he did not go. He walked slowly as he played with the cowry necklace giving to him by Dingane, savoring the image of the city which had been his home and his prison. As he neared the outskirts, he trotted, leaving the memories that haunted his life, fleeing the revelations the past few days had heaped upon him. His hand clenched around the necklace, and with a sudden jerk he ripped it from him neck and flung it into the darkness. By the time he reached the grasslands he was running, tears streaming down his cheeks, a vow forming in his mind and his heart. He would return and Selike would burn.

10

The harvest season was upon Abo. Farmers labored in the small fields surrounding the city, gathering the bounty of a successful season. It was good that the crop was abundant, for Abo was a growing city. Mawena tradesmen traversed the grasslands, deserts and forests, trading goods with distant cities and returning with the bounties of other nations. All around him Oba Noncemba watched his people prosper, the forest giving way to new homes and new problems. But it was one growth that was the most perplexing to the wise oba, one problem he never seemed able to solve.Noncemba sat on his gilded stool flanked by his guards. His graying head rested in his palm, his eyes following Kumba as he paced across the floor.

"I tell you my oba; this boy ties me in knots! No matter what I do, he responds with total indifference!"

"Maybe it is because he is indifferent," Noncemba responded.

Kumba stopped his pacing and glared at the oba, an expression Noncemba dismissed. Kumba was allowed a certain leeway because of his family rank, a privilege he used at every opportunity.

"It doesn't matter how he feels," Kumba said. "What matters is his duty as a Mawena and as a member of the royal house."

"Don't explain duty to me," Noncemba replied. "Obaseki is well aware of his responsibility. His interests at the moment lie elsewhere."

"And that's another thing," Kumba continued. "He spends too much time with Fuluke. The boy should be training as a warrior, not as a medicine priest."

"We cannot deny Obaseki his calling or his wishes," Noncemba reminded Kumba. "Remember, he is one of twins, a meji, and we cannot displease him lest bad luck befalls our clan. He has special talents that only Fuluke can develop."

Noncemba paused to scratch his beard. "Meji or not, Obaseki should spend more time with you. When he returns, I will discuss this matter with him."

Kumba almost smiled, the closest Noncemba had seen him to happy in months. He turned to leave the room. "I will expect him in the morning."

Obaseki was far away from the conversation deciding his fate. He had grown into a tall, broad-shouldered man, resembling his grandfather in many ways. He was deep in the forest, close to the area known to the Mawena as Tepula, the land of the hidden ones. He moved with the grace of a gazelle, walking the narrow, wet path as if he'd walked it for many years. In a way, he had. These woods were filled with spirits, and Obaseki had a way with spirits.

Fuluke raised his hand and Obaseki obeyed, halting in the middle of the path. The sun's light barely penetrated the green canopy overhead. The glade was alive with sound, a natural symphony that comforted both men.

"I think this is the place," Fuluke said. "It has been many years." He turned to Obaseki. "What do you see?"

Obaseki looked into the forest to a clearing off to his right. "There," he said. He entered the underbrush, clearing a path for Fuluke with his machete. They halted at the edge of the clearing.

"It is a small village," Obaseki remarked.

"There are at least twenty huts. I don't recognize the people. They are not Mawena."

"They called themselves Noke," Fuluke replied. "Do you recognize the chief's hut?"

"Yes," Obaseki replied, "near the center."

Obaseki saw a spectral outline of the hut. "I see something near the fireplace. It glows like a spirit, but it is not."

Fuluke nodded. "So it has not been discovered."

"What is it?" Obaseki asked.

"Go see," Fuluke replied.

Obaseki hesitated. This place was powerful. The spirits were clearly defined, as if they'd all just passed into the Zamani, though he knew this not to be true. Never before had he encountered such a thing and it frightened him. He looked back to Fuluke.

"Go on, Seki," Fuluke urged. "You of all people should have no fear of this place.

Obaseki entered the site humbly, aware he violated sacred ground. Crouching above the fireplace, he dug with his spade, each shovel revealing more and more of the mystery. The spirits turned toward him, ceasing their empty chores to watch the stranger among them. Obaseki didn't notice; he was immersed in discovering this strange energy.

Obaseki was suddenly overwhelmed by a searing white light. He plummeted past angry faces that shouted at him in unknown tongues. Terror swallowed him as he fell faster and faster, the burning brightness usurped by a numbing darkness that penetrated him like a thousand spears. But then he stopped, hovering in darkness over a single object. It was a horn; it's wide based encircled with a gold and cowry shell ring. At the point was a ringlet of emeralds. Obaseki gazed at the horn, past its surface into the center. The gilded horn held an orisha, the most powerful of all spirits, a messenger between ordinary men and Olodumare. Obaseki expected to feel anger emanating from the spirit; instead he felt contentment. This orisha was apparently where it wanted to be.

Obaseki reached out to the mayembe; to his surprise it rose from its resting place and glided to his hand. It touched his flesh and darkness engulfed him. He seemed to spin as a rush of images passed before his eyes, sights that seemed incomprehensible and yet so familiar. His eyesight returned as suddenly as it fled. He sat on the back of his legs, his hands resting on his thighs, the mayembe warm and pulsing against his palms. Hundreds of tiny lacerations covered his body, blood mixed with sweat forming rivulets all over his body.

Obaseki looked up to see Fuluke. The medicine-priest smiled and nodded his head in approval.

"What happened?" Obaseki asked.

"You have been tested," Fuluke replied. "And the fact that you are still alive means you passed."

Obaseki struggled to his feet, surprised at his weakness. "I don't understand," he said.

"You will, Seki, you will," Fuluke replied. "Come, we have what we came for."

Fuluke grabbed Obaseki by the arm and helped him walk. They made their way back to their horses as nightfall crept slowly across the forest, sealing off the light that filled the gap between the leaves. Fuluke and Obaseki made camp in a clearing not far from the road they traveled, preparing themselves for the night ahead. Their journey to the Noke settlement had taken only half a day; because of Obaseki's condition it would take much longer to return to Abo.

Fuluke searched the nearby woods for the proper herbs and prepared a healing broth for Obaseki. The bleeding had stopped, but the young apprentice was still quite weak. He sipped Fuluke's concoction and felt momentarily refreshed, strong enough to raise himself to a sitting position.

"You said you would tell me about the mayembe," he said to Fuluke.

"Moyo," Fuluke answered. "The mayembe you possess is called Moyo, the Noke word for heart."

"How did it come to be?" Obaseki inquired. "The medicine-priest who created it must have been very powerful."

"Moyo was not made by a medicine priest," Fuluke responded. "No one knows exactly how it came to be. Some say Moyo was cast down from the heavens, that the orisha trapped inside offended the One and was sentenced to eternity within the horn. Jakobi of the Noke was the first to stumble upon Moyo and gained the orisha's favor by promising to find a way to free it from the horn. He used Moyo's power to make his people great, but soon Moyo realized that Jakobi did not intend to keep his bargain. Jakobi was oba of the Noke by then, holding council over his people and many surrounding tribes. But Moyo set a chain of misfortunes upon the Noke, circumstances that ended with Jakobi and his followers being driven from Nokeland. They ended at this site, Jakobi spending the rest of his days trying to free Moyo from the horn."

"If Moyo does not trust men, why am I allowed to possess it?" Obaseki asked.

"Moyo no longer dwells in the horn," Fuluke replied. "When he was cast from the heavens, Moyo became mortal. What is left of Moyo, his ka, inhabits the horn. And you know the ka well."

Obaseki understood. Ka was pure essence, that elemental part of every being closest to Olodumare, responding instinctively to the powers surrounding it.

"I still don't understand why I have been chosen," Obaseki asked.

Fuluke yawned and rubbed his gray-brown eyes. "You won't understand any better tonight than you will tomorrow. Now sleep and rest. We must go back to Mawenaland tomorrow for I have matters to attend to."

Thin threads of light stole through dense leaves, making splotches of light on the forest floor. The canopy rustled with the movement and sounds of birds and monkeys. Obaseki and Fuluke rose early, breaking camp and setting a good pace. By afternoon they entered Mawenaland and Obaseki relaxed. This was familiar ground; the spirits surrounding him were welcomed.

The road became a series of crest and troughs as they approached the highlands encircling Abo. Fuluke's home rested atop a hill about three miles from the city, overlooking the farmland surrounding the city like a cultivated moat. Their pack horses seemed to sense the nearness to home for they climbed the steep path leading to Fuluke's house eagerly despite the long journey behind them. Fuluke and Obaseki were happy to see the old stone building, which appeared abandoned. Herbs grew in profusion; some even grew from the cracks in the stone wall. Unlike the farmer who fought constantly to stead nature's chaos, Fuluke welcomed it, for the morass of flora possessed the magic that healed the sick, changed fortunes and summoned the spirits.

Someone awaited the duo as they neared the house. Obaseki recognized him as one of his grandfather's messengers. The man slept, his head resting on his knees which were drawn to his chest, his arms languishing at his sides. His right hand barely held the royal symbol, a ceremonial sword carved with the shape of a leopard. Obaseki rode up to the man, dismounted and knelt close to his ear.

"Jambo!" he shouted. The messenger yelped and tumbled into the shrubs. Fuluke and Obaseki laughed.

"Calm down, Jela," Obaseki said. "The spirits have not come for you yet."

Jela stood quickly, dusting himself off in an attempt to reclaim his dignity. "My prince, Oba Noncemba requests your presence at the palace immediately."

Obaseki frowned. He'd long tired of the mindless intrigues of the royal court. And then there was Kumba, constantly droning about his duty and continuously attempting to make him an outstanding killer.

"I will be along, Jela," Obaseki replied.

Jela stepped out of the shrubs. "I'm sorry, but I must insist that you return with me at this instant. Your grandfather made it clear that you must not delay. A day has already past."

"Go on, Seki," Fuluke said. "I have wasted enough of your time."

"My time with you is never a waste, Fuluke. I will see you soon." Obaseki turned to Jela. "Let's go."

Jela bowed, and then set off down the trail. Obaseki followed on horseback, his mood shattered by the summons. He enjoyed his grandfather's company, but lately his time was occupied with various complications affecting a city like Abo. As they passed through the farmlands Obaseki watched the farmers working the fields. To his right the construction of the outer wall continued, his grandfather's latest effort to protect his people. So much had changed so fast, too fast for many of the tribal elders. Though Abo was still Mawena, many other people now lived in the city. They were drawn by the stability and safety of Mawenaland and they brought commerce and growth with them. Prosperity also brought jealousy; Mawenaland was under constant threat from nearby tribes anxious to usurp Abo's position as dominant trade city between the forest and the savannah. It was obvious that Noncemba did not need the added aggravation of a truant grandson.

They reached the outskirts of Abo at dusk. Obaseki and Jela crossed the thorn bush moat encircling the inner wall of the main city. The Breast of Mawenaland, as it was called, radiated the energy of an anthill. People rushed about, closing deals and gaining profits with every step. Though most were Mawena, the collage of costumes revealed many different tribes, all merchants hoping to bring wealth and prestige back to their homelands.

Obaseki never saw spirits in the inner city. Abo was not built on ancestral ground; the elders would not allow it. The city was constructed to the east of Mawena tribal land, so as not to draw foreigners to sacred ground. Though he knew the reason, Obaseki felt cold in Abo. There was something unnatural about a land with no ancestors. Fuluke had likened it to an empty vessel waiting to be filled. The city teemed with people; still the young prince doubted if his grandfather had filled it with the right water.

Jela and Obaseki walked the wide avenue leading to the center of the city, the ward of the Mawena. The compound was surrounded by the tallest and widest of the three walls, Atuegbu patrolling the mud brick ramparts. Jela and Obaseki were recognized and the iron gates opened quickly. They shut just as quickly once the duo passed through, the heavy thud chilling to Obaseki's ears.

Within the walls of the ward the wealth of the Mawena was clearly evident. Wide brick streets separated well tended gardens crowded with the fruits and vegetables. Beyond them were the houses of the tenders, neat and tiny structures of a much better quality than those on the outside. The imposing homes beyond the tender's sheds belonged to the ancestral families, those who tradition had passed down the privilege of eldership. In the center of it all, resting on a hill constructed by hand was the palace of Oba Noncemba. Jela stabled Obaseki's mount and the young prince passed quickly through the palace oblivious to the numerous servants and relatives that greeted him as he passed. He deposited his belongings in his room carelessly, with the exception of the mayembe. That he placed in a special compartment beneath his bed, making sure no one watched as he did so. He was leaving his room when he spotted Azikiwe, his uncle. There was a serious look on his face, a look that disturbed Obaseki.

"Uncle!" Obaseki called.

Azikiwe jerked his head towards Obaseki. "What? Oh, hello Seki." He spun about and hurried down the hallway. Obaseki was even more perplexed. Azikiwe was always ready for a conversation.

"Uncle, wait!" he called out, but Azikiwe did not heed his call. In fact, he seemed to walk faster. Obaseki stopped his pursuit, watching his uncle mount his horse and gallop away. Something fell from the horse as he rode off and Obaseki retrieved it. It was a gold coin. Not the kind produced in Mawenaland, but a coin unlike any Obaseki had ever seen. He put the coin in his pouch and went on to see his grandfather.

Noncemba was in his chambers, looking very unlike a powerful oba. He was dressed in the fashion of a desert nomad, his body covered with a white robe, his head topped with a checkered turban which hid his face. It was close to evening and Noncemba was preparing to fulfill one of his many obligations as oba.

"Grandfather," Obaseki said. I have come as you requested."

Noncemba turned to the young man, his eyes stern. "You are a day late. Explain yourself."

"Fuluke and I were gathering herbs," Obaseki replied, his voice timid. Although he hated court life, he hated disappointing his grandfather more. "Jela was waiting when we returned and I came as soon as I received you summons."

Noncemba continued to dress. "Kumba was here two days ago. He said you are neglecting your studies. He also said you haven't paid much attention to weapon training."

Obaseki felt like a trapped bull. "It's true, I haven't been attentive to my studies. I…"

"And that is the problem, Seki," Noncemba interjected. He gestured for Obaseki to sit. He sat beside him.

"I have tried not to interfere while you pursue your way. But you are part of the royal house and you have obligations that must be fulfilled. It's time you started learning your role."

"Why?" Obaseki replied. "Azikiwe has returned and made you proud."

"Azikiwe's situation has not changed. He's accomplished much against the Kossi but the elders are still not convinced. I'm not convinced, but we're not discussing your uncle.

'You are my daughter's son. You of all people should know the importance of tradition and the roles we play. We all have a duty to the survival of the Mawena and we must fulfill them. No one is exempt, not even I."

Noncemba stood. Even in the common robes of a merchant he took on a regal bearing. He went to his clothes chest and removed a similar outfit.

"Put this on," he commanded. Obaseki was startled. "You will come with me tonight. It's time you caught up on your lessons."

Obaseki dressed, his mind swirling with a mix of apprehension and excitement. The oba was required to go on a daily procession, touring the confines of the city and settling any disputes presented to him. But the oba was also obligated to go out secretly among his people alone to hear the grievances of those too timid or pessimistic to talk to him publicly. To Obaseki's knowledge, no one had ever accompanied Noncemba on this most secret aspect of his rank.

Noncemba looked him over. "You make a fine Bedouin. Come, we have many stops to make tonight."

Obaseki followed his grandfather out of the room and into the empty hallway. Halfway down the corridor Noncemba pushed against the wall, revealing a passageway Obaseki never knew existed. At the end of the passageway was a hatch door in the floor. Noncemba unlocked the door, then descended through the opening. Obaseki followed, clamoring down the ladder into a narrow tunnel. They walked for a good distance before finally coming to a halt. Noncemba opened another door, and then motioned for Obaseki to follow. Obaseki stepped from the darkness into more darkness, emerging into the forest outside the farmlands of Abo. Before him were a stable holding two camels and a pair of pack donkeys.

"Our disguise is now complete," Noncemba announced. He strode over to his camel and signaled for the reluctant Obaseki to follow. Obaseki climbed onto his mount and the two set out for Abo.

The first stop was the outer wall. Each person bringing goods to the city was stopped while the value of his goods was assessed and the appropriate tax levied. Obaseki was impressed with how his grandfather handled the minor obstacle, going as far as to argue with the tax assessor about the amount of tax required for his goods.

After they'd passed through the gate, Noncemba gave the tax collector a long look. "He charges more than the law dictates. I will be sure to have a meeting with him soon."

They continued to the section of the city where the foreign merchants usually boarded. There was an inn there, and after they secured their animals they went inside. Noncemba sat close to a group of Kossi merchants engrossed in animated conversation.

"The Kossi are well-traveled," he whispered to his grandson. "They are the best source of information on other cities that might threaten Abo."

They listened while the Kossi traders went on about prices and taxes and other mundane business. Obaseki tired of this conversation quickly, his mind wandering back to his encounter with the mayembe. Images that were blurred during his ordeal became clearer as he thought back on the moment. He remembered a parade of faces as he plummeted, two which stood out prominently.

One was the face of a woman weeping, consumed with grief so deep Obaseki found his eyes watering as he recalled her. The other was a face that unnerved him. It was his own face, but yet not his. This Obaseki wore a hard countenance; the deep creases on his face making him seem much older. But his eyes were what shook Obaseki the most. The brown orbs smoldered with revenge. His lips moved, seeming to repeat the same word over and over, a word the young prince could not decipher. The image scattered suddenly, replaced by the Kossi traders still engaged in tepid conversation. Noncemba still concentrated on their every word.

"Not much today," he finally said. "I think we…"

Noncemba fell silent, his eyes transfixed on the entrance of the inn. Azikiwe entered and was immediately approached by the Kossi traders. Words they could not hear were exchanged and the men followed Azikiwe outside.

Noncemba waited a moment then followed, Obaseki close behind. They exited nonchalantly then walked to their camels. Obaseki searched for his uncle as well as he could in the darkness without seeming obvious. He found him standing with the Kossi before a well. A bukra man had joined them, a white man from across the sea.

They talked by the well for a moment and then moved into the shadows of the nearby buildings. Obaseki saw them approach a cart in the darkness where the bukra lifted a sheet covering the contents. Both his uncle and the Kossi trader nodded in approval.

"Our night is finished," Noncemba said.

"What is going on?" Obaseki asked. "What is uncle doing with those men?"

Noncemba gave Obaseki a stern look. "What you see tonight must stay with you. No one must know, not even Fuluke. Do you understand?"

Obaseki had never seen his grandfather so serious. This was something dangerous, so much so his grandfather seemed to be threatening his life.

"I understand," he replied.

Noncemba grasped his shoulders. "Go back to Fuluke's and stay there until you are summoned by me and me alone. Make sure no one sees you."

"Yes grandfather."

"You must go tonight." Noncemba's eyes had a distant look to them, his mind apparently dealing with the mysterious events of the night. Obaseki hoped for some sign of weakness, but his grandfather's eyes held none. He reined his camel and galloped away, his grandfather headed silently for the hidden corridor. Obaseki got what he wished for, but as he rode through the shadowy streets of Abo, he sensed that the trade-off would be devastating.

* * *

Fuluke put the seeds in the earthen bowl and ground them to a thick paste. He added leaves from the spirit tree, ashes from the bones of a freshly killed goat and a small amount of spittle. After a short chant, he began to grind the mixture.

"This is what works for me," he told Obaseki. "You will discover the same medicines do not always work for every priest. The power of one's ka and his mayembe has much to do with the power to heal."

Obaseki nodded, locked in deep concentration. The two weeks he'd spent with Fuluke was more than he could have dreamed. The time of running errands and gathering herbs was past; Fuluke now taught him the true ways of the medicine-priest. Most of all, Fuluke was schooling him in the powers of his mayembe. He held Moyo in his right hand, the horn pulsating with his body rhythm. It was a living thing, far different from Fuluke's cold and lifeless buffalo horn. He was sure his teacher's horn contained a spirit; Obaseki had seen it in use enough to be respectful of its power. But it was nothing like Moyo.

"This should be applied to the sick person's chest," Fuluke continued. "Your mayembe will do the rest." The old priest scooped the paste from the stone gourd and put it into a smaller gourd, closing it tightly.

"Now, are you ready, Seki?" Fuluke grinned.

Obaseki stood with Moyo in his hand. "I am, teacher."

Fuluke chuckled. "Bring the horses about and we'll be off."

Their destination was the home of Ayinde Duruji, a farmer and friend of Fuluke. Ayinde's wife, Halina, had fallen ill three days ago. What Fuluke thought to be a minor sickness grew more serious, causing the medicine priest to believe unsettled spirits were involved. Ayinde performed the proper libations, but Halina's condition remained the same. It was time for more drastic actions.

Ayinde was a prosperous farmer and it reflected in the size of his farm. His fields were filled with yams and millet; just beyond the hills cattle and goats grazed upon dense grasses. The farm was tended by young bachelors from Abo working to earn enough cowries for a decent dowry for marriage. A group of such men met Fuluke and Obaseki and led them to Ayinde's house.

When the duo entered the house, Ayinde was kneeling before his ancestors shrine performing libations. They remained quiet until he finished. When Ayinde finally greeted them, his smile was one of relief tinged with fear.

"I thank you for returning," he said. Worry lines etched Ayinde's broad forehead. "She's worse. I think she is going to die."

"Don't give up yet," Fuluke replied, patting his old friend on the shoulder. "A spirit sits on your wife's head, and we are here to remove it."

"A spirit?" Ayinde wrung his hands. "That is possible. A man like me is bound to have enemies. I am not an easy person."

"It's not your fault," Fuluke advised. "The reason such things happen are not important." He looked at Obaseki. "Come, let us begin."

They followed Ayinde to the adjoining room. Halina lay on the bed, tended by their daughters, Eshe and Nafuma. Nafuma resembled her father, tall and thin with a face too bird-like to be considered attractive but still pleasant enough. Eshe resembled her mother; soft, brown eyes with a delicate face almost regal in appearance if not for the creases on her forehead from hard work in the fields. Obaseki didn't notice himself staring at her. She did, and she turned away.

Halina was bound to the bed. At the moment her face was solemn, as if she slept. Obaseki went to her side. Her eyes opened suddenly in a blank stare and Obaseki felt Moyo stir in his pouch. He reached for it and Fuluke grabbed his wrist.

"Not yet," he said. "The poultice will ease the removal of the spirit. If you use your mayembe now it might tear her ka free as well."

Obaseki nodded and removed the poultice pouch instead. He spoke to the sisters, but his eyes fell on Eshe.

"Pull her shirt back so I can apply this poultice to her chest." The sisters did as he asked, gently pulling back their mother's shirt. With nervous hands Obaseki applied the poultice, following Fuluke's instructions. As he did so an image began to appear, one he knew only he could see. A white aura outlined Halina's form, the sign of the spirit intruding upon her. The spirit took form as the poultice did its work, the aura expanding from outline to coherent form across Halina. Obaseki watched, fascinated at the transformation.

"Do you see it?" Fuluke asked.

"Yes, I do." Obaseki's voice shook with excitement. "I know him."

Everyone looked at each other nervously.

"It is Kafele Gamba, Ayinde's great grandfather."

Ayinde stepped back, his hand against his chest. "Great grandfather, what have I done to offend your memory?"

Fuluke went to Ayinde and placed a hand on his shoulder. "Spirits are like us, my friend. Who knows what might cross them?"

Fuluke looked at Obaseki. "It is time."

Obaseki removed Moyo from the pouch. The horn was hot in

his hands, but he dared not drop it. He held it directly over Halina then moved it back and forth over her body. Kafele followed the horn with his eyes, a smile slowly forming on his face. His form shimmered and became incoherent again, reduced to the glow of the spirit. The glow lifted from Halina, her chest heaving with its exit. It hovered over her body for a moment then settle into Moyo. The heat subsided and Obaseki felt suddenly tired. He slumped to the floor. Every cell in his body ached from what seemed like an easy effort.

"It is done," he said, his voice weak. It took every effort to put Moyo back into his pouch, draining what little energy he had left. Turning to Fuluke, he was swallowed by blackness and fell to the floor.

When his eyes opened, Obaseki rested in Halina's bed. He heard the sound of dripping water and turned to its source. Eshe stood there, wringing out a wet cloth over a gourd. She turned to him and smiled.

"You have come back to us," she said.

Obaseki managed to sit up. His head ached and his stomach cramped with hunger.

"How long have I been here?"

"A week," Eshe replied. She came to him, placing the cloth on his forehead and gently forced him back down on the bed.

"You passed out after releasing mama from Kafele."

"How is she?"

"She is much better," Eshe answered. She dipped the cloth in the water gourd. "She is back to bossing baba around." She laughed and Obaseki found himself laughing also. She was a beautiful woman with radiance from within. It was like seeing a spirit.

"The medicine priest returned to his home," Eshe told him. "Baba will send a man to tell him you are well."

"I thank you for your kindness," Obaseki replied.

Eshe smiled and turned away. "I will get you something to eat. I know you are hungry."

Obaseki spent the next few days under Eshe's watchful eye.

His strength increased rapidly; soon he was about the farm, helping the other workers with daily chores. He should have been spending more time with his herbs but he'd not gone near his bags since raising the spirit from Halina. He was terrified, not of the herbs, but of his mayembe. Fuluke said he was ready, but he was not. He found himself lost in its vastness, drowning in the essence of a spirit over which he had no control. The horn was too powerful. When Fuluke returned, they would go back to the old village and bury Moyo, leaving it for another medicine priest more worthy.

Fuluke returned two weeks after his recovery. Obaseki had gone to the pasture with the young boys, watching over the grazing bovine. The rainy season was coming to an end, the clearing sky and rising temperature heralding the change. Fuluke found the young prince leaning against a tree, his hands wrapped around a herding staff.

"Teacher! It is good to see you."

"You look well, Seki," Fuluke said. "Your interest in Eshe hastened your recovery, I suspect."

Fuluke's words embarrassed Obaseki. "Is it so obvious?"

"Only to me," Fuluke replied, "And probably to Eshe."

"She is a special woman," Obaseki said. They sat beneath the shady tree branches. "I've spent so much time learning the ways; I haven't had the time to notice many women."

"Take the time," Fuluke advised. "Otherwise you'll end up old and mean like me." He looked at Obaseki intensely. "Where is Moyo?"

"Back in the hut," Obaseki replied.

"You left it alone?"

Obaseki saw the concern in Fuluke's expression and looked away. "Teacher, I am not worthy of such a thing. When I used it to raise the spirit from Halina, I was totally lost within it. I had no control over it."

"No one can completely control Moyo," Fuluke answered. "You must remember you possess the ka of an orisha. Even though its state is elemental, it still has its own will." Fuluke laid a hand on his shoulder. "You have the gift of a meji. If anyone can handle Moyo, it is you. Doing so could mean great things for the Mawena."

Obaseki was not sure of Fuluke's last statement. What could a medicine priest do to create greatness among a people? The arts of healing and appeasement were essential to any tribe, but paled to the power held by the oba and his council of lineage elders. Fuluke must be showing his age, he thought. A horse and rider appeared over the hill from the direction of the farmhouse, galloping frantically towards the herd. Obaseki came to his feet, straining to make out the rider's identity. A group of horsemen appeared soon afterwards, bearing shields and lances. Obaseki recognized the white turbans and uniforms and his heart raced. They were Kossi warriors, and they were pursuing Eshe.

"Everyone to the forest!" Obaseki shouted. Fuluke was on his feet, his herb knife in hand.

"Come, Seki," he urged.

Obaseki ignored him, running for Eshe. The world went silent around him, his senses filled by the sights and sounds of Eshe riding towards him, her pursuers closing the gap with every second. Some of the riders broke away, chasing the herdsmen or going after untended cattle. Three warriors continued to pursue Eshe, their lances lowered towards her horse.

Eshe reached him, slowing her horse just enough for him to leap on it. They galloped to the forest edge and Eshe jumped off. She looked at Obaseki in terror.

"Go!" he said. Obaseki reined the horse about and charged towards the Kossi. He veered his mount to his closest attacker, deflecting his lance thrust with his staff and striking the man across the face in one motion, toppling the Kossi from his mount. The others tried to converge on Obaseki simultaneously, but the young prince darted between them. It was not his intention to fight, only to draw the raiders away from the others hiding in the woods. Riding erratically across the fields, he harassed other groups of Kossi until they all pursed him. Obaseki led them away from the fields and toward the road. As he fled he saw plumes of smoke rising throughout the farmlands. This was not just a raid. A battle was taking place around Abo, he was sure, and the Kossi pursuing him were just a glimpse of what was occurring in the city.

Obaseki saw Ayinde and the rest of the workers running towards him, each man armed with spears and bows. The Kossi broke off their pursuit, galloping across the yam fields to the main road.

Ayinde ran up to him. "Where is my daughter? Where is Eshe?"

"She is safe," Obaseki assured him. "She hides in the woods with Fuluke and the herdsmen."

Ayinde relaxed for a moment, but his anxiety quickly turned to anger. "Kossi bastards!" he shouted. "Oba Noncemba will kill you all!"

The mention of his grandfather spurred Obaseki into action. "Ayinde, I need to use this horse."

"Take it," Ayinde replied. "Do what you must."

Obaseki rode to the house and quickly gathered his belongings, hesitating as he reached for his herb bag. He could feel Moyo from a distance, the green glow radiating from the seams of the bag. He finally grabbed the bag, mounted his horse and set out for Abo.

Obaseki knew better than to ride the main roads. Instead he cut through the forest searching for the glade hiding the secret passage to the palace. He passed burned homes and trampled fields, frantic farmers racing back and forth with buckets of water, trying desperately to quench the fires that seemed endless across the horizon.

He finally reached the glade. He wandered about for a moment, making sure he had not been followed. Pushing aside the thicket hiding the entrance, Obaseki charged into the tunnel like a madman, running until he reached the main tunnel that angled upward to the palace. He heard commotion above him and his hands began to sweat. Pushing the iron door under the hall chest open, he climbed into the palace, crept across the room and peered into the hallway. Servants darted about, carrying valuables to load in royal wagons waiting in the courtyard. Obaseki stepped into the hallway and was almost ran over by Jela. The guard went for his sword.

"Fool! Get out of my way! Can't you see…"

Jela's words froze in his throat as he recognized Obaseki and fell to his knees.

"My prince, I am so sorry! Forgive me." The guards shocked expression transformed to puzzlement. "How did you get into the palace?"

Obaseki ignored the question.

"Where is my grandfather?" Obaseki asked.

"He's at the gate. I will take you to him."

The two men ran through the palace. The building was in chaos as servants dashed about amid the babble of panicked voices. They hurried to the stables, mounted and galloped to the gates. The roads of Abo swelled with refugees, many who had entered the city before the gates were shut. Obaseki worked his way through the horde the best he could. He cursed, frustrated with his slow progress, and jumped from the horse. He surmised he could make better time on foot, and he was right. Pushing his way through the mass he soon heard the clamor of battle before him and stopped. He was afraid, far more than he'd ever been in his entire life. It was the true reason he avoided Kumba's instruction, why he never wanted to fight. Obaseki did not want to die. He'd seen all his life what death meant, wandering as an aimless spirit, slowly becoming nothing more that a speck of life. Other men must know what he knew, but still they sang songs of battle and sought its glory. To Obaseki, war was a sinister wall which he wished not to climb.

His hand found Moyo. The mayembe pulsed in his palm, it's heat seeping into his arms then moving through him like a lazy stream of awareness. This was not the possession he feared, nor was it the fall into blackness he experienced before. This was a union, a bond that filled the void of fear in Obaseki's heart. All his senses sharpened, his mind moving in a blur as he watched the chaotic scenes around him. He moved forward again, not with the timidity of fear, but with the confidence of experience.

Mawena archers lined the ramparts of the third wall, delivering their poison arrows with lethal precision. The Kossi screamed and fell in scores but more stepped forward to take their place. Obaseki wondered how their attackers had breached the first two walls. Then he remembered the night in the tavern, the meeting of his uncle Azikiwe, the Kossi and the bukra man. Could his uncle have conspired so? Obaseki pushed the thought from his mind. He had to find his grandfather first. The answers would come later.

The battle raged with unrelenting fury. Women dragged the wounded and dead away from the walls, tending the injured the best they could. Obaseki searched for his grandfather among them.

"Obaseki!" someone shouted. The young prince looked to see one of the palace guards running to him. He was Zubeki, smiling despite the carnage around him.

"My prince, the oba will be happy to see you! We thought the Kossi killed you!"

Obaseki ignored Zubeki's remark. "Where is my grandfather?"

"Follow me."

The duo worked through the confusion to the western section of the wall. Horsemen gathered there, mostly Mawena but also a large number of warriors from the surrounding tribes. They all knew the value of Abo to the stability of the entire region and were ready to give their lives to preserve it. The horsemen surrounded a score of Atuegbu resplendent in their green kapok uniforms and golden trimmed helmets. They held double-headed lances in their hands, gold pommel swords at their sides. At the center were Kumba and Oba Noncemba.

Zubeki yelled over the commotion and waved his lance. The group parted and Noncemba rode up and dismounted, a broad smile on his face.

"My grandson returns," he shouted. "How to you like the celebration?"

"I don't think this is the time for jokes," Obaseki replied as he hugged his grandfather.

"Then maybe you should sit on the royal stool," Noncemba said.

Obaseki turned to Zubeki. "Get me a horse and a lance."

"No," Noncemba said. "You will stay inside until this is over."

"My place is with you," Obaseki protested.

"You don't have the training," Noncemba countered. "This is no game, Seki."

Kumba interrupted their argument. "My Oba, we must strike now. The Kossi are massing a final assault."

"Stay here," Noncemba ordered.

"I'm going with you," Obaseki said.

"Let him come," Kumba agreed. "If he does not live, he never deserved to take your place."

Noncemba glared at Kumba. "Come."

Zubeki returned with a fine roan stallion and a chain mail breast plate for Obaseki. The prince tied Moyo around his waist then donned the mail, covering it with his traditional kapok padding. Zubeki gave him a lance and a sword. Obaseki mounted then rode to join the cavalry.

Obaseki reached the warriors as his grandfather made a final inspection of his remaining forces. Nodding his approval, the oba signaled for them to gather around him. Obaseki rode beside him, with Kumba flanking the Oba's opposite side. The guard fell in behind them, followed closely by the rest of the cavalry. The men on the ramparts watched, waiting for the horsemen to reach the gate. On the Oba's signal they raised the gate. A deep drum sounded and the cavalry charged.

The horsemen wheeled left to confront the main group of Kossi scaling the walls under the cover of archers. Noncemba's attack threatened to pin the Kossi between his cavalry and the wall. The Kossi would have no choice but to retreat. Surprise was the key; despite their valor the Abo's elite cavalry was small. If the Kossi did not falter in the initial engagement they would all be killed.

Noncemba knew this, Obaseki realized. As Oba, he could only survive with victory. Defeat meant he was no longer the strongest link between the Mawena and Olodumare, that he was not strong enough to protect the tribe from its spiritual and physical foes.

They lowered their lances, galloping over the last strides between them and the marauding Kossi. Obaseki felt detached; the scene before him some sort of morbid dream over which he had no control. The bravery was not his but Moyo's, fueled by what he felt as a sense of pleasure. This was what made Obaseki fear the mayembe. Moyo thrived in what he feared the most.

They were almost upon the horde when it began to rain Kossi arrows. Obaseki flinched as a projectile raked his cheek, leaving a thin, red welt in its wake. He rode on, bending low against his horse. He managed to glance back and witnessed a terrible sight. The Atuegbu still rode with him, but the remaining cavalry faltered under the onslaught. The Kossi took advantage, leaping down from the roofs with swords held high. Ahead more Kossi broke away from the assaulting mass to meet the charge. The element of surprise was lost. They were no longer fighting for Abo; they were fighting for their lives.

The Mawena cavalry crashed into the Kossi, Obaseki driving his lance into a man before him. He let the lance trail behind him before pulling it from the man's body and returning it level. He had no time to think, no time to realize that this was the first time he'd taken a life.

Another Kossi appeared before him, this one on horseback. Obaseki charged forward; the Kossi knocked the lance down with his sword. The lance went into the horse instead; the beast screeched in pain and collapsed under its rider. The Kossi leapt from the horse and slammed against Obaseki and they both fell to the ground. The impact stunned them for a moment; Obaseki was the first to regain his composure. He pulled his sword and brought the hilt down on the Kossi's head, knocking him senseless. He stepped away with a moment's respite, the battle swirling around him in a haze of dust, blood and smoke.

Obaseki ran to the Atuegbu. The warriors formed a semi-circle against a section of the second wall that still stood. Kumba stood in the center, his shield and sword working furiously against the endless Kossi onslaught. Obaseki could barely see Noncemba behind Kumba, his sword at the ready. He ran to them knowing he would not make much difference, but determined to be at his grandfather's side. As he ran to his grandfather, Obaseki spotted a group of ten Kossi warriors charging in his direction on horseback. He recognized the lead horseman; it was his uncle Azikiwe dressed in Kossi robes. A group of Atuegbu broke ranks and charged the horsemen, shields and lances at the ready. The horsemen pulled short of lance range and lifted what seemed to be some type of club to their shoulders in unison. Azikiwe raised his sword, his eyes on the advancing Atuegbu.

He sliced his arm downward and Obaseki's ears exploded with a deafening roar. He blinked with pain, his eyes opening to a confusing scene. The horsemen were shrouded in a gray blue haze as they worked the sinister clubs that caused the terrible sound. Before them the Atuegbu lay broken, some not moving while others cried in pain. The Mawena were stunned, frozen wide-eyed by the scene. His grandfather and Kumba stood alone, their faces solemn to what would happen when the Kossi horsemen raised the strange clubs to their shoulders again.

Obaseki reached for Moyo, extracting the horn from the pouch. Maybe there was something the spirit could do that he could not. Before he had used the mayembe only to heal, but he knew the horn could kill. He knew the killing chant, the words that transformed the mayembe into a kifaalu, a death spirit. As he ran to his grandfather, he let the words escape his lips.

Moyo exploded, consuming Obaseki in blinding white light. The kifaalu became a ball of white fire with Obaseki in the center, fiery tendrils lashing out indiscriminately at the warriors surrounding him. A tendril struck Azikiwe, lifting him off his horse, his wide eyes filled with terror. The tendril jerked away and his ka was ripped from him, his body falling lifeless to the ground as his spirit was consumed by the burning light. Moyo the kifaalu cared not who became its victim. Mawena fell as quickly as Kossi. Obaseki realized the horror he'd unleashed and struggled to control it, shouting the words to return the kifaalu to the docile mayembe. But Moyo fought back, moving slowly towards the Atuegbu, striking down all in its path. The Kossi fled in terror, screaming to their cohorts of the terrible death approaching. The onslaught became a confused retreat. But the Mawena behind the ramparts did not pursue. The terrified Mawenabu prayed that the malevolent light would not breach the inner wall.

Obaseki battled to wrest control from Moyo, slowing its advance toward the Atuegbu and his grandfather. One bodyguard jumped from the ranks, his sword high, most of his body hidden by his leaf shield. Moyo lashed out just as quickly and the man fell dead to the ground. Obaseki watched as the man's soul was dragged towards him, the face screaming in silent pain as it was consumed. Obaseki could take no more. He yelled, concentrating everything he could muster into a final grasp for control. The light dissipated and Moyo receded into its material form, clasped tightly in Obaseki's right hand. The prince fell to his knees only a few steps away from the Atuegbu. He tasted blood; his face was drenched with sweat, the pain in his body all consuming. He looked at his grandfather's face, expecting to see a grateful smile. Instead he saw the same fear he'd seen in the face of the Kossi. Obaseki swayed and fell forward, his head crashing into the dirt.

* * *

The pungent smell of healing herbs stirred Obaseki from unconsciousness. He could feel pain, but it was dulled by whatever had been applied to him. He opened his eyes, thankful for the darkness. Torchlight flickered in the distance illuminating uneven shelves packed with countless gourds. He lay in Fuluke's hut, but he did not know how he arrived.

Fuluke appeared above him, a grim look on his face as he

checked Obaseki's wounds. His expression changed when he noticed Obaseki was conscious.

"Seki, always in a hurry," he said.

Obaseki opened his mouth and blacked out for a second. When he focused on Fuluke again, his mentor gave him a sympathetic smile.

"Close your eyes," he said. "The herbs will calm you if you let them."

Obaseki knew better than to talk again, so he closed his eyes and settled into darkness. He dreamed he stood on a grassy plain, a violent wind pressing hot against his skin. A figure appeared in the distance, running toward him at incredible speed. The man carried a shield and an assegai, the spear held high as if to attack. Obaseki tried to run, but his feet were fused into the ground. The man stopped before him and Obaseki gawked at a malevolent version of himself. He looked at himself, a malevolent version of himself. The grass surrounding them began to burn, and the false Obaseki uttered one word as the flames consumed them: Simba.

Sunlight breached the cracks in Fuluke's walls and pulled Obaseki from his disturbing vision. It was a message he was sure, but of what he didn't know. He fought his first battle but showed none of the bravery the Obaseki of his dream possessed. He tried to decipher the image but the details faded rapidly. In moments he could barely remember any detail. Only one word remained in his mind; Simba. He had no idea what it meant.

He was alone. His clothes rested at the end of the cot and he put them on, feeling better the more he moved about. Gingerly he stood and his legs held firm. Standing alone in good health, it was hard to imagine he'd experienced the terror of battle.

He heard footsteps and turned to the door. Fuluke entered with a smile on his face. Obaseki was pleasantly surprised to see Eshe with him.

"Again I amaze myself," Fuluke bragged. "How does it feel to be back from the dead?"

"Good," Obaseki replied. "Hello, Eshe."

Eshe turned away slightly, her smile like the sun. "My father sent me when he heard of your condition. I brought you food and fresh milk."

"Thank you and your family," Obaseki replied. "I will mention your kindness to my grandfather when I return to Abo."

"You cannot go back," Fuluke said.

"I feel fine, really I do," Obaseki replied.

Fuluke and Eshe glanced at each other. "That is not the reason, Seki", Fuluke said. "The council has barred your presence in the city."

Obaseki sat slowly on the cot. "Why?"

"You unleashed a power never seen before, and it terrified them."

"I was trying to save my grandfather," Obaseki defended.

"You killed many men, Seki, Kossi and Mawena. You killed your uncle."

"My uncle deserved to die," Obaseki spat. "He betrayed us. He led the Kossi against us and tried to kill Grandfather!"

Fuluke nodded in understanding. "You also killed the son of Abasi Kanata."

Obaseki stiffened at the mention of the elder's name. Abasi held the highest position on the tribal council. His family was the oldest of the Mawena, and one of the most powerful.

"I...I didn't mean to." Obaseki dropped his head to hide his watery eyes. "I couldn't save grandfather alone. I thought I could control Moyo, but it was too strong. By the time I had it under control..."

"You don't have to explain anything to me," Fuluke said.

"Or to me," Eshe agreed.

Fuluke sat beside Obaseki on the cot. "You must understand what you possess, Seki. A medicine priest holds the power of life and death in his hands. We heal the sick and placate the ancestors. We are responsible for the harmony between the Mawena and the Zamani. We are not obas because our lineage does not allow it. But you are special. You have the power of a medicine-priest and the lineage of an oba. Most of all, you have Moyo."

Fuluke placed his hand on Obaseki's shoulder. He calmed as he looked in his mentor's eyes.

"You threaten the hiearchy of the tribe, and the elders know this. When you unleashed the power of Moyo on the Kossi, you also unleashed the power of the elders on yourself. This is a flood not even your grandfather can stem."

"I don't want to be oba," Obaseki replied. "You know that."

"I know, I know," Fuluke replied. "But the elders do not."

Obaseki asked the question that mattered to him the most. "What does my grandfather think?"

Fuluke's face looked grave. "Your grandfather loves you, but he fears for you. He doesn't understand the power you possess."

"So I must be judged," Obaseki concluded. "I could save everyone the trouble and leave."

Eshe's eyes went wide on hearing Obaseki's words, but Fuluke remained calm. Obaseki knew his decision was rash, but he was angry. Not at the elders, but at his grandfather. He unleashed Moyo to save him! What was so hard to understand?

"What should I do?" Obaseki asked his teacher.

"You must answer that question," Fuluke replied. "You have taken the first step to learning your place in this world. You will never be the priest you can be if you stay in Abo. You can't learn here what you must to control Moyo while appeasing the local spirits. You have destiny that began the day you were born a meji. You must go out into the world to discover you path."

Obaseki could not believe what Fuluke suggested. Abo was his home!

"But where would I go?" Obaseki asked.

"Moyo will lead you," Fuluke answered.

"Forgive me, Teacher, but I think you are wrong," he finally said. "I know the elders well. They are all my uncles. They have no reason to think I would harm them. I made a terrible mistake releasing the kifalu. I know I need time to master Moyo, but when that day comes, I will use my power to help, not harm."

"It is your decision," Fuluke replied. "You are Mawena. But think long on it, Seki."

Fuluke left Obaseki alone with Eshe. He wished she'd not been present to hear what was said, but he was pleased she stayed. Seeing her was comforting and she seemed to sense it. He lay back on the cot and closed his eyes, his mind spinning. The jumble of questions was dashed aside by Eshe's sweet humming. She looked at him, smiling as she hummed. She was preparing a meal for him.

He moved closer to her. "Eshe, why did you come?"

"Because my father sent me," she replied

"Why did you come?" Obaseki asked again, his voice firm.

Eshe looked at him directly. "I came because I am interested in you. You are a strange man."

Obaseki was offended and turned away. "So you see me as a spectacle?"

"No, I did not mean strange in a bad way. You are not like most men. I sense the spirits about you, like I did with my mother. But they do not harm you."

Obaseki did not understand at first why he was having this conversation. His mind should have been on the council and his impending banishment. But that situation was beyond his control, firmly in the hands of Olodumare. This, however, was something he could deal with, and he needed it desperately.

"So you wished to see the odd one," he said.

"At first, yes. But I sensed your ka, and I see you are a man full of kindness and I became sad."

"Why?"

"Because I sense your ka is not whole. Every man has evil within him, whether it manifests itself or not. The good and evil constantly struggle but neither wins, for both are useful in one's life. But you have no evil. Your ka only knows one way. That is why Fuluke took you to the mayembe, I think, and that is why he feels you should leave Abo."

"I dreamed of my evil," he said. "I saw a man with my face,

but with a different ka. He is a warrior, ruthless and terrible. He said Simba. I don't want to find Simba, Eshe. I am terrified of what would happen if I did."

Obaseki looked into her soothing eyes.

"Will you go with me?" he asked

Eshe smiled with the glow of sunshine. She moved her mouth as if to answer him, then abruptly handed him his meal.

"This will make you better," she said, then quickly exited the hut.

Obaseki ate slowly as he contemplated his decision. Abo was his home, a sanctuary of wealth, power and spirit. He had enemies among the elders now, but he felt he could convince them he meant no harm. Abasi Kanata had always been stern to him, but his grandfather was very close to Abasi and could sway him. He finished his meal and left the hut.

Fuluke and Eshe sat outside, their conversation halting when they noticed him.

"I'm going to Abo," he announced.

"You should wait," Fuluke advised. "Let the memory of what happened grow cold in their minds before you confront them. A boiling pot does not cook any meat."

"No," Obaseki replied. "If the council wishes to exile me let them do it now. The pain will be no less now than tomorrow."

"The guards at the gate may not let you pass," Fuluke said.

"They don't have to," Obaseki replied. He turned his attention to Eshe. "Are you going with me?"

Eshe nodded.

"Good, then let us go." Eshe went to the tie post for the horse. Obaseki followed but was stopped by Fuluke's hand resting firmly on his shoulder.

"Be careful, my son," he said. "Whatever happens, it is not worth your life."

Eshe returned and Obaseki mounted the horse. Eshe wrapped her arms around his waist and they trotted down the steep path leading towards the city.

They rode for a day, covering as much ground as they could before nightfall. Obaseki discovered he was not as well as he thought; the jostling of the trail wore him down quickly, forcing them to set up camp long before dark. They stopped at the forest's edge, only a few strides from the beginning of the farmland that surrounded Abo. Once they entered the obadom, a confrontation was imminent. He wanted to be strong when that happened, and the only way to insure that was to stop and rest.

Obaseki began to build a fire but Eshe stopped him.

"You must rest," she said. "Take this cot and find a place with many leaves. It will be the most comfortable. I will start a fire."

Obaseki obeyed eagerly. He found a spot like Eshe described and quickly fell asleep, the first dreamless slumber he'd experienced in days. When he awoke Eshe lay beside him, her warm body pressed against him. Carnal thoughts rushed in his head but he pushed them away. He admonished himself for thinking in such a way, struggling against his urges until he worried himself to sleep.

They broke camp at sunrise and headed for the glade that hid the secret entrance to the palace. The duo arrived about midday, thankful for the shade of the ironwoods standing guard. Obaseki searched for and found the entrance buried under the leaves. He cleared the brush away and called Eshe to him. She hesitated, fear in her eyes.

"Don't be afraid," he said. "This tunnel will take us directly to the palace."

He took her trembling hand and they descended into the tunnel, making good time in total darkness. The ground angled upward through the layers of rock and soil, pierced by the tunnel that eventually led to the hallway outside Oba Noncemba's bedroom. Obaseki pushed against the hatch sealing the door and slid it open. His grandfather's room was empty. No sounds emanated from the other rooms close by. He helped Eshe out of the tunnel. Obaseki helped Eshe out to the tunnel and into the room. She seemed awed by the opulence, her eyes wide and watery as she scanned the room's treasures of gold, ivory, cowry shells and precious stones.

"What do we do now?" Eshe asked.

"We wait." Obaseki walked over to the stool at the foot of Noncemba's bed and sat. Eshe sat on the floor beside him, laying her head on his thigh. No sooner had they settled did they fall asleep. The arduous journey had left their bodies drained.

They awoke to the clamor of footsteps. The door to the room swung wide and Noncemba strode in followed by two Atuegbu. He wore his riding clothes, the dust from the trail still heavy on his garments. His sword hung loosely from his shoulder, its golden scabbard beating against his waist. Noncemba stumbled back into his bodyguards when he saw Obaseki and Eshe. He raised his hand just in time, halting the mortal assault of his bodyguards.

"Leave us," he commanded. The guards left, glancing malevolently over their shoulders.

Noncemba's face remained stern until the Atuegbu were gone. A broad, joyous smile broke across his face and his arms went wide. Obaseki ran to his grandfather and they embraced like father and long lost son.

"Seki, it is dangerous for you here," Noncemba admonished.

"It is dangerous for me not to be here," Obaseki countered.

His grandfather held him at arm's length. "You look well. That is good." He turned to Eshe who was kneeling, her head touching the floor.

"This is Eshe, daughter of Ayinde," Obaseki said.

"Stand up, woman," Noncemba commanded. "You have taken care of my grandson and I am grateful."

"Thank you, oba," Eshe replied.

"Grandfather," Obaseki interrupted. "Why was I banished?"

Noncemba's face took on a gloomy shadow. He sat heavily on his stool.

"Abasi wants it, and you know he is a powerful elder. Your mayembe killed his son, a loss that even our years of friendship cannot heal. He has bent the judgment of the elders, using your uncle's betrayal against our family. He has even gone so far as to question my rule. He cannot usurp me; I have done the Mawena well as oba and our lineage gives us the right to rule. So he has gone after you."

"I must speak to the elders," Obaseki said. "I will not be banished without the chance to defend myself."

"You are right, Seki, but now is not the time. We must wait until wounds have healed. Abasi was not the only one in the city to lose a loved one to your magic. That is why he wields so much power at the moment."

"No, it must be now," Obaseki retorted. He saw the look of disapproval on his grandfather's face and felt sorrow. It was never his wish to defy him, but this had to be. If what Fuluke said was true, then the outcome was already known. But even if he did not change the minds of the elders, he would be satisfied if he said how he felt.

"You are too old to be so impatient," Noncemba replied. "Give it time before you make any rash decisions."

Obaseki was not to be swayed. "Grandfather, I need to see the council. Will you grant me this?"

Noncemba sighed and slumped in his stool. "I will convene the elders. I will not, however, let them know you will be at this meeting. They would refuse to come."

"Thank you, Grandfather."

Noncemba rose. "Wait here until I send for you. The servants will bring you and Eshe food. Eat well and rest. You will need all your strength."

The servants brought a feast to the room, all of them happy to see him back at the palace. They were enchanted by Eshe, and the women fell upon her like joyful captors, dressing her in the finest of Abo and reworking her braids in a fresh and attractive pattern. Obaseki was never in doubt of Eshe's beauty, but seeing her prepared by skilled hands affected him more than he could imagine. She was truly a special woman, worth the dowry he was contemplating if he was allowed to stay in Abo. He realized with those thoughts that he really wanted to stay. Despite Fuluke's prophesy, he was afraid to leave home. Fuluke would one day give up his responsibilities as medicine-priest, and who better to take his place than Obaseki? Fuluke himself said that he would never be allowed to be oba. Even without the fear of too much power in one hand, the stigma of Moyo's slaughter had done enough to eliminate that option. If he convinced the elders that the terrible power they witnessed could be used for the good of the city, Obaseki believed there would be no banishment.

His thoughts were broken by the entrance of the royal messenger to the room. He looked at Obaseki intensely; his true feelings clear despite his submissive tone.

"My prince, Oba Noncemba requests your presence at the meeting tree," he said curtly.

Obaseki stood and turned to Eshe, extending his hand. Eshe eyes flashed with curiosity.

"What do you want?" she asked.

"I wish you to come with me."

A collective gasp filled the room. Eshe hand came to her chest as it heaved with heavy breath.

"I cannot go to a council!" she shrieked. "I was not summoned."

"I am asking you now," Obaseki replied. "You have helped me unselfishly, and I would feel much better before these great men with you beside me."

Eshe smiled broadly. "I will be with you as long as you wish."

Obaseki turned to the messenger, his resolve strengthened knowing that Eshe would accompany him. "We are ready," he said.

They followed the messenger out of the palace and into the streets. A human fence bordered the avenue leading to the center of the city and the meeting tree. The city was void of sound with the exception of the whistle, moans and calls of animals. Mawena eyes focused on the duo, showing a mix of fear, admiration and hate. Obaseki tried his best to ignore them, clutching Moyo under his shirt as it pulsed with heat. Grasping Eshe's hand, he looked toward the tree, striding regally like the son of the oba. They walked for an eternity, the streets he grew up to know suddenly alien and hostile. As they neared the tree, he saw the elders sitting around its base with Noncemba seated on the gilded stool. Abasi sat nearby, his face showing none of the emotion of which his grandfather warned him. The other elders were just as stoic. He approached until he was among them, his grandfather stepping forward with the ceremonial sword gripped in his right hand.

"I have called you together to hear the plea of Obaseki of the Buhari. He has come to address his issue of banishment before your sacred council to explain his actions and beg for reconsideration of his sentence. Will you grant his request?"

Abasi looked directly into Obaseki's eyes. "We grant his request."

Obaseki watched as his grandfather took his place on the stool. "You may begin," he said.

Obaseki fell to his knees, his arms outstretched and finger spread wide.

"Great elders, I humble myself before you to ask for reconsideration of my sentence. On the day of my transgression, our city swarmed with Kossi, a scheme devised and aided by my uncle. Their numbers seemed vast, and with the weapons they possessed our situation seemed dire."

Obaseki paused a moment to study the elders' faces. Some nodded in agreement, while others frowned. Abasi remained unreadable, staring at his folded hands resting in his lap. Obaseki glanced at his uncle, who motioned for him to continue.

"The pain and anger in my heart was great, but it became greater still when I saw my grandfather and his warriors surrounded by Kossi. Having no other choice, I summoned the spirit of my mayembe to protect my grandfather and Abo."

"There was another choice," Abasi countered. "That choice was to raise your sword like the warrior you where trained to be, a warrior like my son." The elder had raised his head, his eyes on

Obaseki. Though his face remained calm, Obaseki saw the malice in his stare.

"That is true, Elder Abasi," Obaseki acknowledged. "But my sword would not save my grandfather or our city. It was my hope that my mayembe would."

"So you unleashed a power that you could not control, costing us many warriors," Abasi finished. "Better that you die a warrior's death at your grandfather's side than to foul this city with evil."

"The boy meant no harm," Abegunde interjected. "Any one of us would have done the same if we possessed such an item." He turned to face Obaseki. "Your failing was you tried to use the mayembe before you mastered it."

"Which is why he must be banished," Abasi said. "This boy must learn the penalty for immaturity. He caused the death of many that day. Granting him leniency disgraces the memory of those who died for nothing."

"You are an elder," Chinzira replied. "Though the loss of your son is one I can only imagine, you cannot let it influence your judgment at this council. Obaseki attempted to save his grandfather and this city, which none of us here can deny. He succeeded, but at a great cost." Chinzira stood, a tall, powerfully built man whose word usually swayed the vote of the majority of the elders. "Obaseki should suffer banishment, but only for a time. Hopefully he will use this time to master his abilities for the betterment of our people. This should please the spirits of those wrongly slain."

"My spirit still burns!" Abasi hissed. "If this is the judgment of the elders, then I renounce my place among you. The Chuma family will not live among those who condone murder!"

The scene was engulfed in an explosion of noise. Elders leapt to their feet in protest of Abasi's words. Others joined in with Abasi's demands, threatening to bring about the fall of Mawenaland. His grandfather stood, yelling for order. In trying to save Abo Obaseki had done more damage than the Kossi could ever imagine.

"Elders, elders, please listen to me!" he shouted. The ruckus went on unabated. Obaseki extracted Moyo and held it high over his head.

"LISTEN TO ME!" His voice thundered throughout the city like the roar of a thousand storms. The elders stumbled away, eyes wide in shock. Even Noncemba cowered as he looked at his grandson. Obaseki gazed at them all, elders and citizens alike and finally saw the truth in Fuluke's words. What he possessed was beyond their comprehension as well as his own. He would find no understanding here, only suspicion and fear.

"I never meant to harm anyone. Abo is my home, but if staying causes the separation of the families that make the Mawena great I have no choice."

He looked at Abasi directly, trying his best to project the sympathy he felt. "I accept the council's first judgment of banishment. I will be gone before first daylight."

Obaseki didn't allow for any further words. He turned quickly and strode away, Eshe trotting to catch up with him and join his side.

"Are you sure this is what you want?" she asked.

"It's not want I want. It is what I must do."

"Then you are the man your grandfather wished you to be," Eshe replied.

Obaseki looked into Eshe's eyes and grasped her hand. Together they walked to the palace between the silent throng, disappearing behind the gilded walls.

Meji Glossary

Name	Pronunciation	Meaning/Relationship
Abo	AH-boh	Mawena capital city
Alamako	ah-lah-mah-koh	A city near Ifana
assegai	A (as in at)-say-guy	spear
Ata	ah-tah	first born of twins
Atsu	AT-soo	second born of twins
Azikiwe	Ah-zee-kee-way	Obaseki's uncle
Celu	SAY-loo	Ndoki's mayembe spirit
Diaka	DEE-ah-kah	the slave people
Dingane	DEHN-gah-nee	Father of the twins
Fuluke	FOO-loo-kay	Mawena medicine-priest
Gamba	GAHM-bah	Sesu warrior
Husani	HOO-sah-nee	Shani's bodyguard
Ifana	EYE-fah-nah	City of ghosts
impi	EHM-pee	a group of Sesu warriors
Inkosi	N-koh-see	Sesu for king
Jelani	JEH-lah-nee	Husani's brother
kimbia	KEHM-bee-ah	Sesu for "march"
Kossi	KOH-see	Mawena traditional enemies
kraal	krahl	cattle enclosure
Mawena	MAH-weh-nah	Shani's people
mayembe	MAH-yehm-beh	A animal horn containing a spirit
Moyo	MOH-yoh	Obaseki's mayembe spirit
Mulugo	MOO-loo-goh	Sesu medicine-priest
Ndoki	N-doh-kee	The medicine priest of Ifana
Ndoro	N-doe-roe	Obaseki's brother
nganga	N-gahn-gah	Sesu for medicine priest
ngwena	N-gweh-nah	crocodile
Noncemba	NOHN-kehm-bah	Shani's father
Obaseki	OBAH-se-kee	Ndoro's brother
Olodumare	olo-doo-mah-ray	Mawena main god
orinka	OR-ring-kah	war club
Oya	O-yah	an orisha - minor god or spirit
Paki	PAH-kee	a boy
Selike	SEE-lee-keh	Sesuland capital city

Sesu	SAY-soo	Dingane's people
Shani	SHAH-nee	The twins mother
Shumba	SHOOM-bah	Diaka for lion
Simba	SIM-bah	Sesu for lion
Songhai	SAHN-high	people of the Sahel
Soninke	SAH-nin-kee	another name for the songhai
Tacuma	TAH-koo-mah	Enemies of the Diaka
Themba	TEHM-bah	Shani's handmaiden
Tuareg	TOO-ar-rehg	people of the desert
Unkulunkulu	oo-koo-loon-koo-loo	Sesu main god
Zuwena	ZOO-weh-nah	nursemaid

ABOUT THE AUTHOR

Milton Davis poses as a chemist by day in order to pursue his true identity as a fantasy and science fiction writer in the evenings and on weekends. He is married with two children and resides in Fayetteville, GA. Meji is his first novel. He can be reached at *mv_media@bellsouth.net*, or by visiting *www.mvmediaatl.com*.